PURRFECT SHARK

THE MYSTERIES OF MAX 91

NIC SAINT

PURRFECT SHARK

The Mysteries of Max 91

Copyright © 2024 by Nic Saint

All rights reserved. No part of this book may be reproduced in any form by any electronic or mechanical means including photocopying, recording, or information storage and retrieval without permission in writing from the author.

This is a work of fiction. Names, characters, places, brands, media, and incidents are either the product of the author's imagination or are used fictitiously. The author acknowledges the trademarked status and trademark owners of various products referenced in this work of fiction, which have been used without permission. The publication/use of these trademarks is not authorized, associated with, or sponsored by the trademark owners.

Edited by Chereese Graves

www.nicsaint.com

Give feedback on the book at: info@nicsaint.com

facebook.com/nicsaintauthor
@nicsaintauthor

First Edition

Printed in the U.S.A

PURRFECT SHARK

Hot Dog!

Marge and Tex had won a two-week stay at the Hampton Cove Resort & Spa and planned to make good use of the opportunity. Unfortunately the resort was being plagued by a thief who enjoyed robbing its guests. Fortunately Gran and Scarlett were on the case. Since the police department was struggling with manpower issues, they had offered the services of the neighborhood watch and were keen to catch the thief. Unfortunately before long one of the guests was found dead on the beach, seemingly the victim of a shark attack. Fortunately the shark that had been seen in the waters wasn't to blame. Unfortunately it soon became clear that the victim had been murdered in quite a gruesome way. Fortunately Odelia and Chase arrived to look into the case. Unfortunately they asked me to talk to the shark…

CHAPTER 1

Kimmy and Kitty Davis were most definitely NOT having a good time. In fact, what they were living through was probably the WORST time ANYONE could have—EVER! The twins had been lured into babysitting duties at the Hampton Cove Resort & Spa by their mom, who pretty much ran the resort with her sisters and Grandma, as a way to make a little money during the summer holidays. Though secretly, Kimmy suspected Mom simply wanted to keep them close so she could keep an eye on them.

Originally, they were supposed to travel to Europe with their dad and his new girlfriend, but since they hated the woman, they hadn't been keen. And so when Mom suggested they spend the summer at the resort, they had jumped at the chance. They got to stay at the big house with Grandma Bea, which was always fun, and had pretty much hoped to spend a leisurely and relaxing time lounging around at the pool, meeting boys, and partying every night, all night. Instead, Mom and Auntie Grace, who was the general manager of the resort, had them on babysitting duties and animator-slash-entertainer for the older kids, a job they pretty much HATED! Those kids were BRUTAL! In fact, the only one who hadn't made their lives miserable was a little girl named Grace Kingsley.

Grace's grandparents were staying at the resort and also her great-grandmother, who was a real pistol. Kimmy had met the family and had to say that she liked Marge Poole the best, and also her husband Doctor Poole. The couple had won a competition and the prize was a two-week stay at the resort. The funny thing was that they actually lived in Hampton Cove, so they were already familiar with the resort. In fact, Kimmy had been to see Doctor Poole once upon a time when she was suffering from persistent stomach pains, and he had been so nice to her—not like the doctors she had met during her time at university this past year. She and her twin sister Kitty were sharing a dorm room, even though they had different majors. They had been inseparable since birth, and even now that they were going to college they were still inseparable.

"I really wish Mom would change her mind," she told her sister as they took a break from their grueling schedule. The kids were playing in the pool and even though they should be keeping them busy with games and whatnot, they did NOT have the ENERGY!

"She shouldn't have done this to us," Kitty agreed. "She shouldn't have tricked us into this lousy job."

"Even the pay is lousy."

"I don't care about the pay. I care about my mental health," said Kitty. "If this keeps up much longer, I'm not going to survive, I can tell you that right now!"

"You're right. This is child abuse and we should probably sue Mom. Take her to court."

"They'll side with her. Judges ALWAYS side with the parents. It's SO not fair!"

Kimmy closed her eyes for a moment. Lying on the chaise lounge was all she was capable of right now, and she was glad for the respite. "I think we should tell Dad."

"Tell him what, exactly?"

"That Mom tricked us! And then he can talk to her and…"

"And what? Do you really think Mom will listen to Dad, of all people?"

Their parents had recently split up, after Dad had decided that he wanted to be a rock star. It hadn't gone well, and in the end he had to abandon his crazy dream and find himself another job since he had left the well-paying one he had to move to Nashville. What he hadn't counted on was that he didn't have one ounce of talent. He couldn't sing, he couldn't play an instrument—nothing. He figured most rock stars didn't play an instrument either, and that you didn't have to be able to sing to make a career as a singer. It was the most ridiculous thing, and Mom hadn't taken kindly to Dad's midlife crisis. Since the big crisis in their marriage, Dad had come to his senses and had begged Mom to take him back, but Mom had been implacable and so now the couple's divorce was final, and both parents had gone their separate ways, with Mom dating an architect and Dad dating a woman ten years his junior who also had dreams of being something—the girls didn't know what exactly, but if you heard her explain, she was going to make it big.

Well, good for her. As long as she didn't bother them with it, it was fine with the girls.

"Will you look at that," said Kitty.

Kimmy opened her eyes. "What?"

"It's Grace's crazy great-grandmother. She and that funny-looking friend of hers."

Kimmy glanced in the direction her sister was pointing and saw that Vesta Muffin and her friend Scarlett Canyon had dressed to impress, Scarlett with a skimpy bikini that didn't leave a lot to the imagination, and her friend in the kind of bathing suit that used to be popular in the nineteenth century. It didn't show one inch of skin and covered the woman from head to toe. She looked like a penguin. Kimmy grinned. "We should take a picture. Add it to our Insta."

She and Kitty had started an Insta chronicling their summer from hell, with pictures of all the amazing things they encountered at the resort. Their mom had told them they couldn't post pictures of people without their permission, but that hadn't stopped the girls from going ahead and doing exactly that.

"This is too cool," said Kitty as she discreetly snapped a couple of pictures of the strange pair. "I can't believe they're friends. They're so different."

"They're the exact same age," said Kimmy. "Can you believe it?"

"If I were allergic to the sun, like Grace's great-grandma is, I'd simply stay inside."

"Now where's the fun in that?" said Kimmy with a grin as she snapped a couple more pictures and added a video to the mix.

At least they'd have plenty of hits on their Insta if they kept this up. Behind the two old ladies, a very large man came waddling past. He was so red in the face that he looked ready to explode, and Kimmy winced. "Ouch," she said.

Grace came climbing out of the pool and hurried up to them and jumped straight onto the chaise lounge, splashing Kimmy with water from the pool. "Kimmy!" she yelled as she slung her arms around Kimmy's neck.

"Grace!" she yelled back as she hugged the little girl. "Where's your grandpa and grandma?"

Grace pointed to the other side of the pool, where Doctor Poole and his wife were enjoying a leisurely time in the shade of a large umbrella. They weren't taking any chances and had been very diligent in applying sunblock every hour, on the hour, and extending the courtesy to their granddaughter—a wise practice.

"Timmy splashed me," Grace complained.

"Did he now?" said Kimmy, as she sought out the annoying little brat. Ever since Grace had arrived at the resort, the kid, who was a year older than she was, had singled her out for a campaign of harassment akin to bullying. And in spite of numerous warnings from both Kimmy and Kitty, he seemed determined to keep it up until his vacation was over.

"I'll talk to him again, all right," she promised the little girl.

Grace nodded. "He's not nice!"

"No, he certainly isn't," said Kimmy.

"He says I look like a jellyfish."

"Where does he get that idea?"

Grace shrugged and held up her hands in an exaggerated fashion. "I don't know," she said in that comical way of hers.

"If he keeps this up, I'll have to talk to his parents," said Kimmy. "And remove him from the group. He won't like that."

Grace shook her head. "He's the leader of the group. And I'm his slave," she said. "But I don't *want* to be Timmy's slave!"

"Poor girl," said Kimmy. "Who wants to be anybody's slave?"

"Not me!"

"Why don't we talk to him now," Kimmy suggested.

Grace nodded. "Tell him I'm not his slave?"

"I'll tell him that and a lot more," said Kimmy, determined to put an end to this nonsense once and for all.

And so she took the little girl's hand and together they walked to the edge of the pool. She saw Timmy the Menace lording it over a small group of kids, acting all tough and in charge. But when he saw Kimmy standing there with Grace, he piped down quickly. She hooked her finger and told him to get out of the pool. Meekly, he swam over.

"Did you tell Grace that she is your slave?" she asked.

"I did not!" he said.

"You did too!" said Grace.

"And did you tell her that she looks like a jellyfish?"

"Well, she does look like a jellyfish," said Timmy. "In that bathing suit of hers. It's blue and purple, just like a jellyfish."

"Listen here, Timmy," said Kimmy as she crouched down, "you can't say these things, all right? And you can't tell anyone that they're your slave. So are you going to behave from now on, or do you want me to tell your mom and dad?"

The kid got a sort of mutinous look on his face that she knew all too well. "I never said that she is my slave," he insisted.

"You did!" said Grace. "You said I'm your slave and I should do what you tell me to and that if I don't do what you tell me to you're going to punish me by turning me from a jellyfish into a toad!"

He shrugged. "Says you."

"It's true!" A triumphant smile came over the little girl's face. "I've got witnesses."

"Oh, yeah? Who?"

Grace pointed to a pair of cats who were sitting in the shade of the umbrella protecting Grace's grandparents from the blazing sun. "They saw the whole thing!"

Timmy looked incredulous. "They're cats!"

"So? They'll back me up."

"Okay, look here," said Kimmy, who was getting tired of this argument. "If you don't stop harassing Grace, I'm going to talk to your parents, and you won't be part of this group anymore. Is that understood?"

Timmy looked disappointed. "But I don't *want* to be kicked out of the group!"

"Then see that you behave from now on."

He nodded unhappily. "Oh, all right."

"So what do we say?" Kimmy prompted.

The kid grimaced, as if he was being put through the most horrible torment.

"Timmy?"

"I'm sorry, all right?" he said. "I'm sorry I called you a jellyfish."

"I'm *not* a jellyfish," Grace insisted.

"Can I go now?" asked Timmy.

"Yes, but don't make me have to talk to you again."

He shook his head and let himself fall back into the water with a big splash. Moments later, he was playing again with an energy and zest for the game that made Kimmy feel tired simply from watching.

"Thank you, Kimmy," said Grace as she gripped her hand tightly and gave it a vigorous shake.

"You're very welcome, Gracey," she said. "And if he does it again, you come to me immediately, all right? This was his final warning."

She watched as Grace hurried around the pool and jumped up onto her grandmother's chaise lounge, knocking the thick novel Marge had been reading from her grip. "I'm not a jellyfish!" she yelled, causing Marge to give Kimmy a look of bewilderment.

As Kimmy returned to her own chaise lounge, she saw from the corner of her eye that her mom had exited the resort and was on her way over. And so she sighed deeply, made eye contact with her sister, and the two girls took up their position in the pool to do more of that entertaining and monitoring they had been hired to do.

God. This was going to be one LOOOOOONG summer!!!!!!

CHAPTER 2

Vesta had watched the altercation between her great-granddaughter Grace and this annoying little punk with a kindling eye. If it was up to her, she would have dragged that little brat out of the pool and given his buttocks a good thrashing, but since her daughter had told her not to get involved, she couldn't, so she simply simmered. According to Marge, the two girls the resort had hired as monitors had the whole situation well in hand, though Vesta had her doubts about that. Those girls looked like teenagers themselves and seemed to prefer lounging around the pool instead of getting into the weeds with the group of kids they were supposed to be entertaining. But what did she know?

"Those twins are laughing at us," Scarlett informed her. "I just know they are. Every time they see us, they can't stop giggling like crazy and snapping pictures of us."

"So what?" said Vesta. "Let them laugh all they want. Wait till they're our age. Let's see if they will still be laughing."

"It's this bikini," said Scarlett as she inspected the tiny piece of fabric that barely managed to contain her ample assets. "I know I shouldn't have believed Ira when she told me it's the latest in fashion."

"What does Ira know about fashion?" she said. "Have you seen the way she dresses? If that's the latest fashion, my name is Kim Kardashian, and it's not, so it isn't."

"At least it's getting me a lot of attention from Sylvester," said Scarlett.

Sylvester McCade was the yoga teacher, and since he was the hottest male at the resort, they both immediately had fallen for the man. Unfortunately he seemed impervious to their charms.

"I think Sylvester's taken," she informed her friend. "By one of those twins over there."

Scarlett made a face. "What do these girls have that I don't?" she complained.

"Youth, for one thing." It was always the same thing, wasn't it? No matter how old they were, men always preferred youth. But then she had long ago given up on males. It was better that way. Better for her peace of mind, and her friendship with Scarlett.

"I think Sylvester is a fool," Scarlett grumbled. "Hot as hell, but a darn fool."

"I just hope that kid won't bully Grace anymore," she said as she cut a dirty look at Timmy Cooper. He had received a good talking-to from Kimmy, though it could have been Kitty, as the two girls looked so much alike it was impossible to keep them apart.

"He won't bother her anymore," said Scarlett. "I just heard Kimmy tell him that if he doesn't behave, she will kick him out of the group and also tell his parents."

"Mh. Kids like that need more than idle threats to change their ways," she said. "They need a lesson that can only be applied with a flat hand to a receptive bottom."

"Vesta!" said Scarlett with a laugh. "Corporal punishment went out of style years ago, or haven't you been told?"

"Too bad," she said. "I wouldn't mind corporally punishing that horrible little punk to within an inch of his life."

"Well, don't," said Scarlett. "We have more important things to do."

They watched as their friend Denice Sutt came walking up, a pep in her step, carrying that oversized beach bag she always liked to lug around. They had met Denice only a couple of days ago and already Vesta felt as if they'd known the woman all their lives. Which is why they had pretty much from the get-go confided in her about the important mission they had embarked upon at the resort. And since Denice was alone there and seemed bored out of her skull, she had asked if she could assist them in their inquiries.

"So what's new?" asked Denice as she took the third chaise lounge and spread her bony frame with relish.

"Nothing new," said Scarlett.

"No more thieving?" asked Denice, and almost seemed disappointed.

When resort management had asked Vesta's son Alec if he could look into a spate of thefts at the resort, he had unfortunately been forced to decline, citing lack of manpower. But then he'd had a most original solution to the problem that the Wheeler family, who owned the resort, were faced with: a sneak thief who had been robbing their guests at every possible opportunity. And so he had suggested that the neighborhood watch make themselves useful by going undercover at the resort and catching this nasty crook.

Grace Wheeler had agreed, and had offered them the full package: a room all to their own, three meals a day at the popular restaurant, and all they had to do was mingle with the guests and find out who could possibly be targeting the resort's upscale clientele.

In other words: the best assignment ever, and they had Alec to thank for it.

As luck would have it, Vesta's daughter Marge and Marge's husband Tex had won a two-week stay at the resort, all expenses paid, so it was like a family gathering. And now that they had Denice on their team, who was a veteran of staying at the resort, it wouldn't be long before they caught the culprit. Though as Scarlett had told Vesta, hopefully they wouldn't catch him too soon. Not before they had taken full advantage of all the amenities the resort had to offer its discerning guests, of which there were many this season.

"You know what we should have done?" said Scarlett. "We should have told Sylvester McCade that we're wealthy widows. I'm sure it would have made all the difference."

"Who's a healthy widow?" asked Denice, who was a little hard of hearing.

"We should have told Sylvester that we are wealthy widows," said Scarlett, raising her voice, but not too much, lest the hot yoga teacher overheard them talking about him. "Then maybe he would have shown more interest in getting acquainted with us."

Understanding dawned on Denice's face. "He's your fancy man, isn't he?"

"I wish!" said Scarlett. "There's too much competition, Denice."

Pretty much all of Sylvester's pupils were middle-aged or old ladies, and all of them were more interested in watching the man contort his most gorgeous physique into all kinds of strange positions than in actually learning yoga, a sport Vesta didn't know why it was so popular, as it was utterly and completely pointless, not to mention mind-numbingly boring. In fact, it was so boring she had trouble staying awake through most of the movements. If it hadn't been for Sylvester, she would have given up after the first day.

Grace Wheeler had told them to infiltrate as many groups as possible, so they might catch the thief, but so far they hadn't had any luck. Even Denice, who had been coming to the resort for twenty-five years or more, said she was stumped.

The thief always used the same modus operandi. He broke into the rooms of his victims while they were spending time at the pool or on the beach, and absconded with money, jewelry, watches, or phones—anything that he could find that might be of value. So far this season five people had reported being robbed, and if this kept up news might spread that the resort couldn't protect its guests from this persistent and pernicious thief.

"We probably should be patrolling the rooms again," said Scarlett after she had applied lipstick to her lips and checked her appearance in the compact she always carried with her.

Vesta sighed. It was one aspect of the job she didn't like: at all hours of the day and night they were forced to patrol the area where the rooms were located, making sure no funny business was taking place. She had that much in common with Kimmy and Kitty that she'd much rather lie back on her lounger, close her eyes, and let sleep take over.

But since she was a conscientious person, and they were there to do a job, she dragged herself up from the chaise lounge and followed her two accomplices as they set foot into the resort proper to do another tour of the building. The resort had security, of course, and also cameras that covered every nook and cranny, but so far the thief had proven more clever than any security measures management had been able to come up with.

Whoever this thief was, he was definitely a formidable foe, and frankly, Vesta was starting to get really curious to discover who it might be. Her money was on a young man who was limber enough to slither along the roof and slip into the rooms through the windows and then out again—unseen and unnoticed by anyone.

In other words: a cat burglar. Young, craven and absolutely brazen.

Which is why they had agreed with Bea Wheeler that they probably should take up vigilance at night and move their operation to the roof, where the sneak thief preyed on his targets. Now if only she could get enough sleep to last through a night...

CHAPTER 3

When Odelia had suggested that we assist Gran and Scarlett with their investigation at the resort, my first inclination had been to respectfully decline. After all, a beach resort is no place for a self-respecting cat, what with all the water and the sand and all of that—but then Odelia had insisted and said it was very important that the watch have eyes and ears all over the resort so we could catch the thief. And so we had decided we couldn't say no.

Which is how we came to be lounging underneath a pair of chaise lounges occupied by Marge and Tex. It's not just the sun I object to, considering it's probably not a good idea for any cat to bask in those lethal death rays it projects, but also the presence of so many people all traipsing about, not to mention plenty of kids with water pistols and a penchant for spraying unsuspecting people—and cats—with chlorinated water from the pool.

I don't know what it is about a resort that brings out the worst in people, but it does. All around us there was yelling and screaming and people jumping into the water and splashing about as if their lives depended on it. It certainly wasn't the kind of place I would have selected for a relaxing vacation, but Marge and Tex seemed to like it, and so did Grace, and even Gran and Scarlett, even though they were supposed to be on the job.

"Is it just me or are Scarlett and Gran spending way too much time by the pool?" asked Harriet, who had noticed the same phenomenon.

"They should be out there looking for this thief," Brutus grumbled. Like the rest of us, he hated the heat and the noise and the pungent all-pervasive smell of sunblock SPF 50.

"I'm sure they have a strategy," said Dooley. "Knowing Gran, she will have this all worked out, and it's only a matter of time before she catches this horrible thief."

"And I think that she wants to drag this out as much as she can," said Harriet. "After all, the longer it takes to catch this person, the more time they can spend at this five-star resort, all expenses paid."

"Too bad Odelia and Chase didn't win a two-week vacation here," said Dooley. "Otherwise the whole family would have been together."

"And I hope it won't take much longer to catch this thief," I said. "Frankly I'm tired of having to watch kids play in the pool, and bully Grace."

It had been a distressing aspect of our stay at the resort that Grace, our human's daughter, had met her foe in the form of a buck-toothed kid named Timmy Cooper. He seemed to have selected her as the victim of a power game and had called her names no little girl likes to be called: lizard brain, slug head, frog turd were some of the nicer ones. It certainly wasn't what Grace had expected when she joined her grandparents for this vacation. The monitors, a pair of twins named Kimmy and Kitty, had been firm with

Timmy, but not firm enough. The moment their backs were turned, the whole thing started again, and I, for one, didn't like it one bit. Normally, Grace was quite capable of taking care of herself, but this kid was a head taller than she was, and she wasn't equipped to deal with him.

We had already told Marge, and she had been keeping an eye on things, but short of physically removing Timmy from the equation—'whack him,' as Gran had suggested with her usual subtlety—there wasn't a lot even she could do. She had tried to inform the kid's parents, hoping to burden them with the responsibility of restraining the miniature bully, but it would appear they were nowhere to be found, having left their son to the twins, who weren't all that interested in running a tight ship.

"They're leaving," said Dooley, gesturing in the direction of Gran and Scarlett, who had just gotten up from their chaise lounges and were heading indoors. They were accompanied by a third old lady they had made the acquaintance of only days ago. Denice Sutt had quickly become part of the troupe, and it wouldn't have surprised me if Gran was going to formally invite the woman to join the watch. Denice was a veteran resort visitor and knew the lay of the land. In other words, if anyone could offer some practical advice to catch this thief in the act, it was her.

"We should probably follow them," said Harriet with a yawn. Even though we had found a spot in the shade, the heat had caused the four of us to experience a debilitating sense of drowsiness, and even though duty called, I was reluctant to heed its message.

In the end, we decided it was probably cooler inside, and so we trotted off after Gran and her co-watch members, hoping to be instrumental in catching the dastardly thief.

We followed the three ladies into the resort and through

the restaurant, where a couple of happy souls were ordering cocktails before they headed out again to enjoy their poolside experience. Before long, we were traversing the corridors of the resort, where the inmates had been put for their allocated time. It was a tedious job, but someone had to do it. According to the security person at the resort, most of the thefts occurred either during the daytime, when the residents were at the pool or the beach and their rooms were empty, or at night, with the brazen thief sneaking in and absconding with the guests' personal items while they slept. Talk about taking a huge chance. But then this thief had all the hallmarks of a master criminal and had been at this game for weeks. All in all, it was a miracle that he hadn't been caught yet, in spite of the vigilance and the concerted efforts of resort management, which rested in the hands of the Wheeler family: Bea Wheeler and her three daughters Lauren, Jill, and Grace, who ran the place together.

"There has to be a better way to go about this," Scarlett lamented. She had wrapped herself in a fleecy sundress, and with her oversized sunglasses looked the perfect tourist.

Gran, who had bought a bathing suit that covered every possible inch of skin, looked more like a diver, and Denice, with her sensible shoes, sensible leggings, and sensible oversized T-shirt, seemed like the most sensible of all, though the hat she had placed on the top of her head gave her the appearance of a scarecrow—not the kind of fashion statement one wants to make at a luxury resort like the Hampton Cove Resort & Spa.

"I keep telling you we should sleep during the day and patrol the place during the night," said Denice. "It's the only way to catch this thief. He won't show his face during the day because he knows that the watch is keeping an eye out for him. So that only leaves the night, his favorite time to break into people's rooms and steal their valuables."

"It's too hot to sleep," said Gran. "And besides, I can't sleep during the day. It goes against my biorhythm."

"What's a biorhythm?" asked Denice.

"Well, *the* biorhythm," said Gran. "You know."

Denice eyed her strangely. "Is it a vegetarian thing?"

"Can you explain it to Denice, Scarlett?" said Gran, who didn't have the patience to launch into a long explanation on any topic.

Scarlett had taken out her phone and had called up Google, that panacea for any discerning seeker of truth and wisdom. "Um… it's also referred to as a person's biological clock?"

"Oh, I know all about the biological clock!" said Denice, nodding. "Everybody has one, right? And it's important that you don't get it all messed up. Take me, for instance. If I don't go to bed every night at the exact same time, I get very grumpy in the morning."

"Same here," said Gran. "Which is why I don't feel like staying up all night just so we can catch this guy." She gestured to one of the cameras suspended from the ceiling. "This place is full of cameras and still they can't catch this fella? How is that even possible?"

"It's not," Denice agreed. "But he's still at it, so they must be doing something wrong. I mean, are you sure these cameras are even working? Maybe they're just dummies."

"Or maybe they're working, but nobody monitors them," said Scarlett. "It's often the case. They just put them up for show, to scare off potential thieves. But they don't want to pay an actual person to actually monitor all the feeds. Plus, it's a pretty boring job."

"I talked to the guy in charge of security," said Gran. "And he assures me all of their cameras are in perfect working order. So either he's lying or this thief is really, really good."

"Maybe it's the invisible man," Scarlett quipped.

"Or he's using an invisibility cloak," said Harriet. "Like in Harry Potter, remember?"

"I don't think an invisibility cloak actually exists, Harriet," said Brutus.

"I know that, pookie," she said, a little annoyed that he wouldn't have understood she was only kidding. "But there must be some explanation why he keeps breaking into people's rooms and nobody has caught him on camera yet."

"Gran's theory is probably the most plausible one," I said. "He's some kind of cat burglar who scales the walls and enters the rooms through the windows, unseen by the cameras that aren't anywhere inside the rooms."

"Too bad," said Brutus. "They probably should put a camera in every room—or maybe even more than one. That way they'd catch him soon enough."

"It's privacy," said Harriet. "People don't like it when they film them in their rooms."

"They should," said Brutus. "It's only to keep them safe."

"Maybe they can install hidden cameras?" Dooley suggested. "You know, like behind the mirrors and inside the light bulbs and all of that? That way the guests won't even know they're being watched?"

Harriet smiled. "There's such a thing as privacy laws, Dooley," she said. "I'm sure that the moment the guests find out, they'd make short shrift of those cameras."

"But they wouldn't know, would they?" said Dooley. "And so they won't complain."

It all seemed ethically iffy to me, but maybe Dooley had a point. If this thief was so very clever to have been able to steal from people's rooms for weeks without being caught, something needed to be done. Something right outside of the normal rule book. If the thief wasn't going to play fair and square, maybe we shouldn't either. But since it wasn't our call, instead I simply kept up a high level of vigilance, which was a little hard since all I wanted at that moment was to continue my very nice nap.

I may be a detective, but first and foremost I'm a cat, and as a prominent member of the feline tribe, I love a nice long nap!

CHAPTER 4

After their mother had intervened, the twins had made an effort to play some games with the group they had under their wing, but since most of the kids preferred to play in the pool, their good intentions had quickly petered out. Both of them were checking their phones while enjoying ice cream, courtesy of a waiter who had a crush on them—a feeling that wasn't reciprocated since he was definitely too nerdy for either of the girls. Besides, they had known him all their lives since they were the exact same age, and Kitty vividly remembered he had pasted a booger on her cheek back when they were kids together. She still hadn't forgiven him and distinctly remembered the slimy sensation on her cheek, his grubby hand, and his gummy smile. You don't come back from something like that.

As she studied a TikTok video of a frog dancing in the rain with an umbrella, she couldn't help but overhear their neighbor talking on his phone.

"Yeah, I need one, Demetrius," he was saying. "I need a hot dog ASAP. If I don't get one very soon now, I'm going to freak out, you hear me." He listened for a moment. "I know it's not safe," he said, trying to keep his voice down. "But you gotta help me out here, bro. I need it. Capisce? Yeah, I'm still at the resort."

She glanced over and saw that it was Greg Lonsdale, who was something of a minor celebrity. He was staying at the resort with his wife and their son Clyde, who was around the twins' age. Cute but boring had been their assessment, though if it was true that his dad was richer than all the other guests combined, maybe they should have another assessment. Especially as the kid seemed to have the hots for her—or maybe for Kimmy. Like a lot of people, he couldn't distinguish one twin from the other, which was pretty hilarious. Even their own mom sometimes couldn't tell them apart, or their dad.

"Okay, so get me the stuff—and fast," the guy hissed, then hung up, glancing around nervously. He grabbed his tote and got up, possibly to meet his hot dog dealer.

Kitty elbowed her sister. "What?" asked Kimmy lazily.

"Did you hear that?" she whispered.

"Yeah, the guy ordered a hot dog. So what?"

"I'm sure 'hot dog' is simply code for something else entirely," she said. "Did you see how nervous he was and how desperate he was to get his hands on that 'hot dog'?"

Kimmy looked up. "So what do you think he meant?"

"Drugs, of course. And he's going to have it delivered here at the resort."

Kimmy made a face. "I hate it when they do that. Order drugs as if it's pizza."

"Yeah, I'm surprised that he would be into that stuff," said Kitty with a thoughtful frown. "Do you think Clyde knows?"

"That his dad is a drug addict? Wouldn't surprise me if he did. That kid's got layers, Kitty, I'm telling you."

Kitty smiled. "You keep telling yourself that."

"No, but he does. He's like an onion. You can keep peeling away and you'll discover stuff that you never thought you'd find."

"And I happen to think he's as shallow as a tide pool."

"He's a layer cake," Kimmy insisted. "Or an onion."

"I prefer layer cake."

Kimmy grinned. "Don't tell me you've got the hots for Clyde?"

She scoffed. "As if!"

"He's handsome, and he's filthy rich. What more do you want?"

"How about some intellectually stimulating conversation?"

Kimmy shrugged. "You can't have everything. Rich and handsome is good enough for me. If you want scintillating conversation you should date a nerd."

"So if he makes his move you'd go for it, is that what you're saying? With a dad who's a drug addict and a mom who looks as if she fell into a bath filled with Botox?"

Kimmy wavered. "I don't mind the Botox, but I do mind the drugs. Are you sure that hot dog is code for dope?"

"Pretty sure," said Kitty.

"Too bad." She thought for a moment. "Maybe we can ask Clyde himself."

"Better not," Kitty advised. "You don't want to get involved in a family row. I mean, if he doesn't know, and you tell him, it might kick off a big stink."

"Yeah, I guess you're right." She sighed and picked up her phone again. "Is this what our summer vacation is going to look like? Watching guests order dope on their phones and handling annoying brats like Timmy? While a thief is stealing from the guests?"

Kitty sat up with a jerk. Her sister's words had galvanized her. "You know what? You're absolutely right, sis."

"About what? About the annoying brats? The addicts? Or the fact that we're wasting our time while we could have been in Paris right now, having the time of our lives?"

"About the thief. You know what we should be doing? Trying to catch that thief."

"But aren't those crazy old ladies doing that already?"

"Do you really see them ever catching a thief? They're probably in the spa right now, enjoying a facial. No, if anyone is going to catch that thief, it's us. So let's get off our lazy behinds and do something useful for a change. And let's start by looking into Sylvester."

Kimmy's eyebrows shot up into her fringe. "You think Sylvester is the thief?"

"I'll bet he is. Plus, it will give us a chance to get close to the guy."

A slow grin spread across her sister's face. "I like your thinking, sis."

And since the plan seemed solid, they both got up and went in search of the hot yoga teacher. The kids could look after themselves—they didn't need them. And if they did, they had their parents to take care of them.

After all, what could be more important than catching a thief?

CHAPTER 5

The twins had gone in search of Sylvester, but what they found was Clyde. The kid seemed determined to talk to them, and since they couldn't shake him, Kimmy decided to put him out of his misery by giving him five minutes of her time. And so, while Kitty went in search of the yoga teacher, who seemed to have vanished without a trace, she settled down next to the cooling fountain, one of the most popular features of the resort, and let her hand trail in the water. Kids were jumping through the spray and having a grand old time while their parents sat in the shade of a nearby tree and kept an eye on them.

"So what have you been up to?" asked Clyde.

"Oh, this and that," she said as she watched a little girl with braces and glasses getting soaking wet while she hunkered down over the fountain. It was one way to stay cool on a hot day, and she wished she had the nerve to follow the kid's example.

"I saw that you and your sister are on babysitting duty again?"

She grinned. "Yeah, you can say that. Though Mom

prefers to call it entertaining the guests' kids. But babysitting is pretty much what it boils down to."

"I don't think I could do it," he confessed as he studied his sandal, which was of the extremely expensive variety, she saw. Clyde might be boring, but he sure had good taste, and the budget to fund it. "Looking after a couple of brats all day? I couldn't do it."

"I can't do it either," she said. "But needs must and all of that."

"*I* could hire you," he suggested.

She laughed. "Hire us! To do what exactly, Clyde?"

"Oh, I don't know. You could assist my dad. Dad loves a good assistant."

She made a face. "Wrangling your dad sounds even worse than wrangling those brats. So thanks but no thanks, Clyde."

"Fair enough. To be honest I wouldn't want to be my dad's assistant either."

Clyde's dad was a comedian who had mostly made his career on the stage, though he had later branched out by starring in his own TV show and also in a couple of hit movies. Kimmy had to admit that she had never seen anything the man was in, though.

"Is your dad as funny at home as he is on stage?" she asked.

"I wish. He's very strict. Doesn't let me do anything without supervision."

"Supervision! How old are you?"

"Seventeen, but he still seems to think I'm seven, the way he behaves sometimes. He's hyper-vigilant all the time, and doesn't let me out of his sight. Says we've all got targets on our backs because he's so famous and rich and successful, and if we're not careful some bad guys will try and abduct us and demand ransom for our release."

"It's possible," she said. "If he's as famous as you're making him out to be."

"Oh, he's famous, all right," Clyde assured her. "And since he's been doing this for such a long time he knows lots and lots of people in the business, so all of his friends are also actors and comedians."

"Are you a comedian?" asked Kimmy, her interest piqued.

"Nah, I'm not funny at all," said Clyde with a smile. "In fact, my dad doesn't stop telling me I'm probably the least funny person he has ever met. Tells me it's ridiculous for me, the son of a famous comedian, to be this unfunny."

"That's not a very nice thing to say."

Clyde shrugged. "My dad may be one of the funniest people on the planet, but that doesn't mean he's also a nice person. He can be really mean-spirited."

"I saw him just now," said Kimmy. "He was ordering hot dogs. Can you imagine? Ordering a hot dog on a hot day like today?" She watched the kid closely for a reaction.

Clyde winced. "I can't believe he's up to his old tricks again."

"What do you mean?"

"He's got this guy on speed dial. This hot dog guy. He's pretty much addicted to the stuff. Can't get enough of it. Even in a place like this, where the food is top-notch, he has to have his hot dog. Mom keeps telling him it's not normal, but he ignores her."

Kimmy relaxed. So maybe it wasn't drugs after all, but actual hot dogs. She had heard this story about a guy who was crazy about salami, and married to a vegetarian. So when his wife told him to go on a diet and stop eating meat, he started ordering salami in secret and sneaking out of the house to get it. She felt a little guilty about thinking that Clyde's dad was a drug addict now. There was nothing wrong with being addicted to hot dogs.

"Your mom doesn't happen to be a vegetarian, does she?"

"She is," said Clyde, looking surprised. "How did you know?"

"Oh, just a hunch," said Kimmy. "So what I wanted to talk to you about: have you heard about this thief that's been targeting the guests of the resort?"

Clyde's eyes went wide. "A thief? No, I hadn't heard."

"Yeah, this guy has been stealing from our guests for weeks now, and it's proving very hard to catch him. And so now my mom and her sisters have asked these two old ladies to look into it."

"What old ladies?" asked Clyde with a laugh.

"You may have seen them around. Vesta Muffin and Scarlett Canyon. They're part of the neighborhood watch and have caught a lot of crooks. Or at least that's what my mom told us. And so now they're undercover at the resort and will try and catch the thief."

"Your mom must be desperate," said Clyde.

"She is. Pretty much. So you wouldn't happen to have information that might help us catch this thief, would you?"

He shook his head. "This is the first I'm hearing of this."

"And your dad? He hasn't had anything stolen from his room?"

"Nope. Unless he has and he hasn't told me. He doesn't tell me everything."

"Oh, he's one of those, is he?"

"One of what?"

"One of those parents that don't confide in their kids. Kitty and I have one just like him. Our dad doesn't tell us anything either."

"What does he do, your dad?"

"Right now he doesn't do anything. He used to be an accountant, but that was before he quit his job because he wanted to become a rock star."

Clyde laughed. "A what?"

"Don't ask. Mom thinks it's a midlife crisis, but I'm not so sure. He's not even forty yet, so he can't be having a midlife crisis, can he? Kitty and I think he simply lost his mind. I mean, he can't sing. He doesn't play an instrument. And all of a sudden he told Mom he wanted a divorce because he felt she was holding him back from fulfilling his dream."

"So your folks are divorced, huh?"

"Yeah, the divorce came through last year. So now Mom is dating an architect and Dad is dating some woman who owns a diner. It's all one big mess, to be honest." The good thing was that Dad had moved back to Glen Falls, and since she and Kitty were based in New York, they were under no obligation whatsoever to go and pay him a visit. The upshot was that they hadn't seen their dad in months, and as far as she was concerned, it could stay that way. They say that kids often take sides in a divorce, and it was probably true, for she and Kitty had taken the side of their mom when Dad had lost his mind. If they never saw him again, it would be too soon. Then again, they probably couldn't avoid seeing him from time to time, as he was still their dad—much to their chagrin.

"My dad got punched in the face last year," said Clyde, and that made Kimmy look up in surprise.

"Punched in the face? You mean by a street mugger or something?"

"No, on stage, during some big award show. He was cracking a joke at some hapless actor's expense, and all of a sudden the actor mounted the stage and punched him in the face. In front of a couple of million people watching at home. It was pretty surreal."

"Okay, so you win," she said. "Hands down. My dad wanting to be a rock star and moving to Nashville can't hold a candle to your dad being punched in the face."

He took out his phone. "There's a video," he said, and

brought up a TikTok video of his dad on stage. It was just as he had said: all of a sudden this guy jumped the stage and threw a mean right hook. Clyde's dad went down hard. Then, cool as dammit, his attacker buttoned up his vest and returned to his seat and sat down as if nothing had happened.

It was the weirdest thing she had ever seen. Surreal, like Clyde had said.

"Oh, my God," she said as they watched the clip a couple of times. Someone had put a cheerful piece of music to the clip, and it played out like a joke, but she could imagine it hadn't been funny. "Were you in the audience?"

"I was, yeah. And I can tell you that Dad took it pretty bad, even though he acted as if he wasn't affected. You simply don't expect a thing like that to happen, do you?"

"No, I guess not," she said.

She looked up when her sister joined them. Kitty's eyes were shining. "I found him!"

And so she immediately said goodbye to Clyde and followed her twin. Clyde may have proven himself not to be as boring as she had thought he was, but he couldn't hold a candle to Hot Yoga Guy!

CHAPTER 6

After taking a refreshing dip in the pool, Marge decided to head inside to fetch a book from her room. What she loved most about going on vacation was the luxury of lounging by the pool and enjoying a nice beach read. Even though she was a librarian, and as such had a vast selection of books at her disposal, she found that she often didn't have as much time as she would have liked to get lost in a book. And so she had grabbed the top books from her 'to be read' pile to bring along with her to the resort after she and Tex had gotten the news that they had won a two-week stay. It was possibly the first time in her life that she had won anything, as mostly she was never that lucky and neither was her husband.

She headed inside and as she passed reception she was accosted by Hazel Heflin, who was the head of the booking desk at the resort. An elderly woman who was probably older than Marge's own mom, she was a self-declared book nut, and she and Marge had become fast friends in the short time she and Tex had been at the resort.

"I had a great idea, Marge," Hazel said, in that no-

nonsense way that she had. "I want you to organize our library." She placed a deft finger on Marge's collarbone as she said it, and from the forcefulness with which she spoke the words, it was clear that she had made the decision and brooked no contest.

"Okay, great," said Marge therefore. She had seen the tiny collection of books the resort carried and Hazel was right in that it was a pretty pitiful excuse for a library. Mostly it was books that guests brought, finished, and then dumped on the shelf so other guests could enjoy them. An eclectic mix of pretty much the most commercially available and popular stuff, it featured everything from Harry Potter to Nora Roberts, Danielle Steel, Janet Evanovich, and James Patterson, and everything in between.

"I mean, you *are* a librarian," Hazel pointed out.

"That's true," Marge conceded.

"A professional librarian."

"I've got the degree to prove it," said Marge.

"And you've been running the Hampton Cove library for how many years now?"

"Oh, I've lost count," said Marge. "So please don't remind me." Thinking back to how long she had been at the helm of their local library made her feel old, so she preferred not to go there. Not when she was on vacation anyway!

"Okay, so I was thinking that we probably should put some order to the thing," said Hazel. "Now it's basically just a pile of books. So what are your ideas, Marge?" She folded her arms across her ample chest and made Marge feel as if she was applying for a job.

She smiled. "Why don't we tackle this project together, you and I? I mean, I'm sure you've got some ideas, right?"

Hazel's face lit up. "Ideas! Oh, have I got ideas, young lady!"

And so they retreated to the woman's office, which was a

cozy mess, with papers strewn about and pictures of families with kids plastered on every available wall space.

"Looks like you've been doing this for a really long time," said Marge.

"I've been here forever," said Hazel, "and I'm not even exaggerating. I think I was probably one of the first hires when Bea's dad started this place. This was before her husband took over, and before Bea's daughters took over from him."

"So you've been working for three generations of the same family?"

"That's correct. Though I have to say that the latest generation is probably the best. Those girls are amazing. Bea's dad wasn't too bad either, but Lauren, Jill, and Grace have taken things to the next level. They've got the same passion for this place that their granddad had back in the day."

A man walked into the room sporting a bushy beard and a kind expression on his face. He grabbed a measuring tape from Hazel's desk and walked out again without a word.

"Cole Newman," Hazel said. "He's in charge of maintenance around here. And married to the big boss. Grace Wheeler? Now there's a cute story." And so she launched into an abbreviated history of the Hampton Cove Resort & Spa and all of its principals. It was a story fit for a novel of epic proportions, Marge thought, and probably better than the beach reads she had brought. She scratched the red spot on her elbow that had started itching again. And when one spot starts itching, you can bet your bottom dollar that all the others will wake up and start itching also, and that was exactly what happened now. Before long, she didn't have enough hands to scratch all the different spots.

Hazel eyed her with concern. "Bedbugs, huh?"

"Yeah, I don't know," said Marge. "At first, I thought they were mosquito bites, but Tex says they're too small to be mosquito bites. He thinks it's probably bedbugs too. Though when I went in search of the annoying beasts, I couldn't find them."

"They're a pest," Hazel confirmed. "I have the privilege of living in one of the bungalows on the terrain and even I've had to contend with them. Cole got me some bug spray, and since I've fumigated the entire bungalow I've seen a major improvement."

"Maybe you should organize something?" Marge suggested. "I've heard from several guests that they've been dealing with the same problem."

"I know," said Hazel. "And Grace is looking into it. They want to hire a professional exterminator who will take care of this pest once and for all. The problem is that they're so pernicious and hard to kill. You think they're gone, but then they pop up again."

"I hope Grace gets rid of them soon. Before they ruin my entire stay here."

Hazel nodded. "I'll take care of it. What's your room number again, Marge?" And when Marge had given it to her, she made a quick note, then turned to her computer and started typing a message. "There you go," she said. "The big boss has been informed. And trust me when I tell you that Grace is one of those can-do, make-it-happen kind of girls. So you should see some improvement real soon."

She certainly hoped so, for if there was one thing she hated, it was to be used as target practice by a bunch of voracious bugs night after night. She wasn't kidding when she said it was ruining her otherwise pleasant stay at the resort, and she wasn't alone in that.

As she walked out of Hazel's office and reached the lobby, she almost bumped into the wife of that well-known actor and comedian Greg Lonsdale. Elaine Lonsdale gave her a vague smile in greeting and hurried away again. As she did,

Marge saw that the poor woman's back was covered with red spots and remembered that she and Elaine had commiserated over their shared ordeal that morning during breakfast. It looked as if she was suffering from those annoying bugs even more than Marge was.

"Poor woman," Marge murmured and went up to her room to fetch that book she wanted.

CHAPTER 7

So far, we hadn't encountered any sneak thief, but then I couldn't imagine that traipsing along the corridors of the resort was a great strategy to catch a thief. Quite possibly, whoever was behind this crime wave was smarter than that. Otherwise, he would have been caught by now. The three old ladies didn't seem to agree with my assessment, as they were having a grand old time shooting the breeze and talking about the various ailments that plagued them and the possible remedies. Especially Gran was in fine fettle as she rattled off a list of solutions to arthritis after Denice complained that from time to time her right index finger would cramp up and her doctor couldn't suggest a good solution except to tell her she had to learn to live with it.

"I don't think this is very useful," said Harriet after a while. We had been following the three old ladies around for over an hour now, traversing corridors and going up and down stairs, and frankly, we'd all had enough. It wasn't just the fact that I was getting sore paws or that I hadn't had a bite to eat in quite a while, but also that the entire effort was futile. Even Gran herself had admitted it in so many words: no way was this thief dumb enough to steal something in front of a group of witnesses. And even if he was, the moment he clocked a threat, he would be out of there so fast we'd barely see a blur.

"I think we should call it quits," Brutus agreed with his girlfriend. "This isn't a good use of our time, you guys."

"But Gran says we have to patrol," said Dooley. "And Gran knows, since she's the leader of the watch."

"Let's get out of here," I said, deciding to overrule Dooley's minority vote as inconsequential. And besides, I felt a great nap coming on, and I didn't want to lose that window of opportunity.

As luck would have it, a familiar figure reached the top of the stairs, and when she saw us, she was as happily surprised to see us as we were to see her.

"Marge!" said Harriet. "Just the person we need!"

"Hey, you guys," she said quietly, glancing around to make sure nobody overheard her talking to us. "What are you doing here?"

"We're patrolling with Gran," I said.

"So far it's been an exercise in futility," said Brutus.

"But Gran is the leader of the watch," said Dooley, reiterating his earlier point. "And so we should do what she says."

"I'm tired," I said. "And hungry. You wouldn't happen to have a bite to eat, would you, Marge?"

Our human smiled. "Of course I do. Follow me."

And so we followed her.

It wasn't long before she was opening the door to Valhalla: a room where we could have a nice nap and also a bite to eat. It was all I needed at that moment, and frankly, I couldn't care less about this thief, who was probably also taking a nap and gathering his strength for a big night of stealing people's precious valuables.

"I wouldn't lie on the bed if I were you," said Marge as I made to jump onto the bed. "It's full of bedbugs. Unless they managed to get rid of them by now. But I doubt it."

"Bedbugs?" asked Dooley. "What are bedbugs?"

"They're tiny bugs that live in beds," said Marge, and it sounded plausible enough. "And they bite." She showed us her arm, and I saw a welter of small red spots.

"My God!" said Harriet. "What happened to you, Marge?"

"Did those bedbugs do that?" asked Brutus.

She nodded unhappily. "Tex got me a cream, so the itching isn't as bad as it was. But it's still pretty annoying." Then she seemed to get an idea. "Say, you guys couldn't have a chat with these bugs, could you? Maybe convince them to leave me in peace?"

"We could always try," I said, though if these bugs were as ferocious as she seemed to indicate, I didn't know if they would be receptive to our arguments.

But since Marge is possibly the nicest human in the world —with the notable exception of my very own human Odelia, of course, I decided to give it a shot.

And so I walked up to the bed, took a deep breath, and jumped right on top of it. For a moment, nothing happened, but then I spotted a tiny bug that seemed to have taken up sojourn there. It was lodged on the pillow and was probably waiting for an unsuspecting human to place their head there so it could take a nice big bite.

"Hey there," I said by way of greeting.

"Hey," said the bug with a touch of reticence, as if it wasn't all that happy to make my acquaintance.

"My name is Max," I said. "And that woman over there is Marge. She is my human, and she tells me that you've been biting her. Is that a fair representation of the facts, would you say?"

The bug glanced over at Marge and nodded. "It's possible

that I did have a nibble," he said. "Though I have to say I like the other one best."

"The other one? You mean Tex?"

The bug waved its arms. "No names, please. Us bedbugs prefer to use a group noun when referring to people like Marge."

"So what would you call her?"

"Well, food, of course."

"That simple, huh?"

"Personally, I have a slight preference for blood type O, but I'm not averse to any of the other blood types. As long as it's freshly squeezed and warm, straight from the vein, it's all gravy to me." The bug eyed me with interest. "What is your blood type, by the way?"

I recoiled a little. "You're not telling me I'm also part of your preferred foods?"

"Oh, I'm not averse to adding some variety to my diet. I like chicken, for instance, but I wouldn't mind adding cat to the menu. Variety is the spice of life, after all." It approached me with a distinct gleam in its eyes. "You're a nice specimen... Max, you say your name is?"

"Don't eat me!" I cried, suddenly apprehensive.

"I have no intention of eating you," said the bug. "Though if I could have a nibble, I wouldn't mind. I mean, it's one small drop for you, one giant meal for a bug my size."

"I prefer not," I said staunchly. "I don't like it when someone compromises the physical integrity of my body."

"Is that a fancy way of saying you don't like to be bitten, Max?"

"That's exactly right. Don't bite me, bug."

The bug sighed. "See, this is what we get all the time. Nobody wants to be bitten, but then when we can't survive they complain about the lack of biodiversity, and how they should bring back those ancient species that have gone extinct. You don't want me to go extinct, now do you, Max?"

"Well...."

"Oh, for crying out loud!" said the bug. "It's not a good look, Max. I mean, you should be applauding biodiversity. It's good for everyone, and that includes you. It's a richer, more diverse planet that we all want, right?"

"I... guess so," I said.

"Okay, so just a little nibble. I promise you won't feel a thing. I'm very gentle when I take a bite out of a person."

"But then why is Marge scratching herself all the time?" asked Dooley, who had also jumped up onto the bed.

"Is it my fault that she's allergic?" said the bug. "I mean, you can't really blame me for that, can you? She should probably work on her immunity, and not place the blame entirely on my doorstep. And besides, like I said, I prefer her husband, and *he* hasn't been scratching himself silly, has he?"

"I guess not," said Dooley.

Harriet and Brutus also joined the conversation. "Why is that, exactly?" asked Harriet.

"Because your Marge is allergic, and her husband isn't, that's why. So we can bite him all we want, and he won't develop those ugly bumps on his skin."

"So you're saying it's all Marge's fault, are you?" asked Brutus, and he didn't sound all that happy with the bug right now. Which was understandable, as Marge looked as if she had been attacked by dozens of the tiny bugs.

"Absolutely!" said the bug. "All she has to do is make sure her body doesn't react this way. It's all due to her immune system going haywire. And that's through no fault of mine, you guys." He didn't seem all that pleased to see the four of us squatting all over his domain, for he was starting to display signs of nervousness. "Say, you're not going to hang around here for much longer, are you? I mean, this is our territory now, not yours."

"This is Marge's bed," I said. "And since we're her cats, we can stay as long as we like."

The bug smiled. "Okay, fine by me. Maybe the four of you can have a nice long nap on the bed. I'll make sure to tell my friends and family not to harm a hair on your heads."

"Good," I said, well pleased that our little talk was starting to yield results.

"Your blood vessels, on the other hand," said the bug cheekily, "are fair game."

This caused the four of us to gulp a little, and I got the distinct impression that the moment we had lain down and closed our eyes, there would be a kind of free-for-all and we would be bitten to within inches of our lives by this bug and all of its buddies. In other words: it would be cat buffet time!

"How many of you are there?" I asked, glancing around to see if there were more where this bug came from.

"Oh, just a couple dozen," said the bug. "Or maybe more. Look, I was just kidding when I made that crack about your veins being fair game. You've got nothing to worry about. Just lie down, fellas. Have a nice, relaxing nap. Sleep as long as you like. I'll stand watch over you and make sure that none of my friends and family go anywhere near you."

Dooley seemed relieved. "Would you do that for us, bug? That's so nice."

"Absolutely," said the bug. "So just lie down... and relax."

"Don't do it!" cried another little bedbug, who now sprang from behind Marge's pillow. "He's lying! He's a big fat liar. He will—"

"Shut up, Lola," said the first bug viciously. He turned back to us. "Don't listen to her. She doesn't know what she's saying."

"He said you're a liar," I said.

"She's young and stupid," said the bug. "I mean, we've all been young, right?"

"I guess so," I said, eyeing the bug with suspicion.

"The moment you lie down, they'll attack!" said the other bug—the whistleblower, so to speak. "Don't lie down, Max! Run for your lives! Run!"

And since this bug seemed to know what she was talking about, we decided to jump down from the bed.

"Spoilsport!" the first bug hissed viciously. "How many times, Lola!"

"I just don't think this is us, Rico," said Lola. "We should rise above this vicious biting business."

"We're bedbugs!" Rico cried. "We feed on blood! What else are we going to do?"

"We could become vegetarians!" Lola suggested.

"What's next? Are you going to convince Dracula not to drink human blood anymore?"

"Absolutely!" said Lola. "I'm sure there are substitutes that are just as nutritious and full of the necessary vitamins and proteins as human blood—or cat blood in this case."

I gulped, and so did Dooley, Harriet, and Brutus. It looked like we'd had a narrow escape.

"So what's the verdict, Max?" asked Marge. "Have you managed to get rid of the bugs?"

"Um…" I said. "Not exactly?"

"But we did manage to escape from being bitten ourselves," said Dooley. "So that's a big win in my book, Marge!"

Marge sighed. "Looks like I will have to keep getting bitten over and over again."

"There has to be a way to get rid of these bugs," said Brutus, who doesn't like to admit defeat. "But how?"

"Bedbugs feed on the blood of mammals," I said. "So maybe we can find some alternatives for them to nibble on?"

"Like what?" asked Harriet. "Unless you want to find an innocent victim and put them here so they'll all go to them and leave Marge and Tex in peace?"

It certainly was a dilemma we were facing. Could we sacrifice one human to save another? It was one of those tough moral choices I wasn't feeling well-equipped to handle. In other words, what we needed right now was a philosopher. A person who could deal with an existential problem and tell us what to do. A wise person. A person like the Dalai Lama maybe, or the Pope. A person with the moral authority to do the right thing.

Just at that moment, the door opened and Gran walked in. "Hey, honey," she said, addressing her daughter. "Our friend Denice here is suffering from corns. You wouldn't happen to have a remedy, would you?"

Okay, since the Dalai Lama wasn't available, and neither was the Pope, we decided to consult with Gran. I mean, sometimes you have to work with what you've got, right?

CHAPTER 8

*E*laine had almost bumped into Marge Poole when she entered the lobby because she had been busy thinking about the tough conversation she had coming up. She had talked to her lawyer on the phone that morning, and he had told her that everything was in place and now all that was needed was for Elaine to finally pull the trigger and tell Greg that she wanted a divorce. And that was exactly the trouble right there: now that the time had come to put things in motion, she was feeling stymied by a sudden case of cold feet.

Chandra had told her that once she put things in motion, there was no going back. The divorce papers would be filed and before long the media would have the story. They'd run with it, and the whole world would know that Greg's marriage was over. Chandra had asked her if she was having second thoughts, and it wasn't that she had second thoughts about the divorce but more about all the attention it would garner—putting the spotlight on her. There would be questions, and she'd be inundated with phone calls from concerned friends and relatives. But more than all of that, what she feared the most was Greg's reaction.

The man had a vicious tongue, and he wouldn't for even a single moment hesitate to paint her in the darkest colors possible and launch a vicious attack on her character. It would affect their son, who wasn't in the best state of mind at the moment, and the whole thing would be like a nightmare that might last for weeks, months, or even years.

She sighed as she walked on, heading to her room so she could have a moment to herself to collect her thoughts. There were practical problems that needed to be tackled: where was she going to live and how was she going to live? Would Greg cut off her access to their joint bank account? Would she still be able to stay at the house or did she have to move out? Even Chandra hadn't been able to reassure her, except to say she was going to do her utmost to land the best deal possible for her client—and for Clyde, of course.

It would have been so much better if she'd been able to build a career. At least she would have been financially independent and wouldn't be on such shaky ground. She had been a successful photographer. But when she married Greg, he had immediately told her that there could only be one star in the family and that was him. He had persuaded her to drop her own career and support his. It had led to him becoming a star, that was true enough, but it had also caused her to become a nobody. An appendage. A mother and wife, which were important roles for any woman to fulfill, but hadn't nearly been enough, especially considering that Greg could be extremely caustic and didn't stint on the insults, jibes, and recriminations when he felt she didn't do enough to shine the spotlight on him.

The truth was that the man was a narcissist. Too bad it had taken her until after Clyde had been born to find out. And by then, she was so thoroughly enmeshed in her husband's life and career that it was difficult to get out. She had worked as his publicist for many years, always staying in the background and making sure she didn't overstep her role. In the meantime, she had borne the sole responsibility for raising their son, something Greg felt was a woman's role, with him adopting a hands-off approach to fatherhood.

Now that Clyde was ready to go off to college and stand on his own two feet, Elaine felt that it was finally time for her to extricate herself from her husband and the toxic marriage she had entered and start her own life again.

Now if only she could work up the courage to tell Greg…

* * *

NEXT DOOR TO ELAINE, and unbeknownst to her, another man was deep in thought about the amazing coincidence of him staying at the exact same resort as his nemesis Greg Lonsdale. Dejuan Daly was the actor who had accosted Greg on stage a year ago, punching the comedian's lights out and in doing so, blowing up his own career. He hadn't had a single work offer since, and would have been in financial dire straits if his girlfriend hadn't taken over as breadwinner, due to her position as general manager of a small but successful chain of whole food stores in Wisconsin. He had been helping her out with the business, and by now had buried his dream of returning to the screen—big or small.

In the wake of the incident, he had lost his agent, his manager, and his reputation, and become the punchline of countless jokes. The punch that he had thrown on that fateful night had been turned into thousands of memes that were ubiquitous now. It had cemented Greg's reputation as a no-holds-barred comedian and sunk Dejuan's career prospects.

"I can't believe this," he said as he paced the room. "Of all the resorts in all the towns in all the world, we have to arrive at the exact same resort Greg Lonsdale is staying at. I mean, what are the chances?"

Tawanna, who had been seated on the bed, didn't seem affected whatsoever by this strange coincidence that was wrecking her boyfriend's equanimity to such an extent. The only thing that was bothering her were the bedbugs that had done a number on her otherwise smooth skin.

"You can't let this idiot affect you, Dejuan," she said, not for the first time. "What's done is done. You need to get on with your life. And that includes facing the guy. So are you ready to walk out there with me right now? Or do you want to lock yourself up in our room the whole trip?"

"Is that an option?" he said, only half in jest.

"No, it is not," she said, shaking her head adamantly. "You need to face Greg at some point, Dejuan. So let's get it over with and get out there, all right?"

Dejuan was standing at the hotel room window, which offered a perfect view of the pool area. His nemesis was lounging by the pool, tapping away on his phone, the busy and wildly successful actor that he still was—probably fielding offers from the big studios to do the kind of movies that at one point Dejuan would have been in the running for.

He was shaking his head. The last thing he wanted was to go out there and face that man.

"Prove to him that your court-ordered therapy paid off," Tawanna urged.

After the punch that reverberated around the world, Greg had filed a complaint against him, and the whole thing had ended up in court, with Dejuan being convicted of assault and sentenced to community service and therapy. It hadn't been as bad as he'd expected, except for the part where his career had crashed with a dull thud. The only good thing that had come out of the entire episode was his relationship with

Tawanna. She had stood by him, even though he had fully expected her to bail on him, just like all of his friends had done. But instead she had pulled him through, which had been quite amazing.

"So you think I should just go out there and face this guy?" he said.

"Of course! Absolutely. Don't you remember what the therapist said?"

He nodded. "That the therapy would only be considered complete when I finally would be able to face my nemesis and he couldn't succeed in getting a rise out of me?"

"Exactly! He did this to you once, babe. Don't take the bait this time."

"Maybe he's changed? Maybe he's not the jerk he used to be?"

"I wouldn't bet on it. In his latest show, he spent ninety minutes lambasting both his wife and his agent. If he abuses the people he loves to such an extent, I can only imagine what he has to say about casual acquaintances and former colleagues like you."

He and Greg had been friends at one point, until the man had walked onstage and used him as the butt of a joke. It was his thing. Greg liked to use his nearest and dearest as the subject of his vicious sense of humor. "He doesn't mean it like that," people said. "Deep down he's a great guy." But Dejuan knew that Greg meant it all too well. It was his raison d'être. He loved insulting people and pushing their buttons. That punch was the culmination of a campaign of years of using Dejuan as the butt of many jokes, and so when Greg had decided to go after Tawanna that time, Dejuan had seen red. Before he could stop himself, he had walked up on that stage and punched the guy's lights out.

In hindsight, and looking at the footage of the incident, he realized that Greg had done it on purpose, and that by punching him he had given the man exactly what he wanted. It had certainly made Greg's career go through the stratosphere, even as it had torpedoed Dejuan's chances of ever working in the industry again.

"Okay, I'll do it. I'll go out there and say hi. I mean, I'm a strong, emotionally resilient man and nobody can do anything to make me lose my cool—not even Greg Lonsdale."

"That's right, babe," said Tawanna as she got up. She stood in front of him and fixed him with an intense look. "You can do this. You know you can."

"I know I can," he murmured, though to be honest he didn't feel as confident now as he had been when he'd done the exercise in his therapist's office so many times. Part of the court-ordered anger management therapy was that he needed to get a handle on his anger when faced with a man like Greg. Unfortunately, they hadn't had access to the real Greg. Instead, he'd had to make do with a poor substitute in his therapist, a wizened old man with a stoop, a limp, and a squint. So when the therapist told him what a loser he was, in that Brooklyn accent of his, it hadn't exactly been the same as when Greg said it.

"Do it now," Tawanna suggested. "Before you lose your nerve."

He nodded and tensed right up, balling his fists and working his jaw muscles into a frenzy. "I'll do it right now."

And before he could get cold feet, he strode to the door and walked out of the resort room. He was going to face the man who had destroyed his life, and he was not going to let him get a rise out of him! He was a strong, confident man in full control of his emotions! And he definitely was not going to allow Greg to goad him into throwing another punch that would send the annoying little jerk flying straight into the pool!

CHAPTER 9

Unfortunately for us, Gran didn't seem to have a clue how to stop these bedbugs from terrorizing Marge and Tex either.

"I don't believe in bedbugs," she claimed. "It's simply a figment of your imagination, Marge. I mean, look at me. I'm sleeping right next door, and do you see any marks on me? Nothing! In fact, I don't think I've slept this well in ages." She stuck her chin in the air. "Probably because over here I don't have to listen to Tex's snoring all night long."

"Tex doesn't snore," said Marge. "Okay, so maybe he snores a little."

"A little! That man probably registers on the Richter scale for earthquakes. When he gets going, it's like a jumbo jet flying over the roof of our house."

"You exaggerate. I've been married to Tex for twenty-five years and have slept next to him for the same number of years, and his snoring has never kept me up at night."

"So you're telling me you haven't been using earplugs?"

"Well, I have," Marge admitted, "but that's not because of Tex. It's just the general noise of the neighborhood. Cars backfiring, people talking on the street, planes flying overhead, dogs barking... I don't know if it's me or if the streets have become a lot noisier over the years, but I can't seem to sleep a wink without my earplugs."

"It's Tex. The older you get, the louder you snore. It's biology."

"It's true," said Dooley. "Gran and I watched a Discovery Channel documentary about snoring, and it said that when men have a tendency to snore, they will only get louder over the years, until their partners can't stand it anymore and murder them in their sleep."

We all stared at our friend. "Murder them in their sleep?" asked Harriet.

"Well, not all of them," he admitted. "But a lot. More than you might think. Probably ninety percent or something like that."

We all gulped and slowly looked up at Marge.

"Why are you looking at me like that?" the woman asked.

"Dooley says there's a ninety percent chance that you will murder Tex," said Harriet.

"Is that true, Marge?" asked Brutus. "Do you feel a very powerful urge to bash Tex over the head with a rock?"

"Or stab him with a knife?" asked Harriet.

"Or shoot him with a gun?" I asked.

Marge smiled. "You guys must have been watching too many horror movies. I have absolutely no intention of murdering Tex."

"I have a strong urge," Gran murmured. But when Marge gave her a penetrating look, she quickly added, "An urge I will never act upon, rest assured."

"Well, I would certainly hope not," said Marge. "Otherwise, I'd have to put some more distance between you and my husband. By moving you into a retirement home, for instance. In Florida," she added for good measure.

Gran's jaw had dropped. "You'd put me in a retirement home?"

"I literally said I was *not* going to put you in a retirement home," said Marge.

"You wouldn't do that to me, would you?" said Gran. "I don't think I would like it. And besides, I'm not old enough to live in one of those places. I still have all of my teeth, see." She took out her dentures and showed them to her daughter.

"Right," said Marge dubiously.

"Please don't put me in a retirement home," said Gran. "I promise I won't try and kill Tex. I mean, even though he tries to imitate a jumbo jet, I love the guy—well, I love him a little. A lot," she quickly amended when her daughter gave her another one of her looks. "I love the guy to pieces. Little pieces," she added as she gave us a wink. "Tiny little pieces, after being pushed through a meat grinder."

"Oh, Ma," said Marge with an eye roll. "Are you going to help me deal with these bedbugs or not?"

"It's an urban legend!" said Gran. "There are no bedbugs. They don't exist."

"Then why do my arms and back look like this?" asked Marge, and showed her mother all the nasty bumps on her arms and back.

"It's all in your mind, honey," said Gran, tapping her forehead. "If you think bedbugs, you'll get bitten—but not really."

"But the cats talked to them. They're right there, in my bed, waiting for me to lie down so they can continue their bloodfest."

Gran glanced over at me. "Is this true, Max? Did you talk to the bedbugs, or was that a fib?"

"No, we literally just talked to them," I confirmed.

"And what did they say?"

"The one I talked to said that he prefers blood type O, but

he's not picky so he will take any blood type. He also said that he wouldn't mind having a taste of our blood as well."

"Hmm," said Gran as she rubbed her chin. "Look, I'm dealing with something very important right now—leading the neighborhood watch in an operation to catch the thief that's been terrorizing the resort. But as soon as I'm done with that, I'll try and think up something to deal with those bugs, all right? If they're real, that is," she said as she gave me a skeptical look.

"They *are* real!" I insisted.

"Says you." And with those words, she was off again, to continue looking for the thief.

"That woman drives me crazy sometimes," said Marge.

"Only sometimes?" Harriet quipped.

Marge laughed. "Okay, fine. She drives me crazy all the time."

"Maybe you *should* put her in a retirement home in Florida," Brutus suggested.

Marge sighed. "I wouldn't be able to forgive myself. She'd hate it over there—far away from her family and friends. Hampton Cove is her home and she's lived here all her life."

"She would make new friends," said Brutus. "And make life impossible for them."

"Now there's something to consider," said Marge as she gave our friend a rub on the head. "And in the meantime, I want you guys to promise me that you will try to find a solution for these bedbugs. Because I'm done with not being able to sleep."

The four of us looked up at the bed and saw that a horde of about two dozen bedbugs had gathered on the edge. "Here, kitty kitty," said Rico. "Give us a nibble."

Yikes!

CHAPTER 10

Clyde had followed Kimmy and Kitty as they stalked off in a hurry. When he saw them fluttering around Sylvester McCade, the yoga teacher the resort had on loan from the Argent, he ground his teeth in dismay and disgust. He should have known. Kimmy talked a great game and came across as interested in what Clyde had to say, but when push came to shove, she was just like all the other girls he knew: she probably thought he was a loser.

It was the story of his life, so he decided to take a walk along the beach. Even though it was pretty hot out, he didn't mind. He had one of those silly hats on his head that protected his face and neck from the worst, and had rubbed his arms and legs with enough sunblock to make sure he didn't turn into a lobster. He set out in the direction of Happy Bays, also located along the coastline, and got ready for a nice long hike.

Walking was the only thing that put his mind at ease these days. He certainly couldn't stand to be around his dad, who was probably the worst human being in the history of the world. His mom had been so nervous, jumpy, and distracted lately that she wasn't much fun to be around either. He didn't know what was going on with her, though it probably had something to do with Dad, who had a knack for getting under people's skin.

Dad was one of those people who had an unsettling knack to discover what triggered a person, and then push their buttons relentlessly. Like that poor guy Dejuan Daly who had punched Dad on stage last year. Clyde had felt for Dejuan, another innocent victim of Dad's jibes and jeers. Only Dejuan had done something about it, whereas most people just took Dad's insults with a forced smile on their faces, afraid of being labeled a sore loser.

Clyde couldn't blame them. Despite the fact that he had been the butt of Dad's jokes since he was born, he'd never done anything about it either. Dad had such an acid tongue that it took a lot of courage to stand up to him, and even then he simply eviscerated you.

Once Clyde had asked his dad not to make fun of him on stage anymore, after his classmates had circulated a cartoon of him as a rain cloud. Dad always referred to him as Clyde McCloud, because according to him, Clyde had no sense of humor whatsoever and always looked sad, like a perpetual rain cloud hanging over his life, ruining things.

The name had stuck, and all through high school, his fellow students had called him Clyde McCloud. He'd heard it so many times he had gotten used to it. His teacher had talked to Dad about it, but the latter thought it was so funny that he had used the story in one of his shows. 'Life under McCloud,' the show had been called, and it had been a great success, full of jokes at his son's expense. People had loved it. Clyde, not so much. Especially when TikTok clips had started circulating. It had led to him being mercilessly bullied, and his mom had asked Dad to stop using his son as the butt of his jokes. After Clyde had come home with a black eye and a broken wrist, after being attacked in the school yard, Dad had finally seen the error of his ways and had swapped out the 'McCloud' material for something else, finding new victims for his mean-spirited 'jokes.'

As he kicked a pebble, he suddenly thought he saw someone familiar seated on the boardwalk. As he approached, he saw that it was his grandad, who had joined them at the resort. After Grandma had died a couple of months ago, the old man had felt lost in the big house he and Grandma Bernadette had occupied, and so Mom had suggested they sell the place and he move in with them. It wasn't as if they didn't have plenty of space, but even so, Dad had expressed his displeasure with having to put up with his old man.

In the end, Mom managed to get her way and Granddad Lloyd had moved in with them, which pleased Clyde to no end, as he was crazy about his grandfather, just as he had been crazy about his grandmother, who was a sweet lady. How two lovely people had managed to produce a curmudgeon for a son was a mystery to anyone who knew them.

"Granddad!" said Clyde as he walked up to the old man.

Granddad looked up in surprise, but when he saw that it was his grandson, a big smile spread across his features. "Hey, Clyde. Whatcha up to?"

"Oh, nothing special," he said as he took a seat on the granite boardwalk, which was hot to the touch after having been blasted by the sun all morning. "Just taking a walk."

"Getting away from your dad, huh?" said Granddad, who was nobody's fool.

Clyde shrugged. "Something like that."

"Was he being his usual charming self again?"

"He was talking on the phone with his agent when I last saw him. They seemed to be having an argument. Something about the agent telling my dad to stop doing whatever it was that he was doing and Dad not agreeing with him."

"When has your dad ever agreed with anyone about anything?" said Granddad, and wasn't that the truth?

"What's that?" asked Clyde, referring to a pot standing next to his grandad. It was about half a foot high and was shiny, with a lid on top. "Cookie jar?" he ventured.

"I wish," said Grandad as he patted the thing and then picked it up to hold in his arms. "This, my boy, is your grandmother."

Clyde's eyes went a little wide. "You mean Grandma's ashes are in that thing?"

"Yup, that's right. She always wanted me to scatter her ashes in the ocean, only I want to do it the right way, by renting a boat and organizing a ceremony. Maybe get a priest involved. Say a few prayers. Only your dad doesn't want to," he added on a sad note.

"What do you mean Dad doesn't want to? How can he not honor Grandma's last wish?"

"You know your dad. He's got some excuse. Claims we need permission to scatter someone's ashes."

"Maybe we do?"

"Nonsense. Who are we going to ask? The Mayor? The Governor? The President? It's just ashes, son. It's not going to do anyone any harm if we scatter them to the winds, the way your grandmother wanted us to."

Clyde eyed the urn with a reverent gaze. "It's hard to imagine that a whole person would fit into such a small thing."

"It is pretty mind-blowing, isn't it? But then I guess that whole 'ashes to ashes' business has got some truth to it after all."

"I guess."

Granddad gazed out across the ocean. "It's probably my fault, you know."

"What is?"

"Well, I pretty much blamed your dad for being responsible for his mother's death."

"And is he? Responsible for Grandma's death?"

"In a way he is," said Granddad. "You know your grandmother was the loveliest and sweetest person alive, don't you?"

"Absolutely. I loved Grandma Bernadette." It had been a real shock when she had suddenly died. Way too young according to anyone he had spoken to. She had been in her early seventies and by all accounts had seemed healthy enough for her age. Until her heart suddenly gave out and she was gone within a couple of hours.

"The thing is, she was never happy with your father's career," Granddad confessed. "Don't get me wrong, she was proud that he made a household name of himself, famous all across the country, and rich beyond anything she or I could ever have imagined. But she didn't like that he made so many enemies. He kept insulting people, and she hated that. Even our neighbors complained about it. Every time he cracked a joke about her, or me, or you for that matter, or your mom, it was like a stake through her heart."

"Yeah, I know what you mean," said Clyde as he dangled his legs. "He got me into a lot of trouble at school with his nonsense."

"I know he did. And he shouldn't have done that. And it wasn't just you. Every person he ever met stood to end up as the butt of one of his jokes. In the end, people were afraid to associate with us, for fear of being made a fool of on national television."

"And you think that contributed to Gran dying?"

"I do, yes. I think her heart finally couldn't take it anymore, and it simply gave up. I told your father, and you can imagine how he reacted."

"By giving you a lot of grief?"

"You know your dad well," said Granddad, slinging an arm around his shoulder and pulling him in. "Look, I know I probably shouldn't have said those things. I know your dad loved his mother very much, and if he hurt her, it wasn't his intention. But that didn't stop her from getting upset every time they aired one of his Netflix specials. In the end, she couldn't even stand to watch him anymore, and neither could I, for that matter."

"I never watch my dad," Clyde confessed. "I've had to look at his clips way too many times over the years, especially when he was still in full Clyde McCloud mode."

"Your grandmother hated that, or when he talked smack about your mom. She even talked to him about it, but he said she shouldn't take it so seriously. It was just jokes, and according to him, jokes never hurt anyone. Not like guns. But I contend that jokes *can* hurt people. They can hurt them something bad, because they take away their dignity and subject them to a lot of ridicule that they don't need." He held up the urn. "So I was thinking that maybe I'll simply rent a boat and scatter her ashes all by myself. Unless…"

Clyde smiled. "Of course I'll go with you, Granddad. You don't think I'll let you scatter Grandma's ashes alone, do you?"

"What about your mom? Maybe she'll want to accompany us?"

"Mom is too busy worrying about her divorce," said Clyde, and immediately regretted that he'd said that.

Granddad looked up in surprise. "Elaine is divorcing your dad?"

"Yes, but don't tell her I said that, all right? I mean,

promise me, Granddad. It's a big secret. I'm not even supposed to know, but I happened to overhear Mom talking to a lawyer one morning, and when I googled her, it turned out she's one of the most famous divorce lawyers in LA. A woman named Chandra Laidens."

"Your dad doesn't know?"

"He doesn't, and I have a feeling Mom wants to keep it that way until she's got all of her ducks in a row."

"She should. The moment your dad finds out he'll go ballistic and it will be full-out war. He'll try to sue her for everything she's got."

"If I'm forced to choose between them, I'll choose Mom," said Clyde. "No question."

A sadness came over his grandfather, and he thought he knew why. No parent wants to see their kid mess up their lives the way Dad had messed up his. To have a son who doesn't want to have anything to do with you is probably the worst thing that can happen to a parent. A clear indictment of their parenting style—or lack thereof, in Dad's case.

"I don't know about you, buddy," said Granddad. "But I'm starting to melt here. How about we take a dip in the ocean, huh? Cool off some?"

He smiled. "How about I race you to it, Granddad?"

"Oh, you're so on, buddy boy."

And as they both started racing for the ocean, Granddad yelled, "Think you can beat your old granddad, huh? Well, think again, son!"

And it was a testament to Granddad's sprightliness that he actually did beat his grandson to the edge of the ocean. And as they dipped their toes into the cooling water, Clyde was glad that Granddad had moved in with them. But then a thought occurred to him. "When Mom and Dad get divorced, where are you going to live, Granddad?"

His grandfather smiled. "With your mom, of course. At least if she'll have me."

He pumped the air with his fist. "Yessss!"

He probably shouldn't be thinking like that, but he was actually looking forward to this divorce!

CHAPTER 11

Greg Lonsdale wasn't in the best of moods. First, his agent called to tell him he couldn't go on like this, indicating he knew all about Greg's hot dog obsession and warning him to 'Just stop, Greg. I mean it.' And then that idiot Dejuan Daly had the gall to walk up to him and say hi, acting as if nothing happened! As if he hadn't punched him in front of the whole world!

And now, to top it all off, his cool cocktail was anything but cool. In fact, it was lukewarm. And if there was anything he hated, it was having to sip from a lukewarm cocktail. Like tasting dishwater!

"Hey, buddy!" he yelled, holding up his glass. "Didn't you forget something?"

The waiter, some young freak with zits all over his face and half-long greasy hair that he had tucked underneath a ball cap, hurried up to him, a confused expression on his face. "I'm sorry, sir. Isn't the cocktail to your satisfaction?"

"No ice!" he yelled as he shoved the glass in the waiter's direction. "How am I supposed to drink this stuff without any ice?"

"I'm so sorry, sir," said the waiter. He held out his hand to take the cocktail glass from Greg, but must have miscalculated, for instead of taking the glass, he slapped it out of Greg's hand, tipping its contents all over Greg's person, soaking him in the process.

"You idiot!" he screamed. "You fool!"

"I'm so sorry, sir!" said the waiter, who seemed to be stuck at that particular phrase. "I'll get you a towel immediately."

"You know what?" said Greg, who was pretty much at the end of his rope by now. "Don't bother. In fact, don't bother coming back here at all. You're fired!"

"But sir!" said the waiter.

He pointed an index finger at the freak. "Get lost, punk. If I ever lay eyes on you again, I won't be responsible for the consequences. Is that understood?"

"Yes, sir," said the kid, and shuffled off in a hurry, probably to complain to his colleagues about the annoying customer. But Greg was serious. As far as he was concerned, the incompetent idiot's career at the resort was over and done with.

He got up to check himself and saw that not only was his shirt soaking with the sticky substance but also his board shorts and even his phone.

"Oh, for crying out loud," he muttered, and only now noticed that all eyes were on him. But since he was used to being the center of attention, he didn't care. If he had cared, he might have noticed that a young woman had been eyeing him pretty intensely for the past ten minutes. Hiding behind a pair of oversized sunglasses and underneath an equally oversized straw hat, he wouldn't have recognized her even if he had noticed, for they had never met before. At least not in person. She had written him plenty of emails, though, and had tried to contact him many times—personally or through his agent. All to no avail.

Which is why she had decided to try a different tack.

*　*　*

Juli Hooton wondered for a moment if she shouldn't simply get a hold of the glass that Greg had been drinking from, but seeing as the man was hyper-vigilant, not to mention fired up after his run-in with the hapless young waiter, she didn't think this was the right strategy at that moment. And so, instead, she decided to go for Plan B.

Elaine Lonsdale had finally come out of hiding and had joined her husband by the pool, so the coast was clear. Juli quickly got up from her chaise lounge and strolled in the direction of the resort. While Greg was engaged in a fight with his waiter, he hopefully wouldn't head upstairs to his room. That would give her ample opportunity to use the key card she had managed to steal from Greg's tote bag and enter his room.

All she needed was some of Greg's hair, and so her immediate target was a brush or comb that belonged to the guy. It wouldn't be hard to differentiate between his comb and that belonging to his wife Elaine. Greg's hair was as dark as Juli's own long mane, while Elaine's hair was a honey-blond hue. There was also their son Clyde, but he took after his mom, so there would be no confusion possible. The idea had occurred to her that she could use Clyde's hair to extract the DNA she needed, but she wasn't sure if that would work. Better to go straight to the source and get some of Greg's DNA instead.

She hurried up the stairs to the second floor and along the long corridor, turning the corner. Greg and Elaine's suite was right at the end, something she knew from the surveillance she had done on the famous actor and comedian.

She glanced around and took the key card from her small

purse. Preparation was everything, and if she was caught inside the room, she had her explanation ready. It wasn't difficult to get the floors confused, and since she was staying one floor up and in the same location, she could simply attribute her mistake to getting the floors mixed up.

She entered the suite and quietly closed the door. Taking a pair of plastic gloves from her little purse, she put them on and glanced around. Greg's lodgings were a darn sight more luxurious than hers. But then he could afford it, being one of the most popular and famous actors in the world. He'd recently signed another deal with Netflix that had reportedly netted him millions, so he didn't have to engage in the kind of penny-pinching she was forced to engage in. Instead, he could live large, and he did.

She made a beeline for the bathroom and started rummaging around Greg and Elaine's personal belongings in search of a comb or brush. It wasn't long before she found what must surely be Greg's comb. Extracting a few hairs, she placed them in the plastic container she had brought along for the occasion and screwed the cap back on.

A smile spread across her face. She'd done it! Now it was only a matter of time before she could prove once and for all that Greg Lonsdale was her dad. He wouldn't be able to ignore her then, would he?

But as she returned to the main part of the suite, the door clicked open, and she found herself face to face with three old ladies. One of the ladies, with fine white curls, wore a triumphant expression on her face. She uttered but a single word.

"Gotcha!"

CHAPTER 12

Turns out that the sneak thief had decided to throw caution to the wind and strike in the middle of the day instead of during the night when all the guests were asleep. Though truth be told, it had been a stroke of luck that had led us to capture the notorious thief. Gran had pretty much been ready to give up and had decided to spend the rest of the afternoon by the pool, in the company of Marge, Tex, and Grace, when she happened to see a young woman behaving suspiciously. The woman had entered Greg Lonsdale's suite. And since Gran knew for a fact that Greg's wife didn't look anything like this young woman, she thought this incursion into the famous actor's suite was highly suspicious.

I told her that it was presumably an assistant of some kind, or maybe the young woman belonged to the resort and was merely placing some pralines on the pillows in the suite, a courtesy only bestowed on the most esteemed guests. But of course, Gran being Gran, she brushed all of my objections aside and sailed in like a ship under steam, bursting into the room with the aid of the master key she had been assigned by

Grace Wheeler, which gave access to every single room on the premises.

As we walked in, I immediately knew that my reservations had been wide of the mark. The girl, whose hair was a bright blue and who sported a tattoo of a butterfly on her collarbone, looked so absolutely guilty that she couldn't possibly be an assistant or in the employ of the resort. She was holding a little plastic jar in her hand, of the kind used to collect forensic evidence or a blood sample, and gulped once or twice, giving a very vivid impression of a deer caught in the headlights.

"I can explain everything!" she said immediately, another clear sign that she was very much guilty as charged.

Gran puffed out her chest. This was her moment, and she intended to seize it with gusto. "My name is Vesta Muffin, and I'm the head of the neighborhood watch. And you, young lady, are busted for stealing!"

"But I didn't steal anything!" said the girl, who was very pretty, I thought, with a sort of tilt-tipped little nub of a nose and cornflower-blue eyes. For some reason, she reminded me of someone, though for the life of me I couldn't quite seem to place her.

"What's that you're holding?" asked Gran, gesturing to the little plastic receptacle.

Caught, the girl immediately tucked the receptacle behind her back. "Nothing," she said, and gulped some more.

"Let me have it," said Gran.

"No!" said the girl. "You can't! I mean, I won't! I mean, let me explain, please!"

She was giving Gran a sort of pleading look now, the kind convicted criminals give the judge when he's about to tell the warden to haul them off to prison for the foreseeable future.

"No need to explain," said Gran. "You gave us quite a challenge, young lady. How many people have you robbed, huh? Dozens, probably. And where is the loot?"

"What loot? What are you talking about?" said the girl.

"Oh, don't give me that," said Gran. She turned to Scarlett. "Hand me those handcuffs, will you, darling?"

"Handcuffs!" said the girl. "You're not actually going to arrest me, are you?"

Gran pointed at her own face. "Does this look like a person who's kidding? No? I didn't think so. You're going away for a long stretch of time, honey. Now give me those wrists of yours, so that I can outfit them with a nice pair of bracelets."

"Maybe you should hear her out first," Scarlett suggested.

"And I say you should arrest her," said Denice. "She's been playing hide and seek with us long enough."

Gran wavered for a moment, but then seemed to feel that it couldn't hurt to give the girl a chance to explain her point of view. After all, the criminal mindset is a fascinating one, and many books and TV shows have been made trying to plumb its hidden depths.

"She doesn't look like a thief," said Dooley. "She looks like a very nice young woman."

"I think she looks exactly like a thief," Brutus grumbled, as he didn't let the girl out of his sight for even a single moment. "A hardened criminal if I ever saw one."

"I'm glad this is over," said Harriet. "I can't imagine having to spend the night on the roof of the resort. I'll bet it's hot up there, even at night. And besides, I need my beauty sleep."

"Same here," said Brutus. "I'm glad she decided to throw caution to the wind and let us catch her. Though I have to say I'm also disappointed that she didn't turn out to be the hardened criminal we all thought she was. She looks more like a juvenile delinquent."

"Look, I'm not a thief!" the girl assured us as she held up

her hands in a gesture of defense. "All I wanted was to get some DNA. Nothing more."

"DNA? What are you talking about?"

The girl sighed deeply. "My name is Juli Hooton, and Greg Lonsdale is my dad."

Gran's frown deepened. "Your dad? I didn't know Greg had a daughter."

"Don't listen to her," said Denice. "She's obviously lying through her teeth."

"Greg has never recognized me as his daughter," said Juli. "He and my mom had an affair, and she ended up getting pregnant. She told Greg, but by then the affair had run its course and he ignored her messages and her phone calls. Mom decided to keep me, and so nine months later I was born." She produced a weak smile. "She only told me last month that my real dad was Greg Lonsdale. She had been keeping it a secret for all those years."

"And so the cup..." said Gran, gesturing to the plastic receptacle the girl was still holding on to for dear life.

"It contains a couple of hairs from Greg's comb," she said. "I want to send it off to the lab for a DNA test. To confirm what I know in my heart to be true: that Greg Lonsdale is my real dad. That way he won't be able to brush me aside as a kook or a freak."

"He did that?" asked Scarlett.

The girl nodded as she bit her lip. "I've been trying to reach him for weeks, ever since my mom told me the big secret. I've sent him messages, emails—tried to get in touch through his agent. All I know is what the agent told me over the phone: that Greg reckons I'm some kind of gold digger, and if I don't go away, he'll file charges against me with the police and I'll regret ever having concocted this crazy story about him and my mom."

"But why would he deny that he is your dad?" asked Scarlett.

"Money," said Denice. "Isn't that right? You and your mom want to bilk Greg for everything he's worth."

The girl got a sort of mutinous look in her eyes. She clearly didn't agree with this assessment of her motivations for going after Greg.

"Absolutely not. I don't want a penny from Greg. All I want is for him to come clean. To accept that he had an affair with my mom when his own wife was pregnant with his son. I want him to apologize to my mom for getting her in trouble and then deserting her. When she discovered that she was pregnant, it got her into a heap of trouble. She was still in high school at the time, and she had to drop out of school for the duration of the pregnancy as her parents didn't want anyone to know. They thought it would create an enormous scandal, especially as Greg was a famous actor, even back then. So they kept her out of school, and then she never got to return and didn't graduate. No college for her, and she was forced to take on minimum-wage jobs to support me."

"And Greg never helped?" asked Gran, aghast at the story.

Juli shook her head. "My grandparents tried to contact him, but he brushed them off and that was it. It hasn't been easy for Mom, and in hindsight, she probably should have terminated the pregnancy. It would have saved her a lot of trouble. But she always told me she was glad she didn't. That I'm the best thing that ever happened to her."

A tear streaked down Scarlett's cheek now, and she wiped it away. "Oh, sweetheart," she said, and surged forward to give Juli a well-meant hug. "What a story," she said.

"You can say that again," said Gran, also wiping away a tear.

"It's all lies," said Denice, who wasn't affected by the story at all. "Search her room. I'm sure you'll find the loot."

"No, you won't," said Juli. "Because I'm not a thief."

"It's easy enough to check," said Gran. "Why don't you show us your room, honey? That way we can clear this up right now."

"But only if you want to," said Scarlett as she rubbed the girl on the back.

"It's fine," said Juli. "I want to prove that I'm not a thief. All I ask is that you don't tell Greg. I don't want him to find out that I stole a couple of hairs from his comb. He might use it against me. That's the kind of man he is. Vengeful, you know. And litigious."

"We won't breathe a word about this," Scarlett promised.

"And that goes for you, too, Denice," Gran stressed.

The old lady rolled her eyes. "Oh, all right. But first I want proof, you hear me? Proof that this young lady is who she says she is. She spins a great yarn, but is she for real?"

And so we all headed to the room where Juli was staying. As it happened, it was located right above the fancy suite where her alleged dad was holed up. It was a simple room, but nice enough. Her grandparents were paying for it, hoping to prove, along with their daughter and granddaughter, once and for all that Greg Lonsdale was Juli's father.

Gran quickly searched the room, along with Scarlett and Denice, but in the end, they had to admit that there was absolutely nothing to indicate that Juli might be the thief we had been looking for.

"Max, she's innocent!" Dooley cried.

"I knew it," said Brutus. "She's got the face of an angel."

I gave him a strange look but decided not to remind him that only twenty minutes before, he had professed that Juli looked like a hardened criminal.

CHAPTER 13

Gran had more or less given up on trying to catch the thief that day. Her plan was to climb on the roof tonight and try to catch the notorious thief that way. It was a plan that the four of us weren't all that excited about, even though cats are supposed to love climbing roofs. I guess we're atypical in that sense, since the last thing I wanted was to go and sit on a roof all night in the faint hope that the thief would show his face.

And since Gran had for the moment dispensed with our services, we decided to go for a stroll along the boardwalk, always a great place to enjoy that light cooling ocean breeze —or so we had been told. As it was, there wasn't a lot of breezing being done and it wasn't long before we regretted having gone down this road.

"We should have stayed at the resort," said Harriet, huffing and puffing like the rest of us. "To think we could be enjoying the miracles of our room's air conditioning right now!"

"Maybe we should venture a little closer to the water,"

Brutus suggested. "It's probably a lot cooler down there. Right?" he added hopefully.

I wasn't convinced, especially since the closer you get to the water, the higher the risk of getting wet, and if there's one thing I hate even more than being hot, it's getting wet. But since I was pretty much melting at that point, I decided to give Brutus's idea a spin. And so it was that we ventured out across what is usually termed a breakwater. The thing was covered with all manner of crustaceans, who clung to it like glue. From time to time, a light mist of brine covered us, and I had to say it was refreshing.

"See?" said Brutus triumphantly. "It's so much cooler over here, isn't it?"

I happened to glance down at the water at that point, and noticed that it was a lot closer than I would have liked. I swallowed away a lump of unease.

"Is that water rising or is it just my imagination?" I asked.

"It's very deep," said Dooley. "And those waves are very high, Max. What if one of those waves washes us away? I can't swim!"

"Of course you can swim," said Harriet. "All mammals can swim. It's in our blood. Even newborn babies can swim, even though they haven't been taught yet."

"I don't know if you've noticed, but we're not exactly newborn babies, are we?" asked Brutus, a note of panic clear in his voice.

Harriet gulped a few times as she clung to the breakwater, for fear of being washed away. "Maybe... maybe we should start heading back. Back to the resort, where it's safe and nice and where our food is and our nice soft sofa in our air-conditioned room!"

"I think that's a great idea," I said, and so we slowly started making our way back.

That's the problem with these breakwaters: you walk and

walk and before you know it, suddenly you're practically in the middle of the ocean, where the water is hundreds of feet deep! Okay, so maybe I'm exaggerating. But not by much!

As we started making our way back, very slowly and carefully, so as not to trip and fall into the water and get swallowed up by those waves, suddenly there was a loud yelling that reached our ears. It almost sounded like, 'Shark! Shark!'

But of course that couldn't be, since there are no sharks on Long Island. Or are there?

As we focused our trained eyes in the direction the screams were coming from, suddenly I saw the telltale sign that there was indeed a shark in the water. It was a fin, and it looked pretty ominous, I have to say.

"That can't be real, can it?" asked Harriet, as she pointed to the fin.

"It looks real to me," said Brutus.

It only added to our general sense of malaise, for sharks are known to eat anything that moves, and that probably includes cats!

"We probably should move a little faster," said Dooley. "Before that shark sees us and decides to have us for dinner!"

And so we put some pep in our step and sped up. It wasn't long before more screams could be heard, and people started thrashing wildly to get out of the water. Kids were screaming, parents were screaming—even we were screaming! I guess this kind of behavior is contagious, and we couldn't help but experience a sense of growing panic as we practically raced across the breakwater and back to the beach, where we would be safe from this monster.

"It looks like a big one!" said Dooley, panting heavily.

"It sure does!" I agreed, also panting liberally.

"It's probably a great big white!" said Harriet.

"What's a great big white?" asked Dooley.

"It's a great big white shark, Dooley!"

"Oh, right," said our friend. He thought for a moment. "But why do they call him that? Great and big, I mean. Isn't that like saying the same thing twice?"

"Probably because he's so big it needs to be said twice!" said Brutus, who wasn't mincing words when it came to an imminent threat to life and limb.

"It just doesn't seem right," said Dooley, always a stickler for *le mot juste*.

"Who cares!" Brutus retorted.

We had finally reached the beach, and we saw that a police presence was already at the scene. The shark must have been circling the tourists for a while, for none other than Mayor Butterwick and Uncle Alec got out of the police vehicle. Uncle Alec raised a pair of binoculars to his eyes and scanned the horizon.

"It's a shark, all right," he said after a few moments. He handed the binoculars to his wife.

"Yep," she said. "That's a shark," confirming the chief's assessment.

These preliminaries having been dealt with to everyone's satisfaction, they proceeded to discuss matters with the representatives of the lifeguards tasked with keeping the beach safe and ensuring that no tourists got harmed while enjoying a fun time in the surf.

"We need to clear these beaches," said the head lifeguard.

"I agree," said Uncle Alec. "We can't take any chances. There might be more than one shark out there."

"He's pretty far from shore," said Charlene with a frown. "I'm sure he won't come any closer as the water is pretty shallow."

The lifeguard gave her a look of incredulity. "Sharks love shallow water," said the lifeguard. "And you know what they love even more? When that shallow water is full of swimmers! It's like a tasty dish! A plate full of delicious goodies they can nibble on!"

Charlene gave him a tight smile. "So you're a shark expert now, are you, Jordan?"

"I'm not a shark expert by any means, ma'am," said the lifeguard, a burly fellow with skin that was bronzed to a nice golden hue. He looked pretty fit, I thought, but it was clear that his opinions irked the mayor. "But I believe in erring on the side of caution. So why don't we get a real expert in, and in the meantime, close down the beaches?"

The mayor seemed exasperated. "It's the height of the season, Jordan! Do you really expect me to close down the beaches all because of one measly little shark? What are the local businesses going to say?"

"The local businesses won't like it if a couple of tourists get chewed up," said Jordan, persisting in espousing his pessimistic view.

"No tourists will get chewed up on my watch," said the mayor adamantly. "And you know why that is? Because I've got the best lifeguards at my disposal." She slapped him on the muscular shoulder. "So why don't we try and keep the panic at bay, and look at this from a rational point of view. It's only one shark, Jordan. Are you telling me that you can't handle one little shark?"

"Pretty sure it's a big shark," said Uncle Alec, who was studying the shark closely—as far as one can study a shark, since most of it is located beneath the waves.

"So now *you're* the expert, is that it?" Charlene snapped. "Look, I'm all for being cautious, but what I'm not prepared to do is sacrifice our town's lifeblood because of the sighting of a single shark. That's just crazy. So let's just keep an eye on that fish and make sure it doesn't go anywhere near the tourists. But in the meantime, I refuse to give in to panic." Her face took on a mulish expression that I had seen many times before. "The beaches will remain open. And that is my final decision."

"Are you prepared to take full responsibility?" asked Jordan.

"Of course. Absolutely. As long as you do your job and make sure that nobody goes anywhere near that shark."

"It's more a matter of the shark not going anywhere near the tourists, ma'am," Jordan pointed out.

"Exactly," said Charlene. She gave the lifeguard a steely look. "You have your instructions, Jordan. Now act on them, is that understood?"

"Yes, ma'am," said the burly lifeguard, but it was clear that he was silently fuming inside, and that he wouldn't have minded countermanding the mayor's instructions if only his job wasn't on the line. Charlene might be a great person, but when it comes to running Hampton Cove, she can be quite ruthless from time to time. But then I guess you need to project forcefulness and leadership when you're in charge.

"I wouldn't like to go in the water right now," said Brutus. "No matter what Charlene says."

"I wouldn't go in the water regardless of that shark," said Harriet with a shiver. "I mean, water is so wet, don't you guys agree?"

"Water is very wet," I agreed, and the others also confirmed that water has a tendency to be very wet indeed.

And since the crisis seemed to have passed, and Uncle Alec and Charlene took off again, we decided not to stick around either. After all, we had an air-conditioned hotel room waiting for us over at the resort. A room that was cool and pleasant, contained our favorite food, but above all, was absolutely shark-free!

CHAPTER 14

We had returned to the resort and saw that our humans were still lounging by the pool, which seemed like a good idea, considering the beach was being terrorized by a huge shark. And so we decided to forgo the pleasure of the air-conditioned room for now and simply find a spot of shade underneath the sun loungers that our humans had selected. I chose Scarlett's lounger, Dooley took Gran's, Harriet selected Marge, and Brutus found refuge underneath Tex's lounger. In other words, a nice distribution of cats along the lines of ownership. Or maybe not quite, as I should have selected Odelia and Brutus Chase. But since they were absent from the scene, owing to not having any vacation days left to spend them idly at the resort, we had to make do with the humans we had at our disposal.

Grace had been playing in the pool all afternoon, supervised by the two monitors, though when I looked around, of the twins there was no trace. And so Grace was forced to fend for herself in her battle against the annoying kid who seemed to have singled her out for his bullying ways. His name was Timmy, and if Marge had told him once that he shouldn't treat her granddaughter this way, she had told him a hundred times. But would he listen? Of course not.

And so it was up to us to keep an eye on Grace and make sure she wasn't scarred for life by the way Timmy kept splashing her with water or trying to dunk her—a very nasty state of affairs if you ask me. I couldn't imagine being dunked—my head held underwater for an indefinite length of time. Talk about the stuff of nightmares!

"We should put a stop to this, Max," said Dooley after Timmy had splashed Grace with water once again, causing the little girl to give him a dirty look. "This can't go on like this."

"I'm sure that Marge has the situation well in hand," I told him.

And it was true that Marge had decided to forgo the pleasure of reading her book and instead focus on keeping Grace safe from harm—a situation that didn't sit well with her, as she loves reading so much.

"Timmy, stop that!" she yelled, a refrain that we had heard a few times before.

"Yes, Timmy, stop bothering my great-granddaughter!" Gran yelled in unison with her daughter.

"We're just playing!" Timmy yelled from the safety of the pool.

"He probably likes her," said Harriet. "When boys like a girl, they like to tease her. It's common knowledge."

"I never teased you," said Brutus. "And I liked you from the start."

Harriet smiled. "No, that's true. You never teased me. Okay, so I probably should amend my statement: boys who are too shy to express their feelings like to tease a girl."

"So what are you saying?" asked Brutus. "That Timmy likes Grace but is afraid to show it, so he teases her?"

"That's exactly what I'm saying. He's very shy, I can tell."

At that moment, Timmy reared up out of the water like some kind of superhero, roaring and screaming, and blasted Grace with a stream from his water gun. It hit her in the side of the head and she did not look pleased.

"He doesn't look shy," I said. "More like a bully."

"It's hard to differentiate sometimes between a bully and a shy person," said Harriet, who seemed to know a lot about this sort of thing.

"I think he's a bully," said Dooley, who had no qualms about calling a spade a spade. "And if we don't stop him, he's going to spoil Grace's fun time here at the resort."

"Timmy!" Gran yelled again. "Stop that!"

Just then, a woman came marching over. Her face was red, and she looked very unhappy with Gran. She stood before her, her fists planted on her sizable hips. "Who are you to yell at my son?" she demanded heatedly.

"Is Timmy your son?" asked Gran.

"He is. And I don't like it when people yell at him. Especially strangers who have no business calling him all kinds of names."

"I didn't call him any names," said Gran, "except his own proper name, which is Timmy, right?"

"Apologize," said the woman, who looked a lot like Timmy, I had to say. The same deep frown on her face and the same rather large nose planted in the center of things.

"Apologize for what?" asked Gran, who was in a pretty mellow mood.

"For yelling at my son!"

This was too much for the old lady, and she sat up a little straighter. Mellow mood or not, she wasn't going to be treated unfairly. "Your son has been bullying my great-granddaughter," she said. "And if he doesn't stop, I'm going to make him stop. Is that understood?"

The woman eyed Gran with astonishment. Clearly, she

had not expected this. "So you're not going to apologize?" she asked, just to make sure.

"He's the one that should apologize. To Grace. He's been squirting her with that water gun of his, and dunking her in the pool, and keeping her head under the water."

"He has done no such thing," said the woman. "All he has done is try to induce that poor little girl to play with the rest of the group."

"That poor little girl would *love* to play with the rest of the group, only your Timmy has been preventing her from doing that," said Gran. "Isn't that right, Marge?"

"Absolutely," said Marge. "Timmy has been a real pain in the patootie, Mrs...."

"Avis," said the woman reluctantly. "So you're all ganging up on a little boy, are you? Have you no shame?"

"We're not ganging up on anyone," said Marge calmly. "All we're saying is that your son shouldn't bully Grace."

"So now you're calling my son a bully?"

"That's exactly right," said Gran. "Because that's what he is: a nasty bully."

The woman blinked. "You know what," she said, pointing a finger at Gran. "You're a terrible person, and I'm going to complain to the manager about you. What's your name?"

"Vesta Muffin," said Gran with relish, rolling the words around her tongue. "And this is my daughter Marge Poole. And since we're on the subject of names, my son's name is Alec Lip and he's the chief of police of Hampton Cove. And my granddaughter's name is Odelia Kingsley and she's a reporter with the *Hampton Cove Gazette*. And you may be interested to know her husband's name as well. That's Chase Kingsley, and he's a police detective. Oh, and my son's wife's name is Charlene Butterwick and she is the mayor of Hampton Cove." She turned to her daughter. "Have I left anyone out, honey?"

"You left me out," said Tex, lowering his newspaper. "I'm Tex Poole, and I'm a doctor. And what your son is doing is very dangerous, Mrs. Avis. Keeping a person's head under the water is a dangerous game that should be frowned upon by the boy's parents. And I'm telling you this as a medical professional."

The woman gulped a couple of times at this litany of names and seemed to have had a sudden change of heart. "I'll tell him not to do it anymore," she said meekly, and hurried off to have a heart-to-heart with her little boy.

Gran grinned triumphantly. "And I didn't even mention *your* name, Scarlett. Or the fact that you're with the neighborhood watch."

We watched as Mrs. Avis practically dragged her son out of the pool and walked off with him, the boy squirming and trying to wrestle free from her iron grip.

Grace came toddling up to us. She seemed relieved that her tormentor had been removed from the scene. "Who wants to play in the pool with me?" she asked.

Gran got up with a groan. "I'll play with you," she said, and Grace yipped. Together, the two jumped into the pool, and before long, they were playing to their heart's content. And since Scarlett needed to cool off, she soon joined her friend and Grace.

"Finally some peace and quiet," Tex grunted, and raised his newspaper. Marge picked up her book again, and for the next few moments, all was well. Across the pool, a man was seated on a chaise lounge, and I recognized him as the man Juli Hooton claimed was her dad. Greg Lonsdale was reading something on his phone and didn't look like a happy camper. Whatever the message was that he had received, he wasn't happy about it, for he suddenly cursed so loudly everyone around the pool could hear him. When he saw that his outburst had been badly received, he held up his hand and smiled. "My apologies!" he yelled so we all could hear him. "Trouble with the old ball and chain!"

If this was supposed to be funny, nobody was laughing. Before long, the 'ball and chain,' as he eloquently put it, came walking up from the resort and joined her husband. Or at least I assumed this was the man's wife. For a few moments, husband and wife conversed in hushed tones, and then all of a sudden Greg screamed, "You have got to be kidding me!"

As everyone looked in his direction once more, I saw that his face had turned a darker shade of puce, and this time he abruptly got up out of his chaise lounge. For a moment he stood glaring at his wife, who seemed embarrassed by her husband's outburst and especially the fact that they were in such a public place. But then he thought better of it and turned on his heel, striding off in the direction of the resort.

"Trouble in paradise?" asked Dooley, who had followed the altercation the same way we all had.

"Looks like it," I said.

And since I was pretty drowsy at that point, my eyes soon drooped closed and I fell into a very pleasant slumber.

Nap time is always the best time.

CHAPTER 15

That evening, the entertainment was being provided by the one and only Greg Lonsdale. But since the four of us weren't all that interested in a comedy show, we decided to watch from the balcony of our room, which happened to overlook the central plaza where the entertainment was being provided. People sat at tables and enjoyed a pleasant evening while Greg stood on stage and practiced his brand of comedy, which was called insult comedy. It mainly consisted of insulting members of the audience, colleagues of his, and members of his family. I wasn't sure if I liked it, especially when he caught sight of the four of us and decided to launch into a long tirade about cats and how we were probably the most horrible creatures in the universe, ranking well below the common cockroach.

It was the first time I had been unfavorably compared to a cockroach, but then I guess you have to take these slings and arrows with a pinch of salt. Insult comedy is a genre, and as such not to be taken personally. Or at least that's what Marge had told us before she had placed a table on the balcony where we could sit and enjoy the spectacle. She and the rest of the family were down below in the audience, along with Odelia and Chase, who had also come out for the occasion, and even Uncle Alec and Charlene.

"I think Greg Lonsdale is a dog person, Max," said Dooley.

"Yes, he does seem to prefer dogs to cats," I agreed.

When we had entered the man's suite earlier that day to catch Julie Hooton in the act of stealing a few samples of the man's hair, I did get a whiff of canine, so I was pretty sure the man had a dog. Only so far we hadn't actually laid eyes on the creature. Not that I was eager to, mind you. We were on vacation, after all, and had already met bedbugs, been on the trail of a thief, seen a shark, almost been washed away by the waves, and seen a bully in action. In other words: too much excitement for one day. Add a dog to the mix and the mixture would have been too rich for my blood, as I like things tranquil and chill.

"Now take this guy for instance," said Greg as he gestured to a man at a table near the stage. "You may not remember this, but he once threw a punch at me during an award ceremony. 'The slap that was heard around the world,' the media termed it. It got twelve million hits on YouTube and then some."

Necks craned and eyes glued to the back of the man's head as he tried to sink a little lower in his collar.

"Dejuan Daly," said Greg. "He used to be an actor. Now he sells second-hand cars. Or so I've been told by people in the know. Second-hand car buyers, I mean." A smattering of laughter trickled through the crowd. "That's what you get when you hit Greg Lonsdale! Life hits you right back. And you wanna know why? Because life has my back!" he roared, applause rising up from the audience. "Smack me, and you'll get smacked back tenfold. That's karma for you. He had the gall to walk up to me this afternoon and demand an apology. For wrecking his life. *I* wrecked *his* life! Listen, Dejuan. You did that all by yourself, with no help from yours truly! And in fact, it should be *me* demanding an apology from *you*! I was the injured party—literally. I was the one that got slapped in the face! Or I should probably say punched." He touched his nose. "My left nostril is still bigger than my right, because of this fella here being determined to land a punch. I mean, if Dejuan gets bored selling second-hand cars he can always try out for the WWE!"

More laughter, and Dejuan was sinking even lower in his seat, though the woman seated next to him was refusing to be cowed and was sitting ramrod straight, something I greatly admired, I have to say. I got the impression that she was eager to follow in her partner's footsteps and give Greg a punch of her own.

"He's extremely belligerent, isn't he, this Greg Lonsdale fellow?" asked Harriet.

"Annoying, you mean," said Brutus. "It's a miracle he only got punched once."

"He's spoiling for a fight," I said. "Probably derives a great deal of pleasure from insulting people."

"That punch was probably the best publicity this guy ever got," said Brutus. "He should have thanked this Dejuan fella."

Having exhausted the subject, Greg moved on and launched into the topic of his wife. "My wife told me today she wants a divorce," he said. "I told her, 'What took you so long?' I mean, did she expect I was going to burst into tears? Good riddance is what I say. Though if she thinks she's going to get her hands on any of my money, she's got another thing coming. She's not getting a single cent. When she told me about the divorce, I gave her the magic word. The word that no wife wants to hear. Prenup! That's right, folks! She signed a prenup, so that means she walks away from this marriage with what she brought into it, which is nothing, bupkis, and zip—nothing whatsoever! Not a single dime!"

He proceeded to call her a few very opprobrious names that made my ears hurt, and I winced, for I thought I had detected the man's wife in the audience.

"She should have divorced him a lot sooner," said Harriet sternly. "No man should talk about his wife like that."

"No, if Chase talked about Odelia like that, he would find himself out on his ear," I said. "And good riddance."

"Chase would never do a thing like that," said Brutus. "He respects Odelia too much. Plus, Chase is a gentleman, and that can't be said about this guy."

After only having endured the show for twenty minutes, I was already starting to dislike this Greg Lonsdale more and more.

"I wonder why he's so popular," said Dooley, who must have had the same experience. "He's not very nice, is he, Max?"

"No, he's not very nice at all," I agreed.

And since I felt I had listened to all the Greg Lonsdale jokes I could stomach, I decided to return indoors and take another nap. If Gran was still adamant to crawl onto the roof that night and go patrolling, I needed to be well-rested and ready for any contingency.

Moments later, I was fast asleep.

CHAPTER 16

In spite of the fact that Gran had expressed her reservations about organizing a stakeout on the roof of the resort, referring to the potential deleterious effect on her biorhythm, we still found ourselves on that self-same roof that self-same night, accompanied by Gran, Scarlett, and Denice, the third member of the neighborhood watch—though if asked, she would probably have denied that she was a member, merely an observer—a bystander, so to speak. Or in other words, what is often termed a tourist.

Denice seemed to derive a lot of pleasure from the experience, though, if her general demeanor was anything to go on, but then she probably had never been on a stakeout, having lived quite the peaceful life in the Midwest, where she originally hailed from.

She and her husband had celebrated their honeymoon at the Hampton Cove Resort & Spa many moons ago, and always said they'd return there one day. Alas it wasn't to be. Until Denice's husband had died twenty-five years ago, and in his honor she had decided to make the trip and had liked it so much she had started coming back every year since.

Contrary to what Harriet had feared, the roof wasn't as hot as we would have expected. Even though it had been a hot couple of days, the nights were much cooler, so when we settled down on the roof, we didn't suffer any ill effects, and the bitumen that had been used for the roof wasn't even sticky to our paws.

Gran had decided that if the thief was going to make his move, he would have to pass by the roof and gain access to the rooms he had selected as his target that way: rappelling down from the roof, as it were, and gaining access to the rooms he wanted to hit.

And since the roof was of the flat variety, we would have no trouble spotting the culprit. Except for a couple of chimneys and what looked like an elevator house or bulkhead, we had a clear view across the entire structure. And since a full moon had decided to lend us its support by illuminating the roof in a pale white light, it was a piece of cake and only a matter of time before we would be able to slap a pair of handcuffs on the dastardly criminal mastermind who had been the bane of the resort for many weeks now, carrying out assault after assault on the personal possessions of its inhabitants.

Gran, Scarlett, and Denice had carried folding stairs up to the roof, and Gran had even managed to convince the kitchen to hand over some supplies for the brave fighters for justice in the form of a cooler filled with all kinds of goodies. She had also thought of the four of us and doled out the meaty nuggets with a generous hand, which did a lot to overcome our initial sales resistance to this latest scheme of hers.

"I think we should be able to see some action real soon," she said as she checked her watch. "According to my son, most break-ins occur between the hours of two and three, so that should give us ample time to get some shut-eye after collaring our target."

"Where do you think he will hit next?" asked Denice, who was munching on a baloney sandwich and loving all of this.

"My best guess is the rooms on that side," said Gran, pointing in a western direction. "So far he hasn't hit those yet, as he seems to have focused on the north side of the building. But since all of the people on that side are very vigilant now after so many of them have been hit, I'm sure he'll try a different tack from now on."

"You know, this is a lot of fun," said Denice. "We don't have this kind of thing back home. Where I come from, we don't even have neighborhood watches and all of that jazz."

"Where you come from, you probably don't have a lot of crime," Scarlett ventured. "But here in Hampton Cove, we do."

"Yeah, the denizens of the criminal underworld keep us pretty busy," Gran said with a sigh. "Night after night, we patrol the streets of this lovely town of ours, and more often than not, we run into these foul creatures of the night, their intention always to separate the hardworking citizens of Hampton Cove from their hard-earned personal possessions."

"I really don't understand how anyone can think that it's a good idea to rob people," said Denice. "I mean, you have to have a twisted mind or something. Is it true that it's got something to do with the shape of a person's head?"

"I think that's a misconception that's largely been ruled out," said Gran, who has watched a lot of shows about crime and criminals in her time. "Though possibly it does have something to do with the way your brain is laid out. The ridges and the folds, I mean. Rumor has it that criminals have a lot less of those ridges. Their brains are mostly just a gooey mass of gloop."

"I did not know that," said Denice. "Just a big mass of gloop, huh?"

"Yeah, no ridges at all," said Gran. "And it's the ridges you want."

"Ridges, good," said Denice, nodding. "Gloop, not good. Gotcha."

"I hope in that case I have plenty of ridges," said Scarlett. "I wouldn't want to have a head filled with gloop, you know. I think I would feel funny if I did."

"I'm sure you've got a beautiful brain, honey," said Gran as she ducked into her cooler in search of something delicious. She came away with a chicken drumstick and put her teeth into it with relish.

"Did you hear about that shark?" asked Denice now.

"A shark?" asked Gran. "What shark?"

"A shark has been spotted. Several people saw it. The mayor and the chief of police even had to come out and consider closing the beach. But in the end, the mayor decided against it. She said she wants to keep the beaches open to protect the local businesses. And also, it was just the one shark, so she didn't think it was that much of a threat."

Scarlett and Gran shared a look of surprise. "Well, how about that?" said Gran.

"I still wouldn't go in the water," said Denice. "Even if it's just a small shark."

"No, me neither," said Gran. "Small or big, these things got big teeth."

"And a big appetite," Scarlett added.

Gran directed a quizzical look at me.

"It's true," I confirmed. "We saw that shark with our own eyes, didn't we, guys?"

"We saw the shark," said Brutus without much enthusiasm.

"I think it was a great big white," said Harriet. "But of course I could be mistaken, as I'm not a shark expert."

"I still think it's a strange habit to call a shark both big and great," said Dooley. "Considering those are synonyms. Unless," he added, his eyes going wide, "great doesn't refer to the shark's size but to the fact that he is, well, great. You know, like majestic."

"Nobody says great big white shark," said Gran before she could stop herself. "It's just 'great white shark.'"

Denice stared at her. "Is that a fact?" she said after a pause. "Great white shark, huh? I didn't know that. No, I did not know that. But aren't they dangerous? I mean, like that shark from Jaws?"

"Great white sharks have been known to attack humans, it's true," said Gran as she gave me a look of caution. The disadvantage of being with Denice was that we couldn't freely shoot the breeze with Gran and have that pleasant back-and-forth that is typical of neighborhood watch stake-outs. Instead, we had to keep our conversation to a strict minimum, which was a little limiting, since the four of us are pretty big on talking, and so is Gran.

"I hope he won't attack anyone," said Scarlett, who was daintily taking a bite from a radish. She's not one for devouring big chunks of meat, mindful as she is about her figure. "I don't think it would be good for Hampton Cove if a shark attacks someone. Or for the resort, for that matter."

"I don't think it would do much to dissuade people from visiting the resort," said Gran. "I mean, we have the pool. And people have already paid for their stay here, so I don't think they'll flee the resort en masse. And besides, people like some excitement, and who doesn't want to see a real live great white shark?"

"I don't," said Dooley. "Unless he's really nice, of course. But seeing as he's out there in the ocean and we're here on the shore, I don't see how we would ever meet."

"Unless we go out there on a boat," said Brutus, "and have

a chat with him." He laughed. "Imagine that. Us having a chat with a shark!"

"Yeah, that would be ridiculous," I said, as my stomach suddenly gave a sort of lurch or spasm. The last thing I wanted was to go have a friendly chat with a great big white shark—or even a great white shark, big or not big. I didn't think we would get along with a species who likes to eat things, whether they be car tires, old bicycles, or humans. He might even like to eat cats. And if there's one thing I'm allergic to, it's to being eaten alive. It would cramp my style, and I think I speak for any cat when I say that steering clear of sharks is probably a good rule of thumb to live by.

With conversation limited to the four of us talking amongst each other, and Gran and her friends talking amongst themselves, time passed by ever so slowly. And when two hours had passed and there still was no sign of the thief, I think I wasn't the only one who felt that perhaps it was a good idea to call it a night and consider the mission a bust.

Gran seemed annoyed that the thief had decided not to respect her plan of catching him in the act. "I don't understand what's taking him so long," she grumbled.

The cooler was empty, and she was running low on both food and patience.

Denice yawned and stretched. "Maybe he's taking a break from stealing stuff?" she suggested. "Even thieves take a vacation from time to time, you know."

"Yeah, maybe he's down at the beach enjoying one of those beach parties," Scarlett suggested.

"What beach parties? He should be here, trying to steal stuff," said Gran. "Now we'll have to do this again tomorrow night, and the next night, until we catch him. And I don't know about you guys, but I need my beauty sleep."

"You mentioned that," said Scarlett. "And you're not the

only one. I also like to sleep. And get up early and have a nice walk along the beach before breakfast." She got up. "So I think I'll call it a night."

"Yeah, I guess I'll also pack it in," said Gran as she folded up her chair and picked up the cooler. "It's not fair, you know. Here we are, all ready to welcome this thief with open arms and a pair of shiny handcuffs, and he decides to go to some beach party."

"Yeah, he could have told us," Scarlett quipped as she gave Denice a wink.

The old lady from the Midwest laughed. "You guys are such a hoot!"

"Hoot or not," said Gran, "let's hope we have better luck tomorrow. I really want to catch this thief. Otherwise, I feel like such a chump, staying here for free and having nothing to show for it."

"It's fine," said Scarlett. "I'm sure the Wheelers appreciate the efforts we're going to to catch this guy. And they know it's not as easy as it sounds. Otherwise, they would have caught him a long time ago."

"Yeah, I guess you're right," said Gran. She gave me a smile. "Are you guys ready for a nap? I know I am."

We got up without delay and trotted off with a spring in our step. "I thought you'd never ask!" said Harriet.

And before long, we were back in our room, safe and sound, and ready to have a nice long nap.

Which is when a tiny voice sounded from the bed.

"Oh, there you are. I thought you'd never get here."

It was Rico the bedbug, and he wasn't alone. On the edge of the bed, dozens of bedbugs sat, and they seemed extremely eager to get a bite out of us!

CHAPTER 17

Steven Lesinske had been working the desk at the Hampton Cove Resort & Spa for as long as he could remember—at least since he'd reached the mature age of sixteen, when he had started working there as a student. He liked it so much that he'd asked if he could stay there indefinitely, and since the feelings of mutual respect and admiration between himself and Old Man Wheeler had been reciprocal, he'd been accepted in his current position at the reception desk and hadn't looked back.

Some people had told him over the years that he could probably make a lot more money working for The Argent, arguably the most prestigious beach resort on the South Fork, but then he'd have to contend with a lot more competition in the workforce, and also—allegedly—the atmosphere at The Argent wasn't much to write home about. 'Pressure cooker environment' and 'toxic atmosphere' were some of the epithets often bandied about when the topic of The Argent cropped up in conversation.

And so he'd much rather stay on at the Hampton Cove Resort & Spa, where the atmosphere was friendly and easygoing, especially since the new management had taken over after Wheeler Senior had kicked the bucket. His widow and their three daughters now ran the resort and did a great job, as far as Steven was concerned. In fact, he couldn't have wished for a nicer employer and knew that all of his colleagues felt exactly the same way, which was why turnover was extremely low—something that couldn't be said about The Argent, where a steady stream of people needed to be hired to replace the ones that left or were canned.

As he sat behind the desk, his eyes slowly closing, he wished for his shift to end so he could go to bed. He didn't often take the night shift, as he preferred to sleep at night rather than stay up and facilitate late check-ins and walk-ins. As a young man, he hadn't minded staying up all night, and there had been times when he had pulled a double shift, but these days he couldn't quite hack it anymore, as he'd fall asleep at his desk if he did. Also, he was a married man now, with a baby on the way, and so he had other responsibilities that demanded a lot of his time away from the desk that had become his second home.

Which is why he was so surprised when all of a sudden a sort of deluge assaulted his sleepy senses and caused him to be wide awake again after a lull in the proceedings.

It started when those three funny old ladies came down from the roof, where they had held some kind of vigil in the hope of catching the thief that had been terrorizing the resort. They had dragged folding chairs up to the roof and had spent part of the night there, but according to the woman in charge, Vesta Muffin, it had all been in vain.

"Almost as if the thief knew we were waiting for him," she complained to Steven. She then patted the desk and said she was going to turn in for the night.

He thanked her for her vigilance and watched the old

ladies head to their respective rooms, followed by no less than four cats. It sure was a curious sight!

But if he had thought that was the only interlude in an otherwise unremarkable night, he was very much mistaken. Before long, his phone started ringing off the hook, and people started showing up at his desk. All of them had but one complaint: bedbugs!

Even the cats returned, this time accompanying Tex and Marge Poole, the latter claiming she was being eaten alive, and if her multitude of red spots were any indication, she wasn't lying. He himself didn't suffer from bedbug bites but a lot of people did.

"An exterminator is coming in tomorrow," he assured all those who complained. And since Cole Newman had stocked up on bug spray, he handed the cans out like candy, impressing upon every single person he dispensed the spray to that they should spray the stuff around in the rooms that had been most affected, then close the door and wait about twenty minutes before heading in again while holding their breath, and immediately opening all the windows and airing the space before they turned in for the night again.

It wasn't going to finish off those dreadful bugs, but at least it would make them sit up and think about what they were doing long enough for their guests to get some shut-eye.

And since he was starting to experience a sudden itchy feeling himself after all of those complaints, he decided to empty a can in the lobby as well. You never knew if they hadn't traveled down with the complainers and were gathering strength to attack him en masse.

He might not be allergic to the bites these beasts delivered, but that didn't mean he should allow them to use him as the main source of their meal.

And as the night progressed, and the number of

complainants dwindled and finally were reduced to nothing, he relaxed and closed his eyes again. If a person showed up at the desk, all they had to do was ring the bell and he'd be on his feet in seconds.

And he'd just been dreaming of a nice evening spent at home with his husband when a noise brought him out of his slumber and he saw that one of the guests hurried out of the resort and into the night. If he wasn't mistaken—and he rarely was, since he knew all of the guests and had a knack for remembering their names—it was that comedian who had made such a big impression that night at the show, Greg Lonsdale. Personally, he wasn't a big fan of Mr. Lonsdale, finding him a little too belligerent for his taste, but he certainly was the kind of celebrity management liked to see at the resort since he attracted a lot of attention and therefore business. And what was good for the resort was good for Steven.

It wasn't long before Lonsdale came hurrying in again, this time tucking a package under his arm. He waved a greeting at Steven and disappeared into the elevator.

Steven checked his watch. It was one o'clock. He wondered what the late delivery might be. Possibly the actor had received his latest script for another hit movie? But since it was none of his business, he closed his eyes again, and wasn't disturbed again until he was relieved by the receptionist taking over at six o'clock on the dot for the morning shift.

And he was just making the transition when a woman in a jogging outfit came running into the lobby, a look of panic on her face.

"Shark attack!" she yelled. "There's been a shark attack!"

CHAPTER 18

I don't normally advocate getting all murderous when dealing with bugs, but these bedbugs really had it coming, and so when Tex and Marge emptied a can of bug spray on the bed and its surroundings, I could only applaud them for their determination in getting rid of the foul creatures. Maybe this would teach those pesky bugs a lesson they wouldn't forget. At the very least, it might make them think twice about trying to drink our blood and vouchsafe a peaceful night for both us and Marge and Tex. Gran, as she had already indicated, didn't seem all that affected by the creatures, nor was Scarlett, but since the bugs had declared open warfare on the rest of us, the game was on!

"We have to do something," said Harriet as we awaited further developments in the case while huddling in the corridor. Tex had done the deed, and now we had to wait until the dust settled, so to speak, before we could enter, as this spray wasn't all that conducive to our good health.

"We *are* doing something," I told her. "Tex has sprayed the good spray and hopefully this will make the bugs take a hike."

"They'll be back," said Harriet, taking the pessimistic

view. "And then what? They'll be twice as angry and hungry and they will take it out on us."

"Yeah, they'll come for us big time," said Brutus. "We form an easy target." He glanced at his mate. "Though maybe not you, snuggle bug. With your long coat of fur, they might have a hard time reaching your skin and extracting your blood."

"Oh, but they're very persistent," said Harriet. "Extremely so, in fact. A little bit of fur won't stop them from trying to have a nibble at my precious corpus." She shivered. "Imagine that. Being eaten alive by a bunch of annoying little bugs. It's not fair, is it?"

"No, it certainly isn't," I agreed.

"And that for a five-star resort. They should have taken care of this problem long before the guests started being devoured."

"Well, they're not actually eating us whole," I reminded her. "Just sucking our blood."

"Vampires!" she cried. "Blood-sucking vampires, that's what they are! And it wouldn't surprise me if they spread plenty of diseases while they're at it."

"Bedbugs aren't known for spreading diseases," said Marge. "They suck your blood, that's true, but they don't spread diseases as such."

"At least there's that," said her husband.

"I don't care," said Harriet. "I know for a fact that I don't want anything or anyone to nibble at me. I mean, I wasn't made to be nibbled on!" She directed a smile at Brutus. "Except by you, of course, snuggle pooh."

Dooley eyed her strangely. "You allow Brutus to bite you?"

"I said nibble, Dooley, not bite. Harriet doesn't allow anyone to bite her, and that includes my sweet prince."

"Who's your sweet prince?" asked Dooley, confused.

"Why this handsome fellow here, of course," said Harriet as she gave Brutus a stroke along the cheek.

As we sat there, all of a sudden that same small voice that had addressed us before now sounded nearby.

"This isn't over, cats," said the voice. "We'll get you for this, you hear me!"

It was Rico, and he and the rest of his family were emerging from the room by crawling right underneath the door. They can do that since they're so tiny.

"You tried to kill us?" Rico said. "Well, I can promise you right now that we will get even with you murderers!"

"We didn't try to kill you," I said, though my words sounded untruthful even to my own ears. "We only want to stop you from eating us alive."

"One tiny nibble!" Rico cried. "All we want is one tiny drop of blood. Is that too much to ask? I mean, you have gallons of the stuff running through your veins, and you can't even spare a single drop? That's very selfish of you, Max."

"I know," I said ruefully. "But it's not a lot of fun being bitten, you know, Rico. Cats, as a rule, don't enjoy it, and neither do our humans."

"I suggest you think long and hard about this selfish attitude of yours," Rico suggested. "Sharing is caring, Max. You've got the blood, we need the blood, and if you don't want to share voluntarily, a time might come when you won't be given a choice."

With these words, which sounded pretty ominous, I thought, he and his family moved along to get away from the deleterious effects of the bug spray.

"What... what do you mean by that?" I asked, not easy in my mind about what to my ears had sounded like a threat.

But Rico wasn't prepared to elucidate his words for my

benefit. Instead, he trekked along to put as much distance as he could between himself and our room.

"Well, good riddance is what I say," said Brutus.

"But… didn't that sound like a threat to you guys?" I asked. "I mean, it sounded like a threat to me."

"Oh, Max," said Harriet. "What can he do? Him and his army of bedbugs?"

"Well, they can gather an even bigger army," I said. "And attack us when we least expect it."

"Nonsense," said Brutus. "This poison is keeping them at bay, and they don't like it. That's why he came over all angry, but in actual fact, there's nothing he can do."

"In other words: we can finally sleep again without having to be afraid of being bitten," said Harriet jubilantly. "Oh, happy day!"

Happy day indeed, I thought, as I glanced in the direction of the retreating army of bedbugs. Something told me this wasn't over. But Harriet was right: at least we'd be able to sleep again.

Before long, the four of us were stretched out on the foot of Marge and Tex's king-size bed and enjoyed a wonderful slumber. But since Marge is one of those people who like to get up early, and so is Tex, it wasn't long before they stirred and rolled out of bed. I wanted to stick around and sleep some more, but Marge didn't see it that way.

"The early bird catches the worm!" she told us while she gave us a vigorous shake.

"I'm not a bird," I told her. "So I don't eat worms."

"Let me sleep," Harriet muttered sleepily.

"You can sleep when we get home. We're on vacation now and that means we're all going for a brisk walk along the beach."

"Brisk walks along the beach are for dogs," I told her.

"Not cats. We don't do brisk walks along the beach—or anywhere, really."

"Well, this time you do," she said. "So up and about, sleepyhead!" And to show us she meant business, she physically picked us up one by one and deposited us on the floor.

It looked like we had gotten rid of the bedbugs but not of Marge's infuriating habit of getting up early and expecting us to do the same. Sometimes I wonder if vacation really is as good for a person as it's made out to be. Back home I never have to get up to go for walks along the beach.

But when Marge has a bee in her bonnet there's simply no way to convince her to drop it. And so ten minutes later, she and Tex were both dressed in leggings, T-shirts, and sunglasses and were raring to go. They had even added walking sticks to their outfit, which I found a very confounding habit. We traipsed along after them, still feeling pretty sleepy after having spent half the night on the roof trying to catch a thief, and the rest of the night worrying about bedbugs and the physical integrity of our precious bodies.

"I don't like long walks on the beach," Brutus announced. "I'm sure it's not healthy to get up this early. Or to do a lot of walking."

"You're preaching to the choir, buddy," I said. "I think beach walks are extremely overrated and possibly even bad for you. They put too much stress on the body."

"Max is right," said Brutus. "Our bodies weren't made for walking."

"We should have slept in Gran's room," said Dooley. "I'm sure she's not as crazy as Marge. She won't get up in the middle of the night to go walk on some silly beach."

But there, it would seem, we had been mistaken. For when we reached the lobby, we found that Gran was waiting for us, dressed in similar garb as her daughter and son-in-law, only in her case more fluorescent. Accompanying her was Scarlett, looking fresh as a daisy, which was quite a feat, considering she had also been up on that same roof with us.

It just goes to show that humans are a pretty hardy species.

Five minutes later we were trailing after our humans, who were setting a pretty fast pace, propelling themselves forward with their sticks, or whatever those things were called.

"It's called Nordic Walking," Dooley explained. "Gran says it's very invigorating. It involves ninety percent of all the body's muscles and is a lot better than simple walking."

"Maybe *we* should get some of those Nordic Walking poles," Harriet quipped.

"Haha," I said, not in the mood for levity. Not at that early hour, at least.

A sort of gathering caught our attention, with several people all standing around some object located on the beach.

"Probably a seal," said Brutus. "They sometimes like to rest on the beach after an exhausting trip across the ocean."

And since any opportunity to take a break is fine with us, we were pleased to find that our humans were as curious as we were to look at the seals.

Only when we got there, it turned out that it wasn't a seal lying on the beach, but a human being. He looked very much dead, and if I wasn't mistaken, it was none other than Greg Lonsdale! Oddly enough, a big chunk of his leg was missing, causing bystanders to whisper those ominous words feared by any beachgoer: "Must have been a shark attack!"

CHAPTER 19

Odelia and Chase had arrived and had been assigned by Uncle Alec to conduct the investigation into the death of the famous comedian. Abe Cornwall, the county medical examiner, had also joined us and was busy doing a preliminary examination of the body. The location where the body had washed up on the beach had been cordoned off, and officers had been dispatched to make sure that onlookers and tourists were kept at bay while law enforcement could ensure that the scene was preserved and that nobody got anywhere near the body. A sort of tent had even been set up to prevent people from snapping pictures on their phones, or reporters from doing the same.

The four of us kept our respectful distance, not just because we didn't want to get in the way of the professionals doing what they did best, but also because I don't particularly like to get too close to dead bodies, especially when they have big chunks of their persons missing, as if after a shark attack.

"Good thing that shark didn't grab *us* yesterday," said Harriet. "It could have happened, you know. One slip on that breakwater and we would have been goners. Once you find yourself in those treacherous waves, you're fish food, especially when a big fish like that shark is circling the waters."

I swallowed a lump of unease, as the prospect of being swallowed up by a shark appeals to me even less than being chewed on by bedbugs. At least bedbugs aren't lethal.

"Shark attack, you think, Abe?" asked Chase after the medical man had studied the body with distinct interest. Every case is different, and Abe likes them all, the epitome of a man who loves his job.

"You'd think so, wouldn't you?" said Abe. "But I'm not so sure."

"What do you mean?" asked Odelia. "He's clearly been bitten. Part of his leg is gone."

"Probably went for an early swim," said Chase, "and got nabbed by the shark, who dragged him under the surface and caused the poor fellow to drown."

"Like I said, you'd think so, wouldn't you?" said Abe. "But look here." He pointed to the wound on the leg. "Neatly sliced off—to the bone. As if someone shaved off pieces with a knife. Not exactly the kind of stuff a shark would get up to. And also, there's a deep stab wound in his chest, and it wouldn't surprise me if that's what actually killed him."

"What are you saying?" asked Chase. "That he was stabbed to death?"

"That's exactly what I'm saying," said Abe. "Stabbed to death and then dumped in the ocean. To make it look as if he was attacked by a shark." But then he threw up his hands. "Now look what you made me do. I'm speculating! All I can tell you right now is that he has a stab wound to the chest and that a piece of flesh on his right leg was sliced off. The rest is speculation, and I for one am not going to engage in that kind of unprofessional behavior." He got up with some effort and gave Chase a smile. "You'll have to wait until I get this poor fellow on my slab. You can expect my full report in due course, detective."

"That stab wound to the chest," said Odelia. "Is it possible that a shark did that?"

"Oh, right," said Chase. "He bit down on his chest and one of his teeth dug a hole into his chest?"

"Absolutely out of the question," said Abe. "If that were the case, he should have corresponding bite marks all over his torso, and there are none. So unless this is a shark with only one single tooth, and a very thin, sharp one at that, I think your theory doesn't hold water, Odelia." He shook his head. "No, I don't think this was a shark attack at all. I think this man was murdered." And with this surprising statement, he gave them a cheerful salute and headed off in the direction of his car.

"Murdered!" said Odelia. "But then how did he end up in the ocean?"

"Dumped, most likely," said Chase, "just like Abe said."

"Which means that this must have happened pretty recently," said Odelia.

"I still don't understand what Abe said about the leg," said Chase as he rubbed his chin. "The meat sliced off, all the way to the bone? Couldn't a shark have done that?"

"It's possible that the poor guy was murdered, and after he ended up in the water the shark got to him and chewed up his leg," said Odelia.

"I think that's a reasonable assumption. And it would explain the wound on the leg."

"We better head down to the resort," said Odelia. "Talk to the people who last saw him."

"He was a comedian of some kind, right?"

"Yeah, he was a famous insult comedian."

"An insult comedian? I didn't even know that was a thing."

"It is, and he was considered a master at it. He loved to come up with ways of insulting people in the most creative ways."

"I guess someone couldn't take a joke."

And since there wasn't a lot more we could do for the man, Odelia and Chase decided to launch into their investigation.

Looked like vacation time was at an end, both for us and for Mr. Greg Lonsdale.

CHAPTER 20

"I don't think it's a lot of fun being nibbled on by a shark, Max," said Dooley as we made our way back to the resort.

"If I understood Abe correctly, he was already dead when the shark nibbled on him," said Harriet. "So that's probably a good thing, since he didn't feel anything."

"I guess you're right," said Dooley, cheering up. "If you're going to be nibbled on by a shark, better make sure you're quite dead first."

"That would be my advice," said Harriet.

It was solid advice, I thought, though it didn't exactly fill me with a sense of warm anticipation. The best thing would be *not* to end up dead and *not* to be nibbled on by a shark. In my personal view at least.

Before long, we had returned to the resort and found a couple of familiar faces waiting for us: Marge and Tex, and also Gran, Scarlett, and their new recruit, Denice. All of them were eager to find out what was going on. And since Odelia may be a police consultant but doesn't have a heart of stone, she decided to share what they had discovered so far with her nearest and dearest. What interested me the most was to find the dog that belonged to Greg. So far, I hadn't really paid much attention to the creature, and I didn't even think we had laid eyes on it, but now that its owner had ended up murdered, it was important we had a chat with the little doggie—or the big doggie, as the case might be.

"We need to find that dog, Max," said Brutus. "The dog is always the key."

I didn't know if that was the case, but it was certainly true that the dog might know stuff. Stuff that could give us a clue as to what had happened to Greg and who killed him.

"We should probably talk to the shark also," said Dooley. When we gave him a look of astonishment, he quickly added, "He's probably the last person who saw the victim alive. Well, apart from the murderer, of course."

Since the last thing I wanted was to talk to the shark, I merely nodded and hoped that the same idea wouldn't occur to Odelia. I like to solve mysteries as much as the next cat, but that doesn't mean I have to take things to the extreme.

Chase had picked the victim's phone from his pocket and was checking it now. "Plenty of messages about hot dogs," he announced as he scrolled through the messages. "He seems to have been pretty crazy about the stuff."

"Odd," said Odelia. "To be a guest at a five-star resort and still wanting to order hot dogs."

"Maybe they don't serve hot dogs at the resort," Chase ventured.

"Where did he order them from?"

"Some person he called the Hot Dog Guy," said Chase.

"Very original," said Odelia with a smile.

"Sometimes I wish *I* had a hot dog guy on call," said Chase. And when Odelia gave him a strange look, he added, "Just when I get a craving, you know. As one does."

"I guess," she said, though I got the impression she wasn't as into hot dogs as her hubby was.

The first person they talked to was the hotel receptionist, a man named Steven Lesinske. Mr. Lesinske was a man in his late thirties or early forties who looked extremely tired. But then he'd been up and about since the night before, as he'd been on night shift. He looked dead on his feet, and I felt sorry for the guy.

"No, I didn't see him leave," said Steven as Chase and Odelia questioned him. "He probably took a different exit. Though it's not unusual for our guests to go for an early walk on the beach or a jog. I did see him around one o'clock, when he stepped out for a moment. And before you ask, he returned safely and went up to his room."

"Was he gone long?" asked Chase.

"Only a couple of minutes."

Chase turned to his wife. "Possibly to meet the Hot Dog Guy."

"The Hot Dog Guy?" asked the receptionist.

"Mr. Lonsdale seems to have had a penchant for hot dogs."

The man smiled. "As one does."

"Right?" said Chase with a grin. But then he turned professional again. "So you didn't see him leave this morning?"

"I did not. I did see your mom and dad take off," he told Odelia. "They said they were going for a walk."

"They're the ones who found Mr. Lonsdale," said Odelia. "And called 911."

The receptionist shivered. "I can't imagine finding a dead body on the beach. Was he badly injured? It was a shark attack, wasn't it?"

"We're not sure yet," said Chase diplomatically. "So what can you tell us about Mr. Lonsdale?"

"Nothing much," said Steven. "I mean, nothing that everybody doesn't know already. He was a famous comedian but not well-liked as he had a habit of rubbing people the wrong way. It was his stock in trade, so to speak, and to make sure that he kept up the habit he managed to get into an argument with one of our waiters yesterday."

"What happened?"

"Mr. Lonsdale's cocktail wasn't cold enough, so he complained about that. And then the waiter accidentally knocked over the glass, and the cocktail ended up all over Mr. Lonsdale's shirt. It was enough to tip him over the edge and demand the waiter be fired."

"And he was fired?"

"Absolutely. When the likes of Mr. Lonsdale demand that a person is fired, he usually gets his way. Customer is king and all of that." He didn't look convinced that this particular customer had been king, I thought. And so I got the impression he hadn't liked him very much. But then if he had gotten a colleague fired, that was only to be expected.

"Anything else you can tell us?" asked Chase as he jotted down a note in his notebook. "Anything out of the ordinary that happened last night or early this morning?"

The receptionist thought for a moment. "There was a whole spate of complaints about bedbugs last night. I ended up doling out plenty of bug spray to a lot of guests, but I don't know if that's relevant," he added when Chase raised a single eyebrow. "Oh, and there was one other thing. I didn't think anything of it at the time, but now with this… death, I do. Someone called early this morning that a room needed to be cleaned."

"Is that unusual?" asked Odelia.

"Yeah, I would think rooms need to be cleaned all the time," added Chase.

"Not in the middle of the night," said Steven. "Mostly

rooms are cleaned after guests check out, not before. But this room was so dirty the guest demanded it be cleaned right away, and not a regular cleaning either, but deep cleaning, which was even more unusual. When I asked why, he said he was unable to sleep since the room was extremely filthy, and if we didn't clean it immediately he would be forced to leave a negative review."

"So did you clean the room?"

"Not me personally, no, but I did ask the person in charge of housekeeping to put it on the list. I'm sure it's been done by now."

Odelia nor Chase seemed to think much of the story but still made a note of it. In a murder investigation, anything and everything might prove important, and so I was sure they'd check it out eventually, even though it sounded like an innocuous enough story.

"Oh, and there was one other thing," said the receptionist. "A different guest made a noise complaint. Said that there was a couple fighting in the room next to his and he wanted me to make it stop as he couldn't sleep."

"A noise complaint," said Chase as he made another note.

"Oddly enough, it was the room next to the one that needed to be deep-cleaned," the receptionist added as he stifled a yawn.

This had Odelia and Chase looking up. "So let me get this straight," said Chase. "A guest complained that a couple were fighting in the room next door. And then another guest complained that his room was so dirty it needed to be deep-cleaned?"

"That's right." The receptionist gave him an apologetic look. "I'm sorry, this is probably not important, but you did ask me to mention anything that happened last night."

"You did the right thing, Steven. When was this? I mean, when did these calls come in?"

"Um…" Steven consulted a document on his desk. "Every complaint is logged," he explained. "And then later we follow up with the guests, making sure that the complaint has been handled to their satisfaction." He slid his finger down the list and stopped on a line near the bottom. "Three o'clock," he said, "was when the call about the noise complaint came in. Room number 336 complained that a couple were arguing in Room 337. It sounded as if they were really going at it," he said with a smile. "One of them was screaming so loud that the guests couldn't sleep."

"But you didn't go up and check?"

"I didn't get the chance. It was around that same time when a lot of people started calling down to the desk and showing up in person, to complain about bedbugs. Suddenly this place was pandemonium. I ended up distributing an entire box of bug spray. By the time I was done, I'd more or less forgotten about the noise complaint, to be honest. And since the guest in Room 336 didn't call again, I assumed that the noise had stopped."

"Okay, and the guest in Room 337 asked for a deep cleaning of his room?"

"That's correct. The guest staying in Room 337 called at…" He consulted his list again. "At four o'clock, demanding that the room be deep-cleaned as soon as possible, since it was filthy and he couldn't possibly stay in a room like that."

"Did he ask to switch rooms?" asked Odelia.

Steven slowly shook his head. "No, he didn't. You're right. That's pretty strange, isn't it? If the room was so filthy he couldn't sleep, he should have asked for a different room and he didn't. But since our policy is that the customer is always right, I simply sent a message to our housekeeping department to take care of it first thing this morning."

Odelia and Chase shared a look. "Do you think the room has been cleaned?" asked Chase.

"I'm sure it has," said Steven. "We run a pretty efficient ship here at the resort, detective." He frowned. "Why? Do you think this business with the room is somehow connected to what happened to Mr. Lonsdale?"

"Can you give us a key card?" asked Chase, deciding not to answer that particular question.

"What's the name of the guest in Room 337?" asked Odelia.

"Um… that would be…" He was checking his computer, then frowned. "That's odd."

"What is?" asked Chase.

"Well, the guest in Room 337 was a Mr. Efrain Simmons. Only he checked out yesterday, after a three-day stay, so he shouldn't have been in the room last night."

"Nobody else checked in?"

The receptionist shook his head. "A couple is arriving today, but the room should have been empty last night." He looked up. "This is all *very* unusual, isn't it, detectives?"

Chase didn't respond, but it was clear that he had his own ideas about what had happened in Room 337.

CHAPTER 21

"Why is this room so important, Max?" asked Dooley.

"It's just a very strange coincidence, that's all," I said. "And in a murder investigation, coincidences are always suspicious."

The look on his face told me that he still didn't understand, so I elucidated, "A man is murdered and dumped in the ocean. A call is made in the middle of the night that an argument has broken out in the room next door. Then later another call comes in from the person staying in that room that the room urgently needs to be deep-cleaned."

His face cleared. "Oh, I think I see it now." But then a look of confusion came over him. "Though actually I don't. Not really."

"Let's just see what we find in the room," said Brutus. "Shall we?"

Chase carefully opened the door with the key card and peered in. The room looked clean enough, not a trace of the kind of bloodbath that I think we all had been expecting—

except for Dooley, maybe, who still didn't understand what was going on.

"We better get the crime scene people in here," said Odelia. "Before we trample all over any possible trace evidence."

"If my hunch is correct," said Chase, "all of that trace evidence will have been wiped away by the cleaning crew that passed through."

"So you think the room has been cleaned?"

"Like Steven said, they run a pretty tight ship here at the resort. Much to our detriment, it would seem, but to the killer's good fortune."

"We better ask the housekeeping people," said Odelia, and took out her phone.

Not five minutes passed before the head of the housekeeping department was answering Chase and Odelia's questions. The woman's name was Heather Davis, and she certainly looked efficient enough. "Yes, I did it personally," she announced. "First thing this morning. According to Steven's message, it was urgent, and the guest had complained that he would leave a bad review if we didn't take care of his complaint immediately."

"So you deep-cleaned the room?" asked Chase sadly.

The woman smiled proudly. "Every last square inch was handled by me personally, detective. Lots and lots of bleach was used, I can tell you that right now. You could eat a meal off this floor and you wouldn't risk a thing. Why? Is there a problem?"

"No problem," said Chase. "You did a great job, Mrs. Davis."

"I take pride in my work," she said.

"You didn't meet the guest who complained?" asked Odelia for good measure.

"No, that was the odd part," said Mrs. Davis. "There was

no guest. Also no personal belongings anywhere. Looked to me as if the guest had already left."

"Yeah, I guess he did," said Chase. "In a hurry, I would say."

"How was the room when you arrived?" asked Odelia.

"It looked fine. Empty, as I said. No personal belongings. It wasn't as dirty as the person had made it out to be. In fact it looked fairly clean to me."

"No... bloodstains on the floor?" asked Chase.

The woman gave him a strange look. "Blood stains? No, I didn't see any blood stains, detective."

"Thank you, Mrs. Davis."

Before long, the crime scene investigators arrived and donned their white protective suits to examine the room. Chase instructed them to use plenty of luminol and look for blood spatter and stains. Luminol will bring out those stains even if they have been washed away. Even bleach won't completely remove the stains, and luminol will bring them out if they're there.

The detective and Odelia patiently waited, and so did we. Before long, the message came that blood had indeed been found in the room. A substantial amount of it had pooled on the floor in front of the bed, and Chase nodded, his face grim.

"Looks like we have found our crime scene," he told Odelia.

"So you think Greg Lonsdale was killed here?" she asked.

"I'll bet my badge on it," he said. He glanced at the CCTV camera in the corridor. "Let's pay a visit to the security people and find out who this mystery guest could have been."

"Detective?" a voice spoke at our rear. It was one of the crime scene investigators. He held up a plastic baggie that contained a knife. "This was found underneath the floorboards," he said. "One of the boards was loose, and it must have dropped down there. We had to pry it loose with a crowbar."

"Now will you look at that," said Chase as he took the baggie and studied the knife. "There's an inscription," he said. "GL."

"Greg Lonsdale?" Odelia suggested.

"So this knife belonged to the victim?"

"Murdered with his own knife," said Odelia.

"How about that?"

It was a long, thin, serrated knife, commonly termed a carving knife, and as Chase handed it back to the crime scene investigator so it could be checked for fingerprints, DNA, and blood traces, he shook his head. "Looks like Abe was right. This was no ordinary shark attack."

The detecting duo headed down the stairs, and the four of us followed in their trail.

"We need to find Greg's dog," I told the others.

"But we haven't seen any dog," said Harriet. "So maybe he didn't bring him along to the resort?"

"I smelled him," I said. "He was definitely in the suite."

"Maybe he's with Greg's wife," said Brutus. "Or his son."

The security cameras were operated from a small room in the administrative wing of the resort, located next to reception. The person in charge of security had been expecting us and greeted Chase and Odelia with a warm handshake. "I figured you'd be paying me a visit," he said. An older man with a fringe of curly white hair around a bald dome, he had been with the resort for a long time, same way most of the regular staff were, which told me that whoever was running the resort must be doing a good job, as people seemed to enjoy working there—always a good sign.

"Looks like one of your guests was murdered," said Chase.

"Murdered?" asked the guy, whose name was Mauricio Whitfield. "But I thought... Steven told me there had been a shark attack, and there was some uncertainty as to when Mr. Lonsdale had left the hotel to go for his morning run?"

"It was definitely murder," said Chase, having less qualms confiding in the security man than he had with the receptionist. "But better not spread the word, all right? Not until we have confirmation."

"Oh, absolutely not," said Mauricio. His kind face registered dismay. "This won't be good for business," he said. "Though on the other hand, it might. It will certainly attract a lot of attention, as Mr. Lonsdale was a pretty famous guy."

"Looks like the murder took place in Room 337," said Chase. "Could we have a look at the cameras in that area? Let's say between one and four o'clock."

"Absolutely," said Mauricio, and took a seat in front of his computer. He fiddled with the keyboard and the mouse, and moments later, the black-and-white footage appeared on the screen. As he scrolled through, for a long time nothing happened, and then all of a sudden a pair of people appeared. He immediately stopped the scroll and returned to the moment the pair moved past the camera. Unfortunately for us, they had been filmed from the back, but there was no mistake: they definitely entered Room 337.

"What time is this?" asked Chase.

"Um... two-oh-five," said the security man.

"Can you scroll through and see if they exit the room at some point?" asked Chase. But no matter how far the security guard scrolled through, the two people never left the room.

"Just what I thought," said Chase. "I think one of those people is Greg Lonsdale, and the other one is his killer. They entered the room at two-oh-five, Mr. Lonsdale was killed, and the body was then dumped from the window. The killer crawled down after it and proceeded to dispose of the body by taking it out to the ocean."

"No cameras that cover that part of the building?" asked Odelia.

"Actually, there are," said the security man. "Let me call up…" He fiddled with some of the controls of the software he used to monitor the camera system, and soon an image flickered to life of the back of the resort, covering the entire rear of the building.

"This is the side that faces the beach, right?" asked Chase.

"That's right. You won't see much, since we switch off the floodlights at night, otherwise people complain they can't sleep. But we should be able to see something."

We all strained our eyes to see, but there wasn't much. Then all of a sudden, there was movement on the screen. It was hard to make out, but something was being dropped from the building.

"There," said Odelia. "That's the body of Greg being chucked out of the window."

"And that's his killer," said Chase as a second figure appeared and quickly lowered himself from the window. Room 337 was located on the third floor, but the killer conveniently managed to jump down from the room's window to the balcony of what I assumed was Room 227 and then make his way down to the ground.

"He's an acrobat," said Mauricio, admiration clear in his voice. "If I tried to do that, I'd probably break every bone in my body."

"Yeah, I couldn't do that either," said Chase, though I had no doubt that he was just being modest for Mauricio's sake.

Once the killer was safe on the ground, we could make out the body being transferred in what looked like a wheelbarrow, before the figures moved out of sight.

"There's no other cameras, I'm afraid," said Mauricio.

"I think it's pretty clear what happened," said Chase. "We probably should find that wheelbarrow. There might be traces that the killer didn't think about removing. Though considering how careful he's been, the chances of that will be pretty slim."

"Clever killer, huh?" said Mauricio, his eyes shining. This was probably the most exciting thing he'd encountered in all the years he'd been in charge of security at the resort.

"Yeah, looks like we're dealing with one smart killer," Chase confirmed. "Covering his tracks really well."

"He must have planned this in advance," said Odelia. "To have a room ready where he wouldn't be disturbed, to lure the victim there, then kill him with his own knife like that."

"So he was stabbed with his own knife, was he?" asked the security man.

Chase smiled and pressed his finger to his lips. "Mum's the word, Mauricio, all right?"

"Absolutely, detective!" said the security man. "Those reporters won't get a word out of me, no way!"

Somehow, I had a feeling that those reporters would get a lot of words out of this man—for the right price, of course.

CHAPTER 22

We were standing underneath the window of Room 337, looking for possible traces of the killer and the wheelbarrow he had used last night. There were plenty of footsteps in the grass underneath the window, but since this area of the resort was very popular, with a path that led straight to the beach, it was safe to assume that most of those footsteps belonged to the guests who used the path to go straight from their rooms to the beach, and so wouldn't yield a lot of information.

We followed the path and as we searched the bushes next to the meandering pathway, suddenly Harriet yelled, "I found it! Oh, my gosh! I found it, you guys!" We all gathered around, and saw that she had indeed found the wheelbarrow in question—or I should probably say she had found *a* wheelbarrow, quite possibly *the* wheelbarrow.

"Good work, Harriet," said Odelia, already donning plastic gloves.

"See that?" asked Chase as he examined the wheelbarrow. "Blood. This is the wheelbarrow that we saw on the footage, all right." He glanced in the direction of the beach, and I could see that he was already reconstructing last night's scene in his mind. "He must have followed this path, his cargo in the wheelbarrow. And then somehow he must have dragged the body into the ocean, hoping that it would be washed away and taken by the current. But he was unlucky, and instead the body washed ashore." He was already pressing his phone to his ear, alerting his team that another important clue had been found, and ensuring that the wheelbarrow was properly investigated.

We proceeded in the direction of the beach, and saw that it was pretty much impossible to trace the killer's path from that point onwards. Footsteps couldn't be seen in the loose sand, and if the killer had left traces in the form of blood, they had been trampled over by the beachgoers who had passed since the killer had been there with his deadly cargo.

"He must have carried the body to the water," said Chase. "No way he could have used the wheelbarrow. The sand is too loose for that. Okay, so he carried the body, then waded into the water and... just let go?"

"I can't see what else could have happened," said Odelia. She then glanced in the direction of a small pier that had been erected nearby. "Unless…"

A boat had been tied to the pier, and as we trudged through the sand to the pier, we found that it wasn't as easygoing as we would have liked. And since Odelia has a heart of gold, and so does Chase, they picked us up and carried us all the way there so we didn't have to ingest a lot of sand in the process of trying to make it to that pier.

The boat was equipped with a powerful engine and was of the relatively uncomplicated variety.

"What do you think?" asked Odelia.

But her husband had already jumped inside the boat and was investigating it closely. "There's more blood here," he announced. "Looks like he took the body out in this boat."

"He really thought of everything," said Odelia.

"I wonder who this boat belongs to," said Chase as once again he pressed his phone to his ear to alert his team of the discovery of the boat.

We didn't have to wait long, for a man came hurrying up to us. "What do you think you're doing?" he demanded as Chase climbed back onto the pier.

He was dressed in navy blue pants, a pristine white shirt, and a captain's cap.

"Is this your boat, sir?" asked Chase.

"That's right," said the guy.

Chase held up his badge, and so did Odelia, and they both introduced themselves. Immediately the guy, whose name was Weston Kerby, piped down considerably. "What is this in connection to?" he asked.

"We have reason to believe that your boat was used in the perpetration of a crime," Chase explained. "So we'll have to confiscate it for the moment as we carry out our investigation."

"Do you rent out your boat, sir?" asked Odelia.

"I do, yes. It's pretty popular with tourists, and since I live right there," he said, pointing to a villa partially obscured by the treeline, "I figured I might as well take advantage of the fact that the beach is overrun with tourists every summer."

"Did you rent out your boat last night?" asked Chase.

"What? No, of course not. Who in their right mind would take a boat out in the middle of the night?"

"How does it work?" asked Chase. "Is there a key or something?"

"No, there's a code you need to punch in and then a button you need to push. It's a very simple mechanism."

"Well, I hate to tell you this, sir," said Chase. "But it looks as if someone took your boat last night to carry a victim of a crime out and dump the body in the ocean."

The man looked properly disturbed by this piece of news. "Oh, my God," he said. "Are you sure?"

"Pretty sure," said Chase. "I'm afraid we'll have to take your fingerprints for reasons of elimination."

"Of course. Who was killed?"

"Greg Lonsdale," said Odelia.

"Not *the* Greg Lonsdale?"

Odelia nodded. "Where were you last night, sir?"

"Um, in bed," he said.

"Can anyone verify that?"

"Well, my wife," he said. His face betrayed his concern. "You don't think I had anything to do with this, do you?"

"This code," said Chase. "How does it work, exactly?"

"Well, my boat is rented mostly by people staying at the resort," he said. "So they have the code and they also handle all the bookings."

"Is it a fixed code or does it change?"

"No, it's a fixed code. So far I haven't thought about changing it. Though I guess maybe now I will."

"For a list of bookings, it's best we talk to the resort?"

He nodded. "They handle everything, and take a commission. All I do is make sure the boat is kept in working order, and the battery charged. It's an electric boat," he explained when Chase gave him an odd look. "The latest model, in fact. Brand-new."

Chase took down the man's information and thanked him for his time. He also told him to report to the police station at his earliest possible convenience so his fingerprints could be taken and entered into the database for elimination purposes. He didn't look happy about it, but then that couldn't be helped.

"Okay, so I guess we have a pretty good idea what happened," said Chase. "But how did the killer get a hold of the code?"

"He may have rented the boat at some point in the past," said Odelia. "And since the code hasn't been changed since Mr. Kerby bought the boat, all he had to do was enter the code and take the boat out to dispose of the body. Easy peasy."

"And then hope the shark would do the rest," said Chase as he scanned the horizon.

Odelia suddenly cut a look down to the four of us, and I had a sinking feeling I knew what was coming.

"No," I told her immediately. "Absolutely not!"

She gave me a sweet smile. "It's just a big fish, Max."

"It's a vicious fish! The kind of fish that eats cats for breakfast!"

"What are you talking about?" asked Harriet.

Brutus grinned. "I have a feeling that Odelia would like Max to talk to the shark. Ask him if he saw what happened last night."

Harriet's face fell. "But Odelia!" she said. "Sharks are dangerous!"

"As long as you don't get too close you should be fine," she assured us. "But it's important that you talk to this shark at some point. We like to cover every possible angle, don't we? And that shark is a potential witness. Potentially a *key* witness, even."

And so we had our task set out for us: at some point, we'd have to talk to that shark.

CHAPTER 23

While Odelia and Chase were searching the victim's suite, I thought it was only prudent to inform Odelia that we had been there before with Gran and her two cronies when we caught Greg's illegitimate daughter going through his stuff, allegedly looking to collect some of the man's hair so she could get his DNA. I wasn't sure if she was a suspect or not, but at the very least, she should be interviewed in connection to the murder.

Odelia agreed with me and wrote the name down on her tablet for later reference. In those hectic early stages of a murder investigation, there is so much that needs to be done and so many people that need to be interviewed that sometimes it's hard to decide what to do first. But at the very least the man's suite needed to be thoroughly investigated before we moved on, as he wasn't the only one who lived there. His family also resided in that same suite, and presumably wouldn't appreciate it if it was off-limits for too long.

We had been clamoring to talk to the man's dog—if he had one—of which I was fairly certain as I had smelled the creature. But that still didn't mean he had brought him along to Hampton Cove. Perhaps his clothes smelled like the dog, but he had left the creature at home. As luck would have it, we found that the dog was indeed in residence when we discovered him hiding underneath the bed.

"Oh, hey, you," said Harriet as she approached the creature. He was a small dog of the Pomeranian variety and seemed exceedingly reluctant to engage with us. I could understand why, as the suite that he considered his home away from home was suddenly filled with a lot of strangers, not to mention four cats.

"My name is Harriet," said Harriet. "And I belong to that nice lady over there. She's a detective, and so am I, and so are my three friends over here." Dutifully, we lined up so the dog could have a good look at us and decide whether he wanted to emerge from underneath the bed. "That's Max over there—he's the stocky orange one. And then there's Dooley, he's small and fluffy, and Brutus is the big, black, gorgeous cat—my boyfriend if you must know," she added affectionately. "And what is your name, my friend?"

"Barney?" said the doggie, as if he wasn't sure about his own name.

"Well, Barney, I think it's pretty cool that you want to talk to us," said Harriet. "And also very important, in light of what happened to your human."

Barney's eyes went wide with fear. "Something happened to my human?"

Harriet could have kicked herself, I saw. But she handled it like a pro. "I'm sorry to have to inform you that your human met with an accident this morning, Barney. He went swimming and unfortunately he didn't make it back to the beach."

Tears sprang to the little doggie's eyes. "You mean... he's..."

Harriet nodded seriously. "I'm afraid so."

"... dead?" Barney managed in a whisper.

"Yep. That's correct. And I'm very sorry about your loss."

"We're all very sorry," I said. "He seemed like..." I was going to say he was a nice fella, but that would have been a lie. "Well, he certainly seemed like a most fascinating man."

"He was," said Barney, as his eyes welled up with tears that soon trickled down his cheeks. "He was a fine man and I adored him." He looked up. "Are you sure he's dead?"

"Afraid so," said Harriet.

We gave the doggie some time to come to terms with what happened, but since time was of the essence and we really did need to talk to him, we couldn't give him the time he probably needed. And so after a respectful silence, I cleared my throat. "There are certain things we would like to ask," I began. "In connection with the accident, I mean." I shot a glance at Harriet, whom I felt probably should have told the doggie straight out that his human had been murdered. Now it would be difficult to backtrack from the accident ruse.

"He was the most wonderful human any dog could ever hope to be blessed with," he said sadly as he sniffled some more.

"No doubt," I said. "No doubt. So, you wouldn't happen to know who Greg met last night, would you?"

The doggie looked up. "Met? What do you mean?"

"Well, he met a person last night in Room 337," I said. "And we would very much like to know who this person is, so we can have a chat with them."

"This person was probably the last person to see Greg alive," Harriet explained.

"I didn't know about a person he met," said Barney. "I know he had a big show last night, and then after the show he returned here and had a drink, watched some television, and then he and Elaine turned in for the night."

"He and Elaine," I said. "The thing is, Greg mentioned on stage last night that he and Elaine were getting a divorce, Barney."

"Did he say that?" asked Barney, looking more and more perturbed. "Did he really?"

"He did. So, are you quite sure he and Elaine turned in for the night together?"

"Maybe I'm mistaken about that," he admitted. "Yes, now that I think of it, Elaine slept in one bedroom while Greg slept in a different one. I was wondering why that was, but I figured that maybe they'd had a fight. The atmosphere seemed a little tense."

"And what about Clyde?" I asked.

"What about him?" asked Barney with a frown of concern.

"Was he also here last night? It's just that Greg didn't seem to have a lot of good things to say about him."

"Clyde is staying in a separate room. The same suite, but a different room. And so is Lloyd."

"Who is Lloyd?" asked Brutus.

"Lloyd is Greg's dad. He's also staying in the suite, but has his own room as well. There's plenty of rooms to go around," he said, then suddenly burst into tears again.

"Oh, you poor thing," said Harriet, and reached out to pat the doggie on the back. But instead of finally emerging from under the bed, he decided to retreat even further, which made the interview a little fraught with difficulty, as we could hardly see him. Tough to interview a dog you can't see, but then we've faced bigger challenges, of course.

"Okay, so Clyde is staying at the resort, and also Elaine and Lloyd," I said. "But you wouldn't happen to have seen Greg leave at some point last night, would you? Around, let's say, two o'clock?"

"No, I was fast asleep by then," said Barney. His voice

sounded strained. "I... I better come clean to you guys. I... I didn't sleep in Greg's room last night. I slept in Elaine's room!" He broke into loud sobbing wails. "Oh, the shame! The betrayal!"

"There's no shame in preferring one human over another," said Harriet quickly. "Just look at me. I like one of my humans better than the others, and that's fine. We all have our preferences."

"Is that true?" asked Brutus. "Who do you like most?"

"Why, Marge, of course," said Harriet. "She's the nicest one of the bunch."

"I guess so," said Brutus. "Though I have to say Chase is also pretty great."

"He *is* great, but I happen to prefer Marge," said Harriet.

"I like Odelia," I confessed.

"And I like Gran," said Dooley. "She's the warmest, nicest, most loving human being I've ever met."

We all looked at him, and I think we were all wondering the same thing: was he talking about a different Gran than the one we knew? But then I guess you can't account for taste. The same was the case with Barney, apparently, who liked Elaine better than Greg.

"And so Elaine was in her room all night?" I asked, hoping to establish at least one alibi.

"She was," Barney confirmed. "If she had left, I would have noticed."

"And what about the others?" asked Harriet. "Greg, Clyde, Lloyd?"

"They were in their rooms, so I'm not sure what they were up to last night," said the dog.

"You didn't hear anyone leave the suite at some point?" I asked.

The doggie shook his head. At least I thought he did. It was a little hard to see since he had retreated to the farthest side of the bed, right up against the wall where light didn't penetrate.

"Okay, Barney," I said finally, deciding to stop tormenting the canine. "If you can think of anything that might be important to the investigation into the death of your human, please don't hesitate to get in touch, all right? We're in Room 415, along with our own humans Marge and Tex Poole."

"And also Vesta Muffin and Scarlett Canyon," Dooley added. "Though they're in Room 419, right down the hall from Marge and Tex. They're with the neighborhood watch," he explained. "Looking for a thief. But it's all hush-hush. Nobody is supposed to know about that."

"I won't tell anyone, Dooley," Barney promised.

I had a feeling the dog had a lot more to tell us, but maybe later, when he'd had time to recover from the shock of discovering that his human was dead. After all, we might be detectives, but in a sense, we're also psychologists, and at that moment my gut instinct told me to leave the doggie be for now.

And so we joined Odelia and Chase as they checked the suite for any sign of what could have brought this calamity to the house of Lonsdale. There wasn't all that much to find, apart from the man's phone and laptop, which might yield a clue or two. And as I checked the small selection of books on the man's nightstand, I saw that he seemed to have a particular interest in Victorian-era England, if the titles of the books in his collection were anything to go on. Charles Dickens, but also William Buckland and others.

Quite the history buff, in other words, and it made me wonder if perhaps he was preparing a show that dealt with that period. We'd probably never know, as he wouldn't be able to share his considerable talent with the rest of the world anymore.

"Odelia!" Chase suddenly yelled. We all came running,

and saw that Chase was clutching a leather case that contained a set of carving knives. They all looked exactly like the carving knife that had been found stuck under the floorboards of Room 337. All of them had the man's initials carved into them, and as Chase pointed to an empty space in the set, it was clear where the carving knife that had killed the man had come from.

"Murdered with his own knife," said Brutus, shaking his head. "Oh, the disgrace."

"Poor guy," said Harriet, shaking her head.

Behind us, suddenly a cry of despair sounded, and when we turned around, we saw that Barney had followed us and was staring at the set of knives, a look of horror on his face. Then he turned on his heel and hurried off again.

"Darn it," said Brutus. "What a way to find out his human has been murdered."

Harriet decided to go after the doggie, but when we made to follow, she said, "Better let me handle this. He seems to trust me."

And so we watched her go off after the Pomeranian.

CHAPTER 24

It didn't take Harriet long to find the little doggie, who had opted to hide underneath the bed of his master again, possibly because he felt closer to him that way.

"I'm so sorry you had to find out like that," she told him as she lounged on the edge of the cavernous space that yawned before her. It was a pretty big bed, and she wondered if they shouldn't have broken the news to the Pomeranian immediately, instead of trying to cushion the blow.

For a moment, the dog didn't speak. Then a weak voice sounded from the recesses of the space under the bed. "Was he really... murdered?"

"I'm afraid so," she said.

"With... his own knife?"

"That's what it looks like."

"But who would do such a thing? He was such a wonderful person!"

"I'm sure he was," she said. "Had you been with him long?"

"Since the day I was born," said Barney. "Well, maybe not exactly the day I was born, but very soon after. He'd had a dog just like me before, you see, and he missed him so much he decided to try and find a replacement. Though I like to think I was so much more than just a replacement." He paused. "My predecessor's name was also Barney, so that's what Greg decided to christen me. But over the years we developed a strong bond. We were never apart, and we traveled everywhere together."

"You traveled a lot, did you?" she asked as she stretched out on the floor. She thought she could see a glimpse of the dog as he hid right up against the wall, staying well out of sight. He probably felt safer that way, where he couldn't be reached.

"We did," said Barney. "We traveled all across the globe. Greg's work took him to China, South Korea, the Philippines, Thailand, Laos, Vietnam, Cambodia, Indonesia, all the fifty states, and of course Europe, where he was just as big a star as he was over here in the States. He toured all the time and spent most of his time in hotel rooms. Though when he was home we also hung out, and he always made sure to walk me personally and never even once hired a dog walker, like other celebrities sometimes do when they don't want to be bothered with the drawbacks of owning a dog."

"He sounds like a wonderful master," Harriet conceded.

"He was," said Barney. "The absolute best."

"How about Elaine? Did she treat you all right?"

"Elaine is all right," said Barney. "Though she's not as much into dogs as Greg was. Greg was a dog person, and Elaine isn't." He sighed. "Do you think I'll have to go and live with Elaine from now on?"

"Or Clyde," said Harriet. "He's also in your life, isn't he?"

"I guess," said Barney, and it didn't sound as if he was all that excited about having to spend the rest of his life with either Elaine or Clyde. "Or Lloyd. He's not too bad. I actually like him better than Clyde or Elaine."

"Who's Lloyd again?" asked Harriet.

"Greg's dad. He's been living with us since his wife died a couple of months ago. He's an odd one, but I like him."

"Odd in what sense?" asked Harriet.

"He likes to lug the ashes of his dead wife along with him everywhere he goes. I'm not sure why. Something to do with scattering them in the right place. Though from the looks of things he hasn't found the right place yet. He'll have two sets of ashes to scatter now, those of his wife and his son."

"Did Greg get along with all the members of his family?" asked Harriet.

"Oh, absolutely. They all got along great."

"That's wonderful to hear," said Harriet. "So nice when you live in a harmonious home, isn't it? No shouting, no fighting. Just peace and harmony all the time."

"That's exactly the way it was with us," said Barney. "All peace and harmony all the time. The perfect home, in other words."

"Okay, I'll leave you to it, Barney," said Harriet, when Max appeared in the door and indicated that it was time for them to leave. She was pretty sure that the big blorange cat had been listening in, and had heard the entire conversation. "If there's anything you need, or if you want to talk about your human, feel free to come find me, all right?"

"I like you, Harriet," said Barney, much to Harriet's satisfaction. "You're very kind."

"I try to be, Barney," she said, swelling up a little. "I try to be."

As she and Max moved into the next room, she saw that their humans were about to leave, and the crime scene people were ready to move in and do their thing. Chase handed Greg's laptop and phone over to the person in charge, and they hurried out of the suite. "So what did he say?" asked Brutus.

"Nothing much," said Harriet. "He said they all got along great, all peace and harmony all the time. Greg was the best human in the world, and the others weren't so bad either. He likes Greg's dad best. His name is Lloyd and he lugs the ashes of his dead wife everywhere he goes, and wants to scatter them at some point. And Greg took great pride in always walking his dog himself and not leaving it to a dog walker. He also traveled extensively for his job, and Barney traveled with him."

"No idea as to who might have been after him?" asked Brutus.

She bit her lip. "Oops. I forgot to ask about that."

"It's all right," said Max. "At some point we'll have to talk to Barney again." He gave her a smile. "You did good, Harriet. Barney seems to really like and trust you. Which is a great thing as he distrusts the rest of us."

"Yeah, I don't know why that is," she said.

"Possibly because you have such a non-threatening personality," said Max. "He doesn't see you as a potential threat."

"But you don't have a threatening personality either, Max," she pointed out. "Or Dooley, who's the least threatening cat in existence."

Max shrugged. "He took a liking to you, and we should be grateful for that." His expression clouded. "Now if only you could do the same thing with the shark, that would be swell." He gave her a sideways look, and she shook her head determinedly.

"Oh, no," she said. "That shark is your responsibility, Max. I'm not going anywhere near that beast. No sharks for me, thank you very much."

"Now how am I going to talk to a shark?" asked Max. "I don't even swim. And even if I did, he'd probably eat me before I got a chance to introduce myself."

"Maybe you have to lure him to that breakwater? What do sharks like, Max?"

"Anything that moves?"

"Pretty much," she admitted. Truth be told, there was very little they did know about sharks.

"We need to find out what makes sharks tick, so we can get under his skin."

"Before he gets under yours, you mean?"

Max didn't even crack a smile. Clearly he wasn't keen on making the shark's acquaintance, and she could see why that was. There are some species of animals you best steer well clear of, and sharks were definitely among them. But since Odelia had asked them to find out what the shark knew, Max obviously felt duty-bound to see his mission through. She just hoped he wouldn't perish in the process!

CHAPTER 25

The first person we sat down with was Elaine Lonsdale, Greg's wife. She had a sort of dazed look in her eyes and didn't seem to be totally there, which was to be expected as Odelia had just broken the news to her that her husband had died. Because the suite where she and Greg had been staying was being gone through with a fine-tooth comb, the conversation was taking place outside, near the big fountain that provided so much joy to the younger segment of the resort population. At this early hour, there weren't a lot of people, and so Odelia and Chase were able to conduct the interview in relative privacy.

"I don't believe this," she said as she fidgeted with her phone, which she had placed on the table in front of her. "Greg is dead? Are you sure?"

"I'm afraid so," said Chase.

"But how?"

"It looks as if he was murdered," said Odelia.

Elaine didn't respond to this as most people would. Instead, there was a sort of delayed reaction. After perhaps ten or fifteen seconds, she looked up in surprise. "Murdered? What do you mean, murdered?"

"He was found on the beach," said Odelia, trying to be as delicate as possible. "So at first we thought that he had drowned. But the medical examiner is convinced that he was stabbed." She had taken out her own phone and showed Greg's widow a picture of the knife that had been found at the crime scene. "Do you recognize this knife, Mrs. Lonsdale?"

She took the phone from Odelia and studied the picture for a moment, then finally nodded. "It's one of a set. Greg takes them along with him everywhere he goes. He's very particular about the way his meat is cut, you see. You could probably make the case that he's the ultimate foodie. Even though he didn't mention it in his shows or his TV specials, his main joy in life was food. Wherever he went, he would insist on sampling the local cuisine. It was what he lived for. And since he traveled a lot, he got to practice his hobby all the time." She frowned. "So what are you saying? That he was stabbed with his own knife?"

"That's what it looks like," said Odelia, taking her phone back. "Though at this point we can't be sure yet. Not until the knife has been thoroughly investigated."

"My God," said Elaine. "Who would do such a thing?"

"Did your husband have a late meeting of some kind?" asked Chase.

"It's possible," she said, shaking her head. "We slept in separate bedrooms, so I really wouldn't know." When they gave her an odd look, she felt compelled to explain. "You'll probably find out soon enough, so I might as well tell you. Greg and I were getting a divorce. I have been in contact with a divorce lawyer, and we were about to file the papers. I actually informed Greg about my intention to do so last night. He didn't take it well."

"We know. He mentioned it in his show," said Odelia.

"Oh, you were here for his show?"

"We were," said Odelia.

"The thing is that our marriage had run its course," said Mrs. Lonsdale with a wave of her hand. "Greg wasn't an easy person to live with. The Greg that people saw on stage was very much the same person as the private Greg. He could be caustic to the point of being insulting, and he never held back." She gave us a bitter smile. "He would never have made a great diplomat. With Greg, what you saw was what you got, and even though I found that refreshing when we first met, over the years it got quite tiresome. I actually wanted out of the marriage a long time ago, but I didn't want our son to suffer the consequences of being shifted from parent to parent, like so many kids are. And so I waited until Clyde graduated from high school to sever the ties with his dad. Clyde is turning eighteen soon, so I felt that the time had come to start divorce proceedings."

"And Greg wasn't happy about it," said Chase.

"I knew that he wouldn't be, which is why I had hired one of the best divorce lawyers in the business. Chandra Laidens. But even though Chandra had prepared me for any contingency, I was still shocked when Greg threatened to cut me off completely. To leave me in financial ruin. We had signed a prenup, you see, that stipulated that in the case of a divorce we would walk away from the marriage with what we had put into it, and since he was the main provider, he said he'd leave me penniless. He was vindictive like that. Though Chandra had assured me that these were all idle threats, and that she would be able to secure me a reasonable divorce settlement if we played our cards right."

"So… Greg threatened to ruin you financially?" asked Chase.

"That's right," Elaine confirmed as she tapped the table

with her long nails. She still didn't really seem to be there, her mind miles away.

"And now?" asked Chase. "I mean, as a widow?"

She frowned. "What do you mean, as a widow?"

"How does Greg's death affect your financial situation?" asked Chase, never afraid of being blunt to the point of being inconsiderate.

She stared at him for a moment, and I got the impression that the temperature had suddenly dropped several degrees. "I'm not sure I like the implication of your question, detective," she said in measured tones.

"Then let me rephrase," said Chase. "Will your husband's death ruin you financially, like your divorce would have, or will you be better off?" When she kept on staring daggers at him, he added, "It's a simple question, Mrs. Lonsdale. So please answer it."

"I don't know," she said finally. "I'd have to consult with my lawyer."

"But I imagine that your husband made a will?"

"I imagine so," she said reluctantly and in icy tones. She was still tapping the table, and I got a feeling that she was about to bolt from the interview to consult with that same lawyer about how she could avoid answering more questions from this annoying detective.

"Can you tell us where you were last night around two o'clock, Mrs. Lonsdale?"

"Next thing you'll be accusing me of murdering my husband," she snapped.

"I'm not accusing you of anything," said Chase. "But I would like to know where you were when Greg was murdered."

"I was in bed. Asleep," she said curtly, and then she did rise from the chair. "I want you to know that I resent your tone, detective. And if you have any further questions for me, I would like to have my lawyer present. Is that understood?"

"One final question, if I may," said Odelia.

The woman executed the perfect eye roll. "What?"

"Greg got a delivery last night around one o'clock. He had ordered a hot dog?"

She nodded. "He had a thing for hot dogs, that's true. But whether he ordered one last night or not, I wouldn't know. At one o'clock I was sound asleep in bed."

With these words, she turned on her heels and stalked off. As she did, she placed her phone to her ear, and I got the impression she was already putting in a call to her lawyer.

"Looks like you made an enemy out of our first suspect," said Odelia.

"She is the perfect suspect, though, isn't she?" said Chase. "She just told us that she stood to lose everything in the case of a divorce, and now that Greg has conveniently been killed, she will probably inherit all of her husband's estate and be able to keep living in the way she has become accustomed. Now if that isn't a motive, I don't know what is."

"She certainly has a great motive," Odelia confirmed. "And if it's true that she was asleep in bed, alone, she doesn't have an alibi."

"Let's put her on the list," Chase suggested, and placed a big dot next to Mrs. Lonsdale's name.

Looked like he had just found his first suspect.

As we waited for the next person to show up for an interview, Harriet seemed to disagree with Chase's theory. "Barney said that all of them got along so great," she said. "He said it was all peace and harmony and all the members of his family loved each other and enjoyed each other's company. Now why would he say that if Elaine wanted to murder her husband so she could get his money?"

"Maybe Barney was lying?" I suggested.

It's hard to believe, but dogs can also make for unreliable witnesses. They love their humans and aren't always eager to talk to outsiders about what really goes on in a household, going so far as to actually lie to keep the truth from getting out.

"But he struck me as being so truthful," she said, looking disappointed. "I really believed him when he said that Greg, Elaine, Clyde, and Lloyd all got along so well. Though I have to say that this Lloyd sounds like a real eccentric. If it's true that he lugs the ashes of his dead wife around with him wherever he goes, looking for the perfect place to scatter them, he's probably not of sound mind and body. So maybe *he* killed his son."

"Sounds like quite the character," said Brutus.

"We should probably tell Odelia," I said, and so I proceeded to put our human in the know of this strange state of affairs.

She looked worried. "If Barney is right, that does sound extremely worrying."

But before she could say more, Clyde Lonsdale arrived, looking sullen and dejected.

Time to have a chat with the kid and find out what he had to say about dear old dad.

CHAPTER 26

"No, I did not like my dad," said Clyde before the first question had been asked. He placed his hands on the table and gave his interviewers a tired look. "He was a bully and a jerk, but that doesn't mean I killed him, all right? And if you want to know, I was in my room last night, talking to a friend on the phone. You can ask him if you want. I have his information right here." He shoved his phone across the table in Chase's direction, who stopped it before it skittered over the edge and smashed to the ground.

"You know that your father was killed?" asked the detective with a note of surprise.

Clyde shrugged and sat back in his chair. "It's all over the internet by now. There's even a TikTok video of his body lying on the beach. Stab wound to the chest, yes?"

Chase stared at the kid. "They showed that on TikTok?"

"Someone was filming on their phone, detective."

Chase shook his head. "It seems that there's always someone filming," he said.

"According to the video, he was stabbed to death with a

knife, and his body was fed to the sharks. Looks like whoever killed him did a pretty good job."

"You don't seem sad," said Odelia.

"Like I just told you, there was no love lost between my dad and me. After all, he had been bullying me since I was a kid, so…"

"Your dad bullied you?"

"He did, yeah. I think I'm probably the only kid on the planet whose dad bullied him for financial gain. He made millions out of using me and the rest of his family as the butt of his jokes." He gestured to his phone. "It's all right there. Most of his stuff is on YouTube. There's videos devoted entirely to me, Clyde McCloud, with all of my dad's greatest hits—and I can assure you that you can take the word 'hits' literally in my case. He may not have been physically abusive, but psychologically he definitely was. And I've got the therapist's bills to prove it. Or at least my dad does, since he was the one who had to pay them. Yes, detective," he confirmed. "I've been seeing a shrink since the tender age of twelve, and it's all my dad's doing." He grinned. "A small sense of satisfaction that he had to spend money to undo the damage he did to make money at my expense."

"I'm sorry you had to go through that," said Odelia with feeling.

"Look, I don't know who killed my dad," said the teenager, "but I'm sure there are plenty of candidates. He was not a very nice person, and he insulted a lot of people over the course of a long and successful career."

"Anyone you can think of in particular?" asked Chase.

Clyde frowned. "As a matter of fact, his most notorious victim is staying here at the resort right now. A coincidence, probably."

"Name?" asked Chase.

"Dejuan Daly? I didn't think you'd need to ask. It's a

pretty famous case and got a lot of attention at the time. He punched my dad at an award show?"

"I remember that," said Odelia, nodding. "Didn't your dad mention him last night, during his show?"

"He did, yeah. Dad can't ever pass up an opportunity to insult a person, and even though Dejuan punched him once, he was probably hoping he would do it again, if pushed hard enough. He got a lot of mileage out of that one punch."

"What happened to Dejuan, do you know?"

"He lost everything, that's what happened. His career, his reputation, his friends. Now if there's one guy who had every reason to kill my dad, it's him."

Chase had noted down the name of the friend Clyde had been talking to last night, and thanked the kid for his time. But when he wanted to offer his condolences, Clyde held up his hand. "Save it for someone who cares, detective," he said, a little harshly, I thought. But then he clearly hadn't lied when he said that he hadn't gotten along with his dad.

* * *

"Poor kid," said Dooley. "To be used by your dad as the punchline for his jokes. That wasn't a nice thing to do, was it, Max?"

"No, it certainly wasn't," I said.

"I think he did it," said Brutus, as he eyed the kid sauntering away from us, his hands shoved in his pockets and seemingly unaffected by the death of his dad. "He hated his father for all the abuse he had piled on him over the years, and so last night things came to a head and he finally stabbed him with his own knife, then tried to make it look like a shark attack. No, he's guilty, all right."

"But what about his friend?" I asked. "He said he was talking to his friend all night."

Brutus made a throwaway gesture with his paw. "Oh, please. They're probably in cahoots, him and his friend. They arranged things so Clyde would have an alibi. Press this friend and he'll cave, I'm sure of it. And so will Clyde himself. In fact, I can tell that he can't wait to tell the whole world what he did."

"He didn't strike me as a killer," said Harriet. "More as a sad kid who wanted desperately for his father to love him, and when he didn't, retreated into his shell."

"I guess we see things differently, snuggle pooh," said Brutus. "Because all I see is a psycho killer, and if he's not stopped he will probably kill again."

"And to think that Barney told me that everyone in that family loved one another," said Harriet. "Peace and harmony, my paw. He was lying through his little Pomeranian teeth."

"You can't trust a dog," said Brutus. "How many times do I have to tell you? Dogs are compulsive liars."

"Not the dogs that I know," she said. "But clearly you're right about Barney. Unless he's one of those dogs that wear rose-tinted glasses when they see the world. Full of self-delusion, you know."

Our next interviewee had arrived, and we welcomed none other than the actor that Clyde had accused of murdering his dad. Dejuan Daly wasn't alone, but had brought his girlfriend Tawanna Kimura along with him. The couple were holding hands and seemed determined to present a united front.

"Whatever you think, I didn't do it," were the first words out of the actor's mouth.

"And I can confirm that," said Tawanna. "I was with Dejuan all night, and he never left the room. So he couldn't possibly have killed Greg Lonsdale. Though he probably should have," she added quite surprisingly.

"Tawanna!" Dejuan said, clearly not having expected this.

"It's true," said the young woman. "The way that man treated you, he deserved everything he got, including being eaten by that shark."

"He wasn't actually eaten by a shark," Odelia pointed out.

"Oh? But on the news they said his leg had been chewed off completely."

"His leg hadn't been chewed off," said Chase with a sigh. He was starting to view the people who had put the footage of Greg lying on the beach online as real pests, spreading a bunch of gossip that wasn't doing his investigation any good.

"What makes you say that your boyfriend should have killed Greg?" asked Odelia.

"That man ruined Dejuan's life, Mrs. Kingsley," said Tawanna. She was an attractive woman in her early thirties, with gorgeous skin the color and texture of honey, and seemed determined to defend her boyfriend. At least one good thing had come out of the man's run-in with the late comedian. "He pestered him and pushed his buttons to the point that Dejuan simply broke down and reacted like any person would: by punching his lights out. And if he hadn't done it, he would have lost his self-respect."

"He may have held on to his self-respect but he did lose his career," Chase pointed out.

"I only had myself to blame," said Dejuan, giving his girlfriend a pointed look. Clearly they had rehearsed what they were going to say, and Tawanna going off script like this wasn't what the ex-actor wanted. "I shouldn't have reacted the way I did and I regret it to this day. It was a terrible thing to do and I have paid the price. I have apologized to Greg Lonsdale and there was no bad blood between us. We cleared all of that up after the fact."

"Didn't he make fun of you last night?" asked Chase. "Try to goad you into giving him another punch?"

"If that's how it came across, I'm sure it wasn't his intention," said Dejuan staunchly.

"Oh, for crying out loud, Dejuan," said Tawanna. "Of course that was his intention. He wanted you to punch him again, considering how much publicity it garnered him last time. It made his career, even as it tanked yours."

"I'm sure he didn't mean it like that," the actor insisted with a dark frown. "Greg and I shared this history, but we had cleared the air and everything was fine between us."

"Sure, everything was fine between you," said Tawanna with a grimace. "That's why he kept referring to you as DeTurd Bailey. Because you bail every time things get tough." Dejuan looked hurt by this comment, and I could tell that Tawanna already regretted her words. "I'm sorry," she said. "I shouldn't have said that. Ever since you've been in therapy, you've made great strides forward."

"You've been in therapy?" asked Chase.

"Yeah, since it happened. At first it was court-ordered," said Dejuan, "but after that ended I've stayed in therapy, as I find it has helped me cope with the fallout from the incident. I like to think I've become a better person and even though my old life is gone and so is my career, I'm very happy with where I'm at right now." He gripped his girlfriend's hand and said with a tight smile, "We're pregnant, you know. And also, I have a new job, moved to a different town, built a house—a family soon. I like the new Dejuan."

"I also like the new Dejuan," said Tawanna affectionately.

"I wouldn't jeopardize all of that just to get back at Greg," Dejuan stressed. "It's true that we hit a rough patch after I punched him, but that's all in the past for me—that Dejuan doesn't exist anymore."

"Can you think of anyone else who may have wished him harm?" asked Odelia.

Tawanna scoffed, "Are you kidding? Maybe it would be

easier to make a list of people who *didn't* want to kill Greg Lonsdale. It would be a lot shorter."

"Anyone in particular come to mind?"

"All the people he insulted in his shows? And that's a long list."

"There was that waiter yesterday," Dejuan said.

"A waiter?" asked Chase.

"Greg got a waiter fired yesterday," said Tawanna. "I know this because I was right there. This was before Greg found out that I was Dejuan's girlfriend. I was at the pool and he got into this altercation with a waiter. Something about his drink not being cold enough or something. According to the guy at reception, he demanded the waiter be fired, and he *was* fired. On the spot. Which just goes to show that Greg Lonsdale was a terrible excuse for a human being, and hadn't changed one bit since he had destroyed Dejuan's career."

"All water under the bridge," Dejuan murmured unhappily.

Tawanna sat up a little straighter. "Now listen to me, Dejuan Daley. If you don't start to stand up for yourself and stop being a wuss, I'm going to tell that therapist of yours that he's not doing a good job. Is that understood?"

"Yes, honey," said Dejuan meekly.

"This is exactly what I mean," she said, planting her hands on her hips. "No backbone whatsoever!"

"Yes, honey."

She gave him a slight shove. "Tell me to take a hike!"

"Take a hike, honey."

"Say it like you mean it!"

"Take a hike, honey!"

"Better," she said. "Maybe *I* should be your therapist. I think I'd do a darn sight better job than the one you have now."

"Yes, honey."

She groaned in frustration, and it was clear that it was the wrong answer.

"I think *she's* the killer," said Brutus, nodding.

"I thought you said the son was the killer?" I asked.

"I was wrong. Clearly this woman is the killer. Just look at those eyes. They're blazing, Max. Absolutely blazing! If she had a knife right now she'd plant it right in her boyfriend's chest."

It was true that Tawanna had a fiery temper. But was that enough to murder a man she hardly knew? And all because he had insulted her boyfriend a year ago?

"She has an alibi," I pointed out. "She was with Dejuan all night."

"That spineless little weasel? He'd say anything."

"That's true," said Harriet. "He would tell us that he was with her all night, even if she was out murdering Greg."

"I don't see it," I said. And when Brutus gave me a dirty look, I added, "I really don't! She didn't even know the guy. Now why would she go and murder a total stranger, just because he once insulted her boyfriend? It's not a strong motive for murder, Brutus."

"She did it," he insisted. "And when Odelia and Chase prove it, don't come crying to me, Max. I called it, and you'd do well to remember when this case is over and she's in prison."

"Fine," I said. "If she is guilty, I will remember that you called it."

"That's all I ask," he said. "To get the credit I deserve."

The couple left the table, and as they walked away, Tawanna was gesticulating wildly, with Dejuan looking dejected.

"Oh, dear," said Odelia. "I hope they'll make up soon."

"They'll be fine," said Chase. "A murder investigation can be tough on people. It's stressful for everyone involved. I'm sure that once this is all over and the killer has been caught, they'll kiss and make up." He checked his notes. "So who's next?"

"I would like to talk to this waiter Tawanna mentioned. The receptionist also said that he was fired, remember? And if that's true, he had every reason to get even with the man." She placed her phone to her ear. "Oh, and we need to speak to Greg's dad Lloyd as well."

I settled down next to the table. Looked like this could be a *loooooong* day. But then part of being a detective's cat is exactly that: spending a lot of time watching your human talk to people and trying to determine who's lying and who's telling the truth.

CHAPTER 27

As we waited for the waiter to show up, we had an opportunity to talk to Greg's dad. Lloyd Lonsdale was a tall man with a full head of white hair and looked a lot like his son. Unlike the suggestion that had been made, he wasn't lugging an urn filled with ashes around with him. He was dressed in baggy cargo pants and a T-shirt that professed his love for the LA Rams, and took a seat at the table looking quite sad. "Such a horrible thing to have happen," he said. "First my wife and now my son. This is really my annus horribilis as the Queen of England used to say. Or am I thinking of a different person?"

"I wouldn't know," said Chase, who isn't a big connoisseur of all things kings and queens. "I'm sorry for your loss, sir."

"Thanks, Detective Kingsley," said the man appreciatively. "So have you any idea what happened, exactly? The internet is rife with all kinds of wild speculation, so I would like to hear it from you." He leaned forward. "Was it a shark attack, as I've seen mentioned?"

"It wasn't a shark attack," said Chase.

"I'm afraid your son was murdered, Mr. Lonsdale," said Odelia.

"Oh, my God," said the man and rubbed his face. "So it's true. I saw my grandson just now, and he told me it was murder. I didn't believe him, but if you're telling me it's true…" His voice trailed off, and he took off his glasses and wiped a tear from his eyes. "I mean, my son was no saint by any stretch of the imagination, but he didn't deserve this."

"Why do you say he was no saint?" asked Chase.

"Well, we all know his reputation," said Mr. Lonsdale. "Calling people names on stage and all of that. He didn't do himself any favors." He gave Chase an interested look. "Do you think it was one of the people he insulted? Like that actor who punched him?"

"I'm afraid we're not at that stage yet, Mr. Lonsdale," said Chase.

"No, I guess it's too soon," said the man. "Do you know if I will have to go and identify the body? Like they do in the movies? Only I'm not sure I can go through with that. I had to do it for my wife, you see, after she collapsed in the street and passed away. It was probably the hardest thing I've ever had to do. Until you see the person lying there, dead so to speak, you can still tell yourself it isn't happening. But once you see them like that…"

"What can you tell us about your son, Mr. Lonsdale?" asked Chase. "You mentioned enemies. Anyone in particular —apart from Dejuan Daly?"

The man thought for a moment. "Can't say that anyone in particular comes to mind. He insulted so many people over the course of a long career… It's something he and I never saw eye to eye over. And neither did his mother. She hated that he put people's backs up like that. And he seemed to enjoy it, too. As if it was some big accomplishment. But I can tell you right now that it's not. I can insult people, but why should I? But Greg felt that it was an art form. He always said that you needed to fit the insult with the person, and once you did, and everything clicked into place, it was such a great feeling."

"So nobody in particular comes to mind?"

"Nah. I'm not involved in Greg's world. All those actors and singers. Most of the people he insulted I had never even heard of. They were all celebrities, but their names didn't ring a bell. I did tell him many times to stop. That it would get him into trouble. Lawsuits, of which he got plenty. Or being attacked, like the Dejuan fella. And now this murder. His mother said the same thing. That he should maybe change his image. Act in nice movies, you know. The kind that we like. Family stuff. It's been done before. But Greg said he'd rather slit his own throat than compromise his artistic integrity, as he called it."

"What about your grandson?" asked Chase.

"Clyde? What about him?"

"Do you think he might have harbored a grudge against his dad?"

"Oh, sure. Clyde hated his dad, that's common knowledge. Heck, the kid's probably been in therapy since he got out of diapers. Strange way to raise a child, but then Bernadette and I didn't want to interfere, though maybe we should have."

"Do you think Clyde might have had something to do with what happened to his dad?"

The old man smiled. "Absolutely not. The kid's as soft-hearted as they come. Couldn't hurt a fly. One summer I decided to take him along with me on a fishing trip. He couldn't do it. Couldn't catch a single fish. Said it was hurting the fishies and told me that I was practicing a blood sport and I should stop." He laughed at the recollection. "He even wanted to set the bait free. Said I was being cruel to those poor worms. It was the last time I took him along, I can tell you that! So no, I don't think my grandson killed Greg."

"Where were you last night, Mr. Lonsdale?" asked Odelia.

"Oh, so now you think *I* killed Greg, do you?" he said with a look of amusement.

"Just a routine question," said Chase.

"Well, I was on the beach," said the old man. "Taking a walk. Couldn't sleep, as often happens since Bernadette left me. So I decided to go for a walk. I find that a deserted beach is the best soporific. Just you and that ocean. The sound of the waves… Beats sleeping pills every time. Only this time the beach was pretty crowded. Plenty of people out and about. Someone even took a boat out, which I found a little odd, but then I guess if you live here on the beach you can take your boat out any time you darn well please."

Odelia and Chase looked up at this. "What time was this?" asked Chase.

"Oh, two o'clock? Two-thirty? Something like that."

"Did you get a look at the boat's driver?"

"Nah, I was too far away. I did see they were lugging something into the boat. Something heavy, I would have thought."

Odelia and Chase shared a look. Now this was interesting! Looked like Mr. Lonsdale had seen his son's murderer, and had witnessed Greg's body being dragged aboard this boat. Odelia and Chase decided not to reveal this to the old man. He had enough to deal with already. And so Odelia changed the subject.

"Your grandson tells us that you want to scatter your wife's ashes, Mr. Lonsdale?"

"He told you about that, did he? Yeah, it's true. Bernadette wanted her ashes scattered in the ocean—didn't matter to her what ocean, as long as it was over the water. And so I decided to bring them along, hoping that we could hold some kind of ceremony while we were all here at the resort. Only Greg didn't seem all that interested, and neither was Elaine." He shrugged. "No matter. Clyde and I have decided that we'll do it together. Just him and me. We just need to arrange for a boat so we can go out there and honor Bernadette the way she deserves." He sighed. "It's a little sad that Greg wasn't interested in honoring his mother's last wish, but then I guess he had other stuff on his mind."

"What do you think he had on his mind?" asked Odelia.

"Oh, well, he had some kind of run-in with some fella yesterday."

"You mean the waiter?" asked Chase.

"Yeah, him, too. But there was this other fellow. They seemed to know each other. I think Greg said the guy used to work for him but he had to get rid of him for some reason. Don't ask me why. Greg's business wasn't my business."

"You wouldn't have a name for this person, would you?"

Mr. Lonsdale thought hard, but finally had to admit defeat. "It's possible that he told me the name, but I forgot. He was tall and very red in the face, that much I remember. I think Greg said he used to be his agent but now he wasn't anymore?" Then he snapped his fingers. "Colin! I think that's what he called him. Colin something or other. He's also staying here at the resort. He must have done something to upset Greg, for he gave him a shove that landed him in the pool yesterday. To cool him off, he said." He smiled. "I think he succeeded, because I haven't seen him around after that."

CHAPTER 28

*J*an Braeman was younger than I had imagined. Nevertheless, he said he'd been with the resort for a long time, starting as a student working weekends and then later in a permanent position as a waiter. He said he regretted having served that cocktail to Greg.

"It wasn't even my fault that his drink wasn't cold. It was Ricky's."

"Ricky?" asked Chase.

"The bartender. He should have known that people want their cocktails served ice-cold on a hot day. He said I should have checked if there was ice in the cocktail." He threw up his hands. "That isn't my responsibility, is it? It's his. *He's* the one who should have been fired, not me."

"So there was no ice in the cocktail," said Chase, trying to speed things along.

"No, there wasn't. And Mr. Lonsdale wasn't happy about it. And then of course I spilled his drink on him, though I can't take all the blame for that either. Mr. Lonsdale made a sudden movement that caused the glass to tip over and fall on him."

"And then he got you fired from your position," said Chase.

The young man nodded sadly. "That's correct. I wouldn't have thought that Mrs. Wheeler would have done it, but she did. Said I'd caused embarrassment to the resort and she couldn't have that. And so I'm out. I still can't believe it. I've been here three years, you know. Three years without incident, and one run-in with this guy and I'm out."

"And now he's dead," said Chase.

The young man frowned. "What's that supposed to mean?"

"Just saying. Greg Lonsdale gets you fired and this morning he was found murdered."

"I'm not sure what you're trying to imply," said Jan, "but if you're suggesting I had something to do with that, you're mistaken, detective. I may not have been Greg Lonsdale's biggest fan, but I'm not a murderer. Whoever did this to him, it wasn't me. And I can prove it. I was on the beach last night, and I wasn't alone."

"Who was with you?" asked Odelia.

"Dejuan Daly," said Jan, quite to our surprise.

"The actor?"

"Well, ex-actor, actually. He had gone for a walk and a smoke. Said his girlfriend didn't like it when he smoked, since she was pregnant. And since my girlfriend is also pregnant, and I also like to have a smoke from time to time, we kinda commiserated and ended up sharing a smoke. We got to chatting, and turns out we had more in common than the pregnant girlfriends and the smoking habit."

"You both lost your jobs because of Greg Lonsdale," said Odelia.

"That's right. He lost his career after he threw that punch on stage, and I lost mine after I accidentally spilled a drink on the guy's shirt."

"So that's your alibi?" asked Chase. "That you met the one man who hated Greg Lonsdale even more than you did?"

"I didn't *hate* the guy," Jan corrected him. "I didn't *know* him well enough to *hate* him. As far as I'm concerned he was just another rude and obnoxious guest."

"Who got you fired. While your girlfriend is pregnant, and you can probably use the money this job brings you."

He sagged a little. "You got that right. I need the money now more than ever. Which is why I was prepared to grovel and beg Lonsdale to retract his complaint and put in a good word for me with Mrs. Wheeler. Convince her to give me back my job. Only now that he's dead I guess that's not going to happen. And so I'll have to go and find another job." Then he brightened. "Unless…"

"Unless what?" asked Chase.

"Well, Greg Lonsdale is dead, right? So that means he can't complain anymore. So maybe if I just grovel enough and beg enough, Mrs. Wheeler will give me my job back."

"What did Dejuan have to say last night?" asked Chase.

"Oh, you know. He complained about Greg. Said the guy had been calling him names again from the stage, clearly trying to get a rise out of him. He hadn't taken the bait, and he was pretty proud of himself, but his girlfriend felt that he should stand up to Greg more. Show the guy that he hadn't been able to destroy him. Only the last thing he wanted was to face the man who had destroyed his life. He'd seen far too much of him already, but his girlfriend was adamant. She figured it was part of his therapeutic process."

"And he didn't?"

"Nah. If he never saw Greg Lonsdale again in his life it was fine with him. It was pure coincidence that he and Greg were here at the same time. He said he couldn't believe it when he saw the guy. And then of course Greg was over the moon. Another chance to use him as the punchline for his jokes. Greg was incorrigible. A nasty human being."

"Yeah, he certainly wasn't Mr. Popular," said Chase, leaning back and dragging a hand through his mane. "You didn't happen to see a boat go out last night, did you?"

"A boat? No, I don't think so. Why, is it important?"

"Possibly," said Chase. "And possibly not." He gave the guy a grin. "Everything might be important, and then again, nothing might. That's what a detective's job is like."

"You wouldn't be prepared to put in a good word for me with Grace Wheeler, would you?" asked the guy hopefully. "I'm sure she would listen to you guys."

"I'm not so sure our word would hold a lot of sway with Mrs. Wheeler," said Chase.

"If you want I'll talk to her," said Odelia. "I really can't imagine she would fire you for such a small thing."

"Thanks, Mrs. Kingsley," said the guy. "That would mean so much to me." He glanced down at the four of us. "Lovely kitties. Are they yours?"

"They are," said Odelia. "My mini-detectives."

"They sure look like detectives to me," said the guy. "Very alert. As if they're listening to every word I say."

"And don't I know it?" Chase grunted.

* * *

DEJUAN DALY WAS BACK, but this time without his girlfriend. He looked contrite. "Okay, so maybe I haven't been entirely honest with you guys."

"Were you or were you not on the beach last night around two o'clock, Mr. Daly?" asked Chase sternly.

"I was," he confessed. "I had snuck out of the room for a smoke, but please don't tell Tawanna. I promised her to stop smoking, but so far I haven't been able to. I mean, I've cut down from a pack a day to no more than half a pack, but she wants me to stop completely, and I'm finding it hard to quit. She says it's bad for the baby, and of course I agree."

"You and Jan Braeman shared a smoke?"

"Who? Oh, you mean the waiter that was fired? Yeah, we met on the beach. Turned out that he and I have a lot in common. A cigarette habit that our pregnant girlfriends hate."

"And Greg Lonsdale."

"Yeah, him," said the former actor with a weary sigh. "Looks like I can't get rid of the guy. He keeps haunting my Facebook feed, and now also my vacation. My one chance to get away from it all, and who has to show up but him—like a bad dream."

"You and Mr. Braeman had never met before?" asked Chase.

"We met yesterday," said Dejuan. "I happened to see how he got into some kind of altercation with Greg, spilling a drink on the guy. And getting fired as a consequence, which I thought was harsh. And then last night we got to talking and he's also going to be a first-time dad soon, just like me. Though he's a lot younger than me, of course. I guess you could say we became fast friends. He asked me to put in a good word for him with the Wheelers, but I'm not sure I carry a lot of weight with the family. I'm not a bigshot, so why should they listen to anything I have to say."

"He asked me the same thing," said Odelia.

"Poor guy needs the work." He gave the detecting duo a cheerful look. "So if there's nothing more…"

"That will be all for now," Chase confirmed. "But please don't leave town, Mr. Daly. In case we have further questions for you."

His sunny smile slid from his face again. "I can't imagine what more information I can give you. Like I told you, I had an alibi. It wasn't the alibi I gave you before, but that's because I don't want to confess to Tawanna that I haven't been entirely honest with her about the smoking. But I promise you that I didn't kill Greg."

"A lot of people have promised us that they didn't kill Greg," said Brutus. "And none of them sound particularly believable. My money is still on Tawanna. Now even more than before."

"And why is that?" I asked as I studied the former actor.

"Don't you see, Max?"

"See what?"

"Tawanna had an alibi, but now she doesn't. Not anymore. The moment Dejuan confessed that he slipped out of the room, he effectively canceled his girlfriend's alibi."

"But he says she was fast asleep," said Harriet.

"We all know that's a load of nonsense," said Brutus, triumphant now that his theory had gained traction. "She was wide awake, all right. And the moment Dejuan slipped out of the room, she put her plan in motion to murder his tormentor. Good riddance!"

There was certainly something to be said for this theory, I thought. But there was still one problem with Brutus's suspect: no motive. To avenge her boyfriend's humiliation didn't feel like a strong enough motive to put her life in jeopardy. Or her future child.

But then of course stranger things have happened.

CHAPTER 29

We found the man that Greg Lonsdale had an altercation with in his room. The door was open, so like any good detective, Chase wasted no time pushing his way in. The man was packing, which immediately made the detective highly suspicious, if the look he darted in Odelia's direction was any indication.

"Going somewhere, Mr. Hackney?" asked Chase.

The man looked up and frowned. "What's it to you?"

Odelia produced her badge. "Hampton Cove Police Department. Odelia Kingsley, civilian consultant."

"Chase Kingsley. Detective," said Chase as he flashed his own badge.

"We should have brought our badges," said Dooley. "Now we can't even produce any ID if people ask us."

"Nobody will ask us, Dooley," I said.

"Max is right," said Brutus. "When has anyone ever asked for our ID?"

"It's true," said Harriet. "Though they should. If humans are obliged to legitimize themselves before peppering a person with a bunch of questions, why aren't we?"

"I find it easier this way," I said. "Dragging those badges along with us wouldn't be a lot of fun."

The man immediately seemed to regret his earlier outburst. "I'm sorry," he said. He gestured to the luggage on the bed. "Yeah, my vacation is over, I'm afraid. It's back to the old homestead for me."

"I'm afraid we'll have to ask you to stick around for a little while longer, Mr. Hackney," said Chase, causing the man to stare at him in dismay.

"But I can't stay," he said. "I have to be back at the office on Monday."

"We're investigating the murder of Greg Lonsdale," said Chase, deciding not to beat about the bush. "And a witness has told us that you and the victim were embroiled in a bust-up yesterday. Can you tell us what that was about?"

The man sank down on the bed. "Just a small thing, really," he said. "Mr. Lonsdale and I had selected the same chaise lounge, and even though I was first, he insisted on taking it and putting down his towel. And so we got into an argument."

"Which ended with you being pushed into the pool."

"Yeah, I guess Mr. Lonsdale didn't like it when I told him I was first and he should select a different chaise lounge."

"And that was the sole reason you and he fell out?" asked Chase, not hiding his incredulity at the explanation the man had given us.

He nodded. "That's right. A silly argument over a chaise lounge, that's all it was. Though of course, I'm very sorry to hear that Mr. Lonsdale was murdered. Shocking," he added, looking mournful. "Extremely shocking. Do you have any idea what happened?"

But Chase wasn't ready for small talk. "How well did you know Mr. Lonsdale?"

"Not well at all," said the man. "I mean, I'd seen him on

television. But we had never met in person, if that's what you mean."

"Yesterday was the first time that you met Greg?"

"That's right. I recognized him from his television specials, of course. It surprised me to discover that he was just as coarse and ill-mannered in real life as he was on the stage. Never meet your heroes, huh?"

"So you admired him?"

"I did, yeah. I thought he was a hugely talented man. But when I was faced with him yesterday I have to say I was sorely disappointed. He was foul-mouthed and ill-tempered and didn't seem to possess one ounce of humor. Plenty of people came up to me later and told me that they sympathized and that Greg was an awful person in real life. A jerk."

"What do you do for a living, Mr. Hackney?" asked Odelia.

"I'm a talent agent," he said. "I work for one of the smaller talent agencies."

"And yet you had never met Greg Lonsdale?" asked Chase.

The man shook his head. "Like I said, I work for one of the smaller agencies. We don't represent talent of Mr. Lonsdale's caliber."

"And yet Greg's dad was under the impression that you used to be his son's agent."

The man smiled. "I don't see how that's possible. Greg has been with the same agent for many years. Quite a legendary figure in our industry. I have never represented him."

"Can you tell us where you were last night between two and three o'clock, Mr. Hackney?" asked Chase.

"Is that when…" He swallowed. "I was in bed at that time. Fast asleep."

"And can anyone vouch for you?"

"I'm afraid not. Although, yes, actually someone can. Or

rather something." He held up his arm and showed us a snazzy smartwatch. "I have one of those sleep apps. If you check, you'll see that my pulse never rose above the level normal for a person who's fast asleep. That should tell you that I never left this room—and most certainly not to go and murder some actor I'd never met before."

"Who shoved you into the pool."

"If I would have to murder every person who ever wronged me, detective, I'd have a full-time job. It was a hot day and it didn't take me long to get dry again and besides, someone working for the resort provided me with a towel and some dry clothes. They're extremely professional and hospitable here. Almost as if they had known that something like this might happen with a man like Greg Lonsdale on the premises."

While the agent talked to Odelia and Chase, I glanced around the man's room. Prominent on the nightstand was a framed picture of a dog, which brought a smile to my lips. Most people like to carry a framed picture of their wife and kids, but Colin Hackney clearly loved his mutt so much he wanted a permanent reminder when he traveled.

Dooley, who had followed me, also studied the picture. "Do you think Odelia would carry a picture of us when she travels, Max?" he asked.

"Somehow I doubt it, buddy," I said. "And besides, when she travels, she usually drags us along, so she doesn't need a picture when she has the real thing to look at."

"I guess so," he said. "Still, it would be nice if she had some kind of picture taken of us and put it up in her living room or her bedroom. Like this guy. I'll bet that back home he has plenty of pictures of this same dog adorning his home."

"Yeah, it certainly looks that way," I agreed.

The framed picture wore a black ribbon, which told me

the dog had died since having his picture taken. It caused my heart to go out to the guy. Clearly, he loved his dog a lot.

"There's one thing I *can* tell you," said the agent. "Greg Lonsdale had a problem with a lot of people. Before yesterday, I thought that was just a part of his image. You know, like his public persona. But obviously, he was a hard man to get along with."

"What makes you say that?" asked Odelia.

"Well, just before we got into this big brouhaha, I saw him engaged in a similar spat with a young woman. She was showing him something on her phone, and it seemed to make him extremely angry, for he slapped the phone out of her hands and told her to buzz off or he'd call security. Lucky for the girl, the phone didn't end up in the pool or on the ground, but it was obvious that his response stunned her to a great extent."

Chase had been jotting down notes. "You wouldn't happen to have caught the name of this woman, would you?"

"No, I didn't. But I don't think she'll be hard to find. She had a butterfly tattoo on her collarbone and bright blue hair. I'll bet there aren't a lot of people answering that description staying here."

"No, there certainly aren't," said Chase as he gave Odelia a wry smile.

"That must be Juli Hooton," said Harriet. "She's the only blue-haired girl we've seen since we arrived here."

"Probably trying to prove to Greg that he was her dad," said Brutus.

"And true to form, he behaved like an absolute jerk."

Looked like Chase and Odelia had just added another suspect to their list—which was getting longer all the time.

CHAPTER 30

For the second time since we had arrived at the resort, we met Greg Lonsdale's alleged daughter, Juli. She seemed a little downcast when we saw her in the resort cafeteria, where she was enjoying a sundae with lots of pink sauce and cherries on top. For a moment, I thought she was celebrating, but when we approached, I saw that she had been crying, for her trademark raccoon makeup had run down. She looked a real sight.

"I'm sorry," she said as she wiped her eyes with a napkin. "You must think I'm crazy. But my recurring dream since I was a little girl was to meet my dad and share an ice cream with him, just like all of my friends did with their dads. Only the chances of that happening have just gone out of the window, haven't they? At least if the stories are true?" She darted a look of hope at Odelia.

But the latter shook her head. "I'm afraid Mr. Lonsdale died last night, Miss Hooton."

She and Chase took a seat in the booth next to the young woman, whose shoulders slumped even more at this sad news. She scooped up some ice cream and put it in her mouth. A dreamy look had come into her eyes. "For years I tried to get in touch with my dad, and now that I had finally found him, and was *this* close to proving that he actually *was* my dad, someone went and killed him. It's just not fair."

"I think Greg himself will probably find it even less fair," Chase pointed out.

Juli looked up. "Oh, I'm so sorry. I must come across as a very selfish person. Of course, it's horrible for Greg and his family. And my heart goes out to them. It really does."

"Is it true that you confronted him yesterday and he shut you down?" asked Odelia.

She nodded. "I did, yeah. At first, I was going to wait for the results of the DNA test, but when I happened to bump into him, I decided to show him a picture of my mom. Surely he must remember her. But he just slapped the phone out of my hand and made a very rude remark. Even if he was my dad, he wasn't the man I had always hoped he was."

"Did you meet him again?" asked Odelia.

"No, I didn't. After he was so rude to me, I called my mom and told her about what happened. She told me to drop this nonsense and come home. She said if she'd known that I had gone off to try and meet my dad she would have put her foot down. She knew what kind of a man he was, of course. And she had told me in no uncertain terms how lucky I was that he hadn't been in our lives. I never believed her, but now I do." She sighed deeply. "But I still wanted him to acknowledge me. To accept that he was my dad."

"It's understandable to feel that way," said Odelia as she took the girl's hand. Juli's ice cream was melting, and I thought that was such a shame. Ice cream should be eaten, not be allowed to melt like that.

"That looks delicious, doesn't it, Max?" asked Brutus, who had followed my gaze.

"It does," I said. "Even though I don't eat ice cream, I can understand the appeal. It's tasty and creamy. But it's probably not good for us."

"I like the colors," said Dooley. "It's like eating a rainbow, isn't it, Max? Or eating fireworks, without the actual fireworks, of course."

"It does look colorful," I agreed.

"Maybe we should tell Odelia to eat it," said Brutus, who hates watching food go to waste as much as any cat does. "But she will have to hurry, before it melts into a puddle."

"Even melted ice cream is yummy," said Harriet. "Or so I've been told, at least," she hastened to add. As everyone knows, for most cats dairy products aren't very healthy, as it might lead to an upset stomach or worse.

Harriet gave Odelia's leg a nudge. When our human looked down, she said, "You have to eat that ice cream, Odelia. It's melting."

But Odelia had other things on her mind, like trying to solve Greg's murder.

"She doesn't want to eat it," said Harriet sadly.

"She probably doesn't like to eat another person's food," said Dooley. "A lot of humans are like that. They hate to eat food that has been touched by another person or been in another person's mouth. It's something to do with cooties."

"I'm sure Juli doesn't have cooties," said Harriet. Then she got a bright idea. "Maybe Chase can eat it? He's a big fella." And so she shoved Chase's leg. The detective hardly paid attention. But since Harriet isn't a cat to be ignored, she simply jumped up on the detective's lap, then hollered into his face, "Eat the ice cream, Chase!"

"They're pretty cute, aren't they?" said Juli with a smile. "I met them when your grandmother tried to arrest me."

"Yeah, she told us about that," said Odelia, even though it had been us who had told her. But then of course she couldn't come out and tell Juli that she talked to her cats.

"She caught me in Greg's room collecting hairs from his comb. I sent them off to a lab that does DNA tests," she explained. "And now I have to wait for the result. I was going to confront him. That way he couldn't deny that I'm his daughter. But now it's too late."

"Where were you between two and three o'clock last night, Juli?" asked Chase as he carefully but decisively put Harriet down on the floor again.

"He's not going to eat it, is he?" asked Harriet, exasperated. "Such a waste."

"I was in bed," said Juli. "Like most people, I guess. Unfortunately, I don't have anyone who can confirm that," she added. But then she brightened. "Aren't these key cards logged or something? If so, you can probably see that I never left my room last night."

"There's always the window," Chase pointed out.

She sagged again. "Oh, yes. The window. Well, I didn't leave my room, and I certainly didn't murder my own dad. Not after I tried so hard to meet him and make him admit that I'm his daughter."

She made a compelling argument, I thought. But was it enough to convince Chase?

Harriet gave Odelia's leg another shove. "Eat that ice cream!" she insisted.

Odelia smiled. "The cats are nervous that you're not eating your ice cream," she said. "They hate food going to waste."

"Oh, of course," said Juli. "I'm sorry, you guys," she said, addressing us. She then picked up her spoon again and put it in her mouth. "I'm going to eat it all, see?" She rubbed her tummy. "Oh, it's so yummy. Do they want some?"

"Better not," said Odelia. "Ice cream isn't good for them."

"It isn't? Oh, I didn't know that. But then I don't have cats, of course. I do have a dog, but he's at home with my mom and dad while I try to find my real dad." She gave us a sad smile. "Looks like my mission failed. So I'm heading home again real soon now."

"Your mission didn't fail," said Odelia. "You'll soon have the evidence that Greg was your dad, and you actually did meet him—however briefly."

"And he proved to you what an absolute jerk he was," Chase said. "So you don't have to think about him ever again."

The girl gave him a bright smile. "You really have a way with words, detective. Have you considered becoming a therapist?"

The look of bewilderment on the cop's face was something to behold and caused both Odelia and Juli to burst out laughing.

At last, we had managed to cheer her up, which was quite an accomplishment.

When we got up from the table and made to leave the cafeteria, two familiar faces stared back at us, eager to have a word with Odelia and Chase. They were Kimmy and Kitty, the twins who had been on babysitting duty.

CHAPTER 31

We hadn't seen the twins since the day before, when they were tasked with keeping an eye on Grace and some of the other kids staying at the resort. They looked excited to see us—or rather, to see Odelia and Chase.

"Is it true that you guys are in charge of the murder investigation?" asked Kimmy—though it may have been Kitty. The two sisters were very hard to tell apart. I'm sure even their mother probably had trouble differentiating one from the other.

"That is true," said Odelia with a smile. She had met the girls in an effort to personally vet them before they took charge of Grace and must have liked what she saw, or she wouldn't have entrusted her daughter to them. "Why? Do you have information for us?"

"Well, yes!" said Kitty—though it may have been Kimmy.

"You probably know this already," said Kimmy.

"The hot dog man," said Kitty.

"Someone must have told you."

"I'm pretty sure it wasn't hot dogs he was selling," said Kitty conspiratorially.

"But drugs!" said her sister in a triumphant tone.

Odelia and Chase looked confused. "Hot dogs?" asked Chase.

"*Not* hot dogs!" said Kimmy.

"Drugs!" said Kitty.

"It must be very confusing to have twins, Max," said Dooley. "For a parent, I mean. Hard to keep them apart and also, you have to make sure you get two of everything. Two pairs of pants, two T-shirts, two phones—two schools. Though maybe not that," he added. "One school is probably enough, unless the twins don't get along, of course, and can't stand to be near one another. They'd have to go to different schools, which is a drag."

"I'm sure these two get along fine," I said. "At least they seem to be great friends."

"Most twins are," said Harriet. "It's in their DNA."

"Unless they're evil," said Brutus. "It does exist," he added when we gave him a skeptical look. "It might be a cliché, but evil twins have been known to exist, and not just in movies or TV shows."

"Well, these girls are anything but evil," I said. "And they seem to have done a great job with Grace."

The little girl now came toddling in our direction. She had become very much attached to the babysitters, for the moment she reached our party, she clutched Kimmy's hand and wouldn't let go.

"You like the twins, don't you, Grace?" asked Harriet.

"Oh, absolutely," said Grace. "They saved me from that horrible Timmy. Ever since they told him what's what, he's been so sweet to me you wouldn't believe."

"I think it was a joint effort of the twins and Gran," I said.

"Gran put the fear of God into Timmy's mom," Harriet explained.

"Whatever she did, it worked," the little girl confirmed. "So good for her."

"Okay, so the man who was murdered was talking on the phone yesterday," said Kimmy when she realized that their story hadn't come across as straightforward and clear as they had intended. "And he was ordering hot dogs. But judging from the way he talked, we think that he was talking to his drug dealer instead, and that hot dogs were simply a code word for some illegal substance."

"Unless he was on a diet," said Kitty, "and his wife wasn't supposed to know that he was secretly ordering hot dogs. But I don't think so."

"No, we don't think so," said Kimmy. "And so we think it's important that you catch this hot dog salesman."

"Maybe they have some information to share about the dead guy."

"Like... *important* information," her sister clarified.

The teenagers' eyes were shining, and it was clear that they thought being instrumental in furthering the investigation was an extremely exciting thing for them to do.

"We'll check Greg's phone," said Chase. "And find out who this hot dog person is. In the meantime, thank you for the assistance, girls. But maybe from now on you'd better leave the investigating to us, all right?"

"Of course, detective," said Kimmy.

"We wouldn't *dream* of trying to find Greg's killer," said Kitty, though I had a feeling that they weren't exactly telling us the truth and that they hoped to find that killer themselves—without any input from the police.

Now wouldn't that be something?

"All I know is that you should rule one person out of your investigation," said Kimmy.

"Oh?" said Chase. "And who is that?"

The girl giggled. "Sylvester."

"Hot Yoga Guy," said her sister.

"He was with me last night," said Kimmy.

"And me," Kitty added.

"Nothing happened."

"All we did was talk."

"About yoga, and other stuff."

"We talked a *lot*! Deep into the night."

"So you see? He couldn't *possibly* have killed Greg."

"And besides, he didn't need to. He's a *lot* hotter than Greg ever was!"

"And we should know! He taught us plenty of techniques —how to be bendy!"

And with these words, they took off, giggling up a storm.

Chase looked dumbfounded. "Who is this Hot Yoga Guy?"

"Beats me," said Odelia. "But looks like we can take him off our list."

"He wasn't even *on* our list!"

"You're not thinking about assisting the twins in their investigation, are you?" I asked Grace. The last thing we needed was for the little girl to put herself in jeopardy just because she felt she owed the twins a debt of gratitude over the way they had handled the Timmy situation.

"Oh, no, absolutely not," said Grace. "I'm on vacation, you guys. So there will be no sleuthing for me. All I want is to play in the pool, enjoy my three square meals a day, and generally have a great old time." She pointed at me. "It's *you* who will be hard at work while I enjoy all the creature comforts this resort has to offer."

"If you put it like that," I said, my face sagging, "it doesn't sound all that exciting."

"No, I wouldn't mind having some of the leisure time and

those three square meals a day," said Brutus. "Especially those meals sound extremely enticing."

"I've noticed that there are a lot of dogs staying at the resort," said Grace. "So maybe it wouldn't be such a bad idea to talk to them. After all, everyone knows there's no better witness than a dog. They see everything, they hear everything, and yet nobody ever bothers to talk to them. Time for you guys to change that."

And with these words of wisdom, she hurried off after Kimmy and Kitty—heading for the pool area, which seemed to be Grace's favorite part of the resort.

"So according to the twins, that hot dog guy Greg met last night…" said Odelia.

"Wasn't really a hot dog guy at all," Chase said. "Though how that ties in with his murder isn't clear to me. Still, we better follow up on that. If Greg was meeting his dealer at one o'clock, he might know something."

"We better schedule a meeting with my uncle," Odelia suggested, "so we don't miss the forest for the trees."

"An excellent idea, partner." But then he spotted Greg's wife and got up. "But first, let's have another chat with Mrs. Lonsdale. If this drugs business is true, she must have known about it."

"And while we're at it, let's ask her about her husband's secret daughter," Odelia suggested.

They waved the woman over, and even though it was obvious that the last thing Elaine Lonsdale wanted was to have another chat with the detective duo, she dutifully wended her way over to us.

She crossed her arms in front of her chest, and growled, "*Now* what do you want?"

CHAPTER 32

"She doesn't seem very forthcoming, Max," said Dooley.

"This is what is usually termed a hostile witness," Brutus announced. "Though in this case, I think it's safe to say we should probably call her a hostile suspect."

"She doesn't look very hostile," said Dooley as he watched the woman closely. But just to be on the safe side, he took a couple of steps back from the table. You never know with these hostile witnesses-slash-suspects!

"Information has come to light that your husband may have been in the habit of using drugs," said Chase, deciding not to beat around the bush but get straight to the point. In his experience, this often worked better than using a circuitous route to get to the heart of the matter.

"Is it possible that the hot dogs you said he loved so much weren't actually hot dogs?" asked Odelia. "But illegal substances?"

"And that the word 'hot dog' was simply a code?" asked Chase.

The woman stared hard at Chase. Obviously, this direct

approach didn't sit well with her. But finally, she nodded curtly. "You're absolutely right. My husband was an addict. And it's also true that he had a person who facilitated his addiction. As far as I know, he was taking steps to deal with this, and he had been going to meetings where we live."

"So what can you tell us about this hot dog dealer?" asked Chase.

"Nothing," said the woman curtly. "Greg didn't involve me in that part of his life, and frankly, I wasn't eager to get involved. My first husband was an alcoholic, and I know from experience that it's extremely hard to kick the habit, and that the people most affected are often the immediate circle of friends and family of the addict. So this time, I simply did not want to know what was going on with Greg. He promised me he'd take care of it, and I believed him."

"Is this one of the reasons you wanted to get a divorce?" asked Odelia.

"One of the many reasons, yes," said Elaine. "I had a feeling that Greg was slipping further and further away from me, and that he hadn't been entirely honest throughout our union. But like I said, I didn't want to get involved, and what little I gleaned of his situation, I decided that I simply didn't want to know." She tilted her chin. "Was there anything else?"

"Well, yes," said Odelia. "We've talked to a young woman who claims that she is Greg's daughter. According to her, her mother had an affair with Greg. She tried to get in touch with him, but he refused to acknowledge her in any way, shape, or form."

"So?" said the woman haughtily.

"So did you know that Greg had a daughter from a previous relationship or affair?"

"No, I did not. Like I said, Greg and I had drifted apart these last couple of years. Frankly, I had no idea what was going on in his life any more than he was aware of what was going on in mine. But it wouldn't surprise me one bit that he did have a secret daughter. Another thing he hid from me," she added bitterly. "And another reason getting that divorce was probably the best decision I ever made. At any rate, a much better decision than the decision to marry the man."

"So you never talked to Greg's daughter?"

"No, I wouldn't know her if I saw her," she said. "Now, if there's nothing else, I really must go. I have a funeral to arrange, and about a thousand other things to take care of."

As she walked away, Odelia said, "Odd that she didn't even ask us about the state of the investigation. Almost as if she isn't interested in who killed her husband."

"Or maybe she didn't ask who killed her husband because *she* killed him?" Chase suggested with a meaningful flicker of his eyebrow.

"I can totally see her taking a knife to his chest," said Odelia. "But climbing down from that balcony, then putting him onto that wheelbarrow and wheeling him all the way to the beach? It takes considerable physical strength to accomplish such a feat. And I'm not sure she has it in her."

"Yeah, I guess you're right," said Chase. "Dragging Greg's body from the room and then transporting him to the beach and onto a boat was no easy feat. Whoever did it must have had a heck of a time with it. I'm not sure even I could manage. If you consider that Greg probably weighed upward of a hundred and eighty pounds—no mean feat."

"I'm sure you could have done it, babe," said Odelia as she patted his brawny arm. "Me, on the other hand..."

"Oh, I'm sure you're much stronger than you look," he said.

"I wonder what the killer did with his clothes. Moving that body, he must have gotten a lot of blood onto him. And he must have spent ages cleaning that room afterward, even before he asked for the room to be deep-cleaned. He must have spent half the night getting rid of the body, the blood and all of the evidence."

"If he killed Greg at two o'clock, and called down to the front desk for the room to be cleaned at four, that gave him two hours. Plenty of time to accomplish all of those things."

Both of them were quiet for a moment as they pictured the details of how the murder must have happened, and that's how Uncle Alec found them when he arrived in the cafeteria and glanced around. When he located the duo he smiled and made a beeline for his loyal detective and his civilian sidekick—and her four feline sidekicks.

When he saw the four of us, his face clouded somewhat, but he decided that he wasn't going to allow his resentment that Odelia liked to lug us around everywhere she went to stand in the way of his appreciation for the work that they had conducted so far.

"I'm hearing great things about the investigation," he said as he took a seat at the table. "So where are you at?" He glanced in the direction of the pool and his face lit up. "I might take a dip in that pool after we're through here. Are my sister and Tex still around?"

"Oh, yes, they are," Odelia confirmed. "They should be out shortly."

"Great," said Uncle Alec. "So? Any closer to identifying Greg Lonsdale's killer yet?"

CHAPTER 33

"I wonder what happened to the bedbugs," said Dooley as he inspected a fly that was buzzing against the window. "I hope they're all right."

The three of us shared a look of surprise. "What do you care about the bedbugs, Dooley?" asked Brutus. "As long as they're gone, right?"

"We should never be mean to a living creature, Brutus," said our friend. "I hope they got out fine last night, after all the guests started emptying those canisters of bug spray."

"We saw them leave," I reminded my friend. "So we know they're fine."

"No, but after that. Did they make it out alive? It was a tricky situation, Max."

"If they knew what was good for them, they would have run for the hills," said Harriet. "Even though those bug sprays are usually a lot less effective than advertised, I can't imagine they're conducive to a long and healthy life."

"I'm sure they don't actually kill the bugs they're supposed to be attacking," said Brutus, more in a bid to assuage Dooley's concerns than out of any scientific knowledge of what bug spray does exactly. "I mean, it's poison, right? But they're not actually going to release a debilitating toxin in a room where guests are going to be sleeping, right? I mean, that would be extremely unethical, not to mention illegal."

"I once read about a couple that died after their room was treated for bugs," said Harriet. "So it probably depends on the kind of bug spray they're using."

We all gulped a little, as one of the rooms that had been treated last night was one where we had also spent the night.

"Maybe we shouldn't sleep in the room anymore," I suggested. "If that poison kills people, it will kill us, and I don't know about you guys, but I'm not ready to die just yet."

"Me neither," said Brutus. "And I have to say that last night, after they sprayed that stuff, my throat was itchy. And I got this strange smell in my nose that I haven't been able to shake." He sniffed loudly. "In fact, I still smell it. So that may have been the bug spray."

"It's all poisonous," said Dooley. "Why else would they spray it? Which is why I hope that the bugs managed to make their getaway last night."

"I'm sure they did," I said, even though I wasn't at all sanguine that this was the case. "They must have decided that the resort had become inhospitable for them and decided to find their luck elsewhere."

And since we seemed to have exhausted the important topic of the bedbugs, we decided to tune into the conversation once again. After all, bedbugs are important, but murder is even more so.

"We've got a long list of suspects," said Chase as he flipped through his notes.

"I've got them all listed here," said Odelia helpfully. "Do you want me to read it out?"

"Please do," said Uncle Alec. He patted his scalp. "I'm just glad that it wasn't a shark attack. Can you imagine the backlash Charlene would have gotten if the guy had been killed by a shark? After she specifically ordered the beaches to stay open?"

"Charlene's very own Jaws moment right there," said Odelia.

The chief gave her a strange look. "Her what moment?"

"Well, a Jaws moment," she said. "From the movie *Jaws*? After a shark has been spotted, Chief Brody argues that the beaches should be closed, but the mayor wants to keep them open, as it's too important for the town and local tourism."

"And then, of course, the shark proves that he doesn't care one bit about tourism," said Chase with a grin, "and attacks anyway."

"Well, be that as it may," said the chief, "I'm glad that the shark didn't kill that poor sap, at least if the crime scene report is anything to go by. And I'm sure that Abe wouldn't confuse a shark attack with a knifing." He placed his phone on the table. "I've received Abe's preliminary report, by the way. But first, let's go through your list of suspects, shall we?"

"Okay," said Odelia. "So there's the wife of the victim, Elaine Lonsdale. She and her husband didn't get along, and she was filing for divorce, with her husband threatening that she wasn't getting a single cent as they had signed a prenup stipulating that each of them would only get out of the marriage what they had brought into it. And in her case, that wasn't a whole lot."

"So she was better off with a dead husband than a divorced one?" asked Uncle Alec.

"That's right. According to her, she was in bed when her husband was killed, with no one to corroborate her alibi."

"I like her for this," said the chief, patting the table. "I like her a lot."

"Next, we have the son," said Odelia. "Clyde Lonsdale and his father didn't get along. Greg had used him time and time again as the butt of cruel jokes in his shows, calling him Clyde McCloud because he hung like a dark cloud over Greg's life, and the kid hated it. He'd been bullied at school because of it, once even came home with a black eye and a broken wrist, and clips and memes of his dad's shows had been circulating online for years. So he certainly bore a grudge against his old man dating back to his childhood."

"He says he was on the phone with a buddy of his, but that's hard to prove."

"Have you checked with the friend?" asked Uncle Alec.

"I did, yeah, and he confirms that he and Clyde were chatting last night. But he can't swear one hundred percent they were still chatting after two o'clock, when Greg was killed."

"So, that's suspect number two," said the chief with satisfaction. "And I like this one a lot, too. Daddy issues. Always a classic."

"Next, we have Dejuan Daly," said Odelia.

"Now, why does that name sound familiar?"

"He's the actor who punched Greg live on stage during an award show," said Chase.

"Oh, right. The slap that was heard around the world."

"It was certainly a slap—or rather a punch—that had a big impact on Dejuan's life," said Odelia. "He was dropped by his agency, his friends deserted him, Greg filed charges against him, and all of his work offers dried up. So effectively, he lost everything."

"Greg taunted him, right?" asked Uncle Alec. "Made some cruel joke at his expense, and the guy snapped?"

"That's right. Greg had been using Dejuan as the butt of his jokes for a while, and when he did the same thing at that show, this time involving Dejuan's girlfriend, he snapped and punched the guy in the face. Unfortunately, millions of people were watching, and of course the entire Hollywood community who were in the room at the time."

"And he's here? At the resort?"

"Bad timing, he called it," said Chase. "He and his girlfriend Tawanna Kimura are on vacation here, and when he ran into Greg, he couldn't believe his eyes. He wanted to make amends, but Greg wouldn't hear of it and was just as belligerent as ever."

"Is it possible the guy snapped again?" asked Uncle Alec.

"Or the girlfriend," said Chase. "Dejuan was having a smoke on the beach and met Jan Braeman, who's also a suspect."

"Jan Braeman," said the chief with a frown. "Not a name that rings a bell. Actor?"

"Waiter," said Chase. "He accidentally spilled a drink on Greg, which got him fired."

"His girlfriend is pregnant, and he can't afford being out of work," said Odelia. "So being fired because of what happened with Greg hit him really hard."

"Another great suspect," said Uncle Alec, well pleased. "Is there anyone in this resort who didn't hate Greg Lonsdale?"

"Not many," Chase conceded. "Looks like the guy had a habit of making enemies of every single person he met."

"Okay, so this waiter? His alibi is that he was sharing a smoke with the actor?" asked the chief.

"That's correct," said Chase. "So they're each other's alibi."

"Which leaves the actor's wife without an alibi," said Odelia. "But as Chase and I have concluded, the murder must have been committed by a person with considerable physical strength. And considering that Tawanna's pregnant, I don't think she would have been able to pull it off, even if she wanted to take revenge for what Greg put her boyfriend through."

"And then we have Greg's dad Lloyd," said Chase.

"Now, why was he upset with Greg?" asked Uncle Alec.

"Lloyd's wife died recently," said Odelia. "And Lloyd had brought along her urn so he could scatter her ashes while he was here. He wanted to rent a boat and take it out to sea to hold a ceremony, in accordance with his wife's wishes. Only Greg wasn't interested."

Uncle Alec's eyes went a little wider. "Greg wasn't interested in scattering his mother's ashes?"

"No, he said he had better things to do."

The chief cursed. "This guy was a horror!"

"He was something, all right," said Chase.

"By now, I'm pretty much ready to kill him myself. What possible important business could he have had that he couldn't take a minute out of his busy schedule to hold a ceremony for his dearly departed mom?"

"That's what Lloyd was wondering, and why he was so upset with his son."

"We also think that Lloyd secretly believes Greg's outrageous behavior and the scandals following him weighed heavily on Bernadette's mind," said Odelia. "And were partly the reason why she died. Every time Greg's name appeared in the paper in connection to some stunt he pulled or some person he insulted, Bernadette got extremely upset and saddened. According to Lloyd, it didn't do her any favors, as she had a heart condition to begin with and should have taken it easy."

"But with a son like Greg, that was a difficult proposition," the chief said, nodding. "I see where you're coming from. Looks like Lloyd had a good reason to take a knife to his son's heart after he did everything in his power to break his mother's heart. Alibi?"

"He was taking a walk along the beach," said Chase. "Alone."

"He actually saw the boat that we think carried Greg's body," Odelia added.

"You weren't lying when you said you had a long list of suspects," the chief grunted. He gave Odelia a nervous glance. "Don't tell me there's more?"

"Oh, yes," said his niece. "There's the woman he had an affair with twenty years ago, who had a daughter that he never recognized. That daughter, whose name is Juli Hooton, is also here, eager to contact her father and prove that he is her dad once and for all."

"She was even caught breaking into his suite," said Chase. "By Vesta, no less."

"Don't tell me my mother is involved in this mess!" the chief cried, much dismayed.

"To the extent that she's been looking for a thief who's been stealing from the guests," said Odelia. "She thought initially that she had caught the thief, but it turns out that all Juli Hooton wanted was to get some hairs from Greg's comb so she could ship them off to the lab for a DNA test. She should get the results any day now."

"Good for her," said Uncle Alec, clearly thinking dark thoughts about his mother. Every time Gran and her friends get involved in one of his investigations, things have a habit of going haywire. "Okay, so how is she implicated? I mean, if she was so eager to prove that Greg was her dad, she's not going to kill him, is she?"

"Greg was extremely dismissive of her and her mother," said Chase. "So it isn't inconceivable that she wanted to get back at him." He shrugged. "It's like you said: the guy managed to turn every single person he met into an enemy."

"It's a miracle he wasn't killed sooner," said the chief. He gave Odelia and Chase an expectant look. "That's it? No more?"

"Well, there's the fact that Greg seems to have been a drug addict," said Chase.

"He had a contact who supplied him with the stuff," said Odelia. "They called it 'hot dogs,' but we think that was probably a euphemism for some illegal substance."

"Elaine Lonsdale confirmed that her husband was an addict," said Chase.

"According to Steven Lesinske, the receptionist, Greg met his supplier last night," said Odelia. "At one o'clock. So we're eager to talk to this person, who may have been one of the last people to see him alive."

"Okay, better get on that. Maybe he couldn't pay for the stuff, and the dealer decided to teach him a lesson that got out of hand." He placed his hands on the table. "That's it?"

"There's one other person," said Odelia, checking her list. "But we don't think he's much of a contender. Colin Hackney got into an altercation with Greg yesterday over who picked a chaise lounge first. Greg won out when he shoved Mr. Hackney into the pool."

"That doesn't sound like a powerful motive to kill a man," the chief grunted.

"Still, it pays to be thorough," said Chase. "So we'll do a background check on him, just to make sure. He claims to have been asleep in bed, and has the sleep app to prove it."

"And does it? Prove that he was asleep at the time?"

"I think so," said Chase. "I mean, I don't know the first thing about smartwatches, or sleep apps, but from what he showed us he seems to have been fast asleep at the time."

Uncle Alec picked up his phone. "Okay, so the crime scene report offers some very interesting reading. For one thing, Abe has confirmed without a shadow of a doubt that the wound on the man's leg wasn't the result of a shark attack. At all," he added, just to make sure we understood that no shark was involved.

"So what did cause that wound?" asked Chase.

The chief wiggled his eyebrows meaningfully. "The skin and meat of his leg was sliced off with extreme skill," he said. He paused for effect. "And then fed to the victim."

We all stared at the chief, who sat back with a look of satisfaction. Finally, Chase was the first to speak. "What?!"

CHAPTER 34

"So first things first," said the police chief. "The blood on the knife belonged to the victim. The fingerprints on the knife belonged to the victim. In fact, the knife itself belonged to the victim. And it was this knife that was used to kill him and also to slice the meat from his right leg, which was then fed to him, as it was found in his stomach."

"He was made to eat his own leg?" asked Chase with a look of astonishment.

"It would appear so," said the chief.

"How sick is that?"

"Pretty sick," Odelia's uncle confirmed. "In fact, I don't think I've ever handled a case quite like it. Whoever killed Greg Lonsdale must have hated the man to a great extent to do that to him." He made a wide sweep of the room. "But then, listening to you, it would appear that there are ample suspects to choose from who would fit into that category."

"What about the room where the knife was found?" asked Chase. "And the boat?"

"I was getting to that," said Uncle Alec. "Blood found in

the room belonged to the victim, but so far, no evidence has been found that points to his killer. There was also blood found on the windowsill of the room and on the ground below, as well as on the wheelbarrow. But again, not a trace of the killer."

"Must have been wearing gloves and a protective suit of some kind," said Odelia.

"It would appear that we're dealing with a person who was well prepared," said Uncle Alec, "and extremely cunning." He tapped the table. "This was no spur-of-the-moment thing, people. This murder was well thought out and meticulously planned in advance. So we're dealing with a very dangerous individual."

"Who was acting alone," said Chase, "if the witness report we received is anything to go on."

"What witness report?" asked the chief.

"Lloyd Lonsdale saw a man dragging a heavy object into the boat and take off last night," said Chase. "Only he was too far away to get a good look at the assailant. But I think it's safe to assume that it must have been the killer, and that it was a person with considerable physical strength if he was able to shlep that body around."

"I guess so," said Uncle Alec. "Though I've known some extremely strong women in my time, so I wouldn't rule out the possibility that this was a woman, not a man."

"Okay, so what do you want us to do next, Uncle Alec?" asked Odelia.

"Considering the number of suspects," said the chief as he studied the list that his niece had made for him, "I'd say you better keep talking to as many people as you can. And keep checking those alibis. Have you interviewed the owners of the resort yet?"

"My officers have talked to the members of the staff," said Chase. "But we haven't talked to the Wheelers yet."

"Get them to sit down for an interview," said Uncle Alec. "Maybe they'll be able to shed some light on possible motives and whatnot. If the Lonsdales have been coming here for years, they probably know them well. And follow up on this hot dog business. Considering the gruesomeness of the murder, it's not inconceivable that we have to look for the killer in the drug milieu." He glanced down at the four of us. "I'm afraid to ask, but what have the cats come up with?"

"So far, nothing substantial," Odelia admitted. "They talked to Greg's dog, who didn't have much of any importance to share."

"Greg's dog, huh?" said the chief, rubbing his chin. "Now there's a prime witness. So the dog wasn't present when the guy met his maker?"

"No, he was in the suite when it happened, fast asleep at the foot of the bed, awaiting his master's return."

"Too bad," said the chief. "Then again, if he had been present, it's extremely likely he would have been killed too. We're dealing with one determined and ruthless killer who won't think twice about targeting a dog if he thinks he might give him away." He got up. "Okay, I'm off to see the mayor—who happens to be my wife—to give her the good news that no shark attack has taken place. Even though she was determined not to close those beaches—a decision I didn't agree with, by the way—she was nervous, I can tell you that. She's still nervous." He then seemed to get an idea. "Have you considered sending the cats to talk to the shark? Tell him to take a hike and leave the Hampton Cove beaches in peace?"

"We have thought about asking the cats to talk to the shark," said Odelia slowly. "Or at least we've asked Max. But so far he hasn't worked up the courage to do so." She focused on me directly. "How far are you with contacting the shark, Max?"

"Um…." I said, breaking out into a cold sweat—insofar a cat can break out in a cold sweat, of course.

"Better get round to it, Max," said Uncle Alec. "No time to waste and all of that. Considering that the victim was found on the beach, it's possible that the shark is a crucial witness and might be able to provide us with a clue to the identity of the killer."

And with these words—which were pretty terrifying, I thought—he took off. A man on a mission: to reassure his wife that no tourists had been hurt so far in a shark attack.

"I'm not sure I'll be able to convince the shark to move away, Odelia," I said the moment the chief had left. "I mean, sharks don't always listen to cats… I think."

"Just do what you can, Max," she said. "Just make sure you don't get too close, will you? This shark may not have attacked anyone yet, but that doesn't mean he would think twice about considering you an appetizer."

I gulped a few times. "An appetizer!" I cried in dismay.

But Odelia had returned to her conversation with Chase, discussing the long list of suspects and what they needed to do next.

"Looks like the fate of the investigation rests squarely on your shoulders, Maxie baby," said Brutus with a grin. "So let's go and meet a shark, shall we?"

I gave him a look of panic. "But how? I can't even swim!"

"You'll figure it out," he said as he patted me on the shoulder. "You are smart, after all. Very smart."

And potentially dead. Very dead!

CHAPTER 35

Okay, I'm not sure if I've mentioned this, but cats don't like walking on the beach. It's all this sand, you see. It gets between your toes and is hard to get rid of. But since Odelia had told me I needed to get a grip and talk to this shark, as he was a potential witness to the murder of Greg Lonsdale, I decided to put aside my abhorrence for anything related to sand and beaches and get on with it. I was glad that I wasn't alone in my endeavor and that my friends were right next to me as I tackled this most difficult and dangerous task.

"We're right here, Max," said Brutus. "So you won't have to face this shark all by yourself."

"I'm so grateful," I said. "I don't think I could do it, you know. I mean, I've never talked to a shark before. They're so big and so dangerous. Not like those nice dolphins." Though truth be told, I had never talked to a dolphin either. In fact, I couldn't remember ever having had a lot to do with any fish of any shape or form.

"I think the shark is very nice, Max," said Dooley.

"You're just saying that to make me feel better, Dooley," I said.

"Well, yes," he admitted. "So is it working?"

I shook my head. "Not really."

I simply could not get the image of being eaten by this giant shark out of my head. Cats are small in comparison with a shark, after all, and for this shark, I would be a mere amuse-bouche—if he even noticed me as he gobbled me up. Like humans who sometimes accidentally swallow a fruit fly while riding a bicycle, he wouldn't even be aware that he'd managed to land a cat in his tummy.

We had decided that our strategy should be to head to the breakwater and try to venture out as far as we could and then somehow attract the shark's attention. That shouldn't pose a problem as sharks are always looking for a bite to eat. If he thought that we were four snacks just waiting for him to dig his teeth into, that should do the trick!

The breakwater was oddly deserted, and so was the beach. It looked like the reports that a shark had been spotted were enough for people to shun the beach and head for the pool instead. There are no sharks in pools, so they felt safe there.

The four of us traversed the breakwater, heading as far as we could before getting our paws wet, and took up position, scanning the horizon for any sign of a shark fin. Mostly, the sight of these strikes fear in the heart of any living creature, and it was much the same for us. But today I couldn't wait to see it—for that would be a sign our mission was a go.

"I don't see the shark, Max," said Dooley.

"No, I don't see him either, Dooley," I confessed.

"So how do we lure him over?" asked Brutus.

I glanced at Harriet and thought I had an idea. "Maybe you can sing a song?" I asked.

From experience, I knew that Harriet's singing carries far, so maybe the vibrations would reach the shark and make him curious enough to take a closer look.

"You want me to sing to the shark?" asked Harriet, putting a paw on her chest.

"Well, yes," I said. "Maybe he'll hear you and wonder what's going on."

Harriet made a face. "Wonder what's going on? You mean like a natural disaster about to strike? Like an earthquake or a tornado?"

I saw that I hadn't chosen my words carefully enough, so I amended my statement. "If I'm not mistaken, sharks are creatures who appreciate beauty," I said. "And so if he hears you singing, he'll be attracted by the sound of your voice and the beauty of your song."

She smiled. "Oh, Max. Those words are like music to my ears." And so she took a deep breath and, as she looked out across the waves, burst into song. It was a good thing that the three of us were located behind her, so our ears were protected from the power of our friend's voice, for she had decided to immediately go for maximum amplitude. It wasn't long before I saw several schools of fish drawing near to take a closer look at this natural phenomenon that is Harriet. But so far, there was not a single trace of the shark.

And then I saw it.

A single fin, slicing through the waves!

"There he is!" I cried, pointing to the ominous sight.

"Oh, dear," said Brutus as he moved back a little more. The thing was that we were on a breakwater, and so there wasn't a lot of space to move back. And besides, it was imperative that we made contact with the shark. And so I decided to stand my ground, even though every instinct told me to run for cover!

The shark came closer, and Harriet, since she had closed her eyes, hadn't even seen him, and was singing louder by the second, as her voice was warming up. She's like those old radios that need a little time to get going. The vibrations of her voice must have carried through the water, for the shark was passing by the breakwater and moving ever closer. Finally, he had reached us, and all of a sudden his large form broke the surface and he glanced up at the four of us with his shark eyes, which were more than a little frightening. Pitch black, they were, and I could see menace in them—and malice!

"Hi, Mr. Shark," I said, by way of greeting. "M-m-my name is M-M-Max, and I would like to ask you a c-c-couple of questions, if I m-m-may b-b-be so b-b-bold."

The shark didn't speak but merely studied us—and especially Harriet, who was still singing. Finally, the last note died away and she opened her eyes. When she found herself gazing straight into the shark's eyes, she produced a little whimper. "Ooh!" she trilled.

"Hi there, gorgeous," said the shark. "That was one amazing performance."

"Why, thank you, Mr. Shark," said Harriet, well pleased. Like any true performer, she doesn't care who her audience is. She's grateful for any compliment. Like the artists who perform for dictators, murderers and maniacs, as long as the money is good, she has no moral scruples. "Do you want me to sing another one? I have an extensive repertoire."

I wanted to stop her, but the shark seemed eager for her to continue. "Please do," he grunted. "I think you've got a lovely voice. What's your name, gorgeous?"

"Harriet," she said, simpering a little. "What would you like me to sing?"

"Do you know any Barbra Streisand songs? I've always been a big fan of the lady."

"Oh, absolutely," said Harriet. "Why don't I sing *Memory?*"

"Love it," said the shark. "One of my all-time favorites."

And so Harriet broke into *Memory*, and this time directed her efforts straight at the shark, who had closed his eyes and was enjoying the private concert tremendously, I could tell. The moment she had finished, he actually smiled, baring all of his teeth, of which there were many! I even saw a few carcasses of dead fishes stuck to them, which told me that the myth that sharks have poor dental hygiene is probably true.

"Amazing," he said. "That was absolutely stunning, Harriet."

"I'm so glad you liked it," she said. "It's always great to meet a fan. What's your name, by the way, Mr. Shark?"

"Bruce," said the shark. "Nice to meet you. So what did you want to ask me, cat?"

"Max," I said, "and the question is very simple, Bruce. A man was killed last night. He was murdered, then taken aboard a boat and dumped in the water, possibly in the hopes that you would have a nibble. So we were wondering if perhaps you saw something?"

The shark grinned. "You want me to give you a witness statement, huh?"

"That's exactly what we would like," I said, happy that the shark hadn't made any move to try and catch us.

"How come you cats are involved in this?" asked the shark.

"Our humans are detectives," Harriet explained. "Odelia and Chase Kingsley. They're investigating the death of this man, and so they've asked us to help them out, since they can't seem to crack this case by themselves."

The shark nodded. "I get it. Humans never seem to get anything done, do they? Always need our assistance. Though I have to disappoint you guys. I didn't see anything out of the ordinary last night."

I felt the sting of disappointment. "No boat?"

"Nope."

"No one dumping a dead man's body overboard?"

"Nope."

"That's too bad," I said, not able to hide my dismay. Looked like Bruce wouldn't be able to fulfill the role of star witness after all.

"Though I did see the dead man lying on the beach—after the fact."

"You did?"

I could see what must have happened: the killer had dumped the body, but the tide had pulled it ashore, where it lay on the beach and must have presented a nice snack to Bruce. Like a piece of meat on a plate, he couldn't resist the temptation to have a sniff.

"There was plenty of blood," said the shark. "And before the guy washed up on shore, that blood had attracted my attention. Unfortunately, by the time I got wise, he was already out of reach. So bad luck for me, otherwise I'd have enjoyed a nice little snack."

"Yeah, bad luck," I agreed. But good luck for the victim, as he would have never been found if Bruce had eaten him.

"I must be losing my touch," said the shark. "But then I'm not as young as I used to be. Take the other day, for instance. Some kid had ventured out, pretty far. I could see his legs wiggling from down below. But as I came up, I got second thoughts. Never happened to me before. I should have snapped him up, just like that, but I didn't. Why? Beats me."

"Maybe you thought of the kid's parents?" Harriet suggested. "Who would have been very sad if their son or daughter had been eaten alive?"

"I never had those considerations before," said Bruce. "But now I do. Though of course, it could be that I'm pretty spoiled for choice. These waters are so replete with fishes of any description that I'm never really hungry. And considering what a lot of trouble a shark can get into when he attacks a human, I just figured it wasn't worth it, you know. I don't know why, but every time we take a snap at one of them, they go berserk and start trying to hunt us down. In the end, it's just not worth the aggravation, if you see what I mean."

"I think you've got your heart in the right place, Bruce" said Harriet. "And you obviously have impeccable taste as well, which is a credit to you. Now if you want me to sing you another song, I'd be more than happy to."

The shark smiled. "Oh, would you? It's never happened to me before that I could enjoy a private concert. I mean, the likes of Taylor Swift or Beyoncé never bother to put on a show for me—but then I guess that's because us sharks have this reputation of being man-eaters. Which is simply not true, I can tell you that right now."

"You don't eat humans?" I asked, quite surprised.

"If there's nothing else on the menu, sure. Unless they can sing as well as you can, Harriet," he added. And then he lay back in the water as Harriet launched into another song.

I also sat back, quite relieved that the shark hadn't eaten me. Even though I hadn't learned anything, I also hadn't died, so that was a win in my book!

But as Harriet wound up her mini-concert, the shark turned to me. "I just thought of something," he said. "Maybe you should talk to the dogs."

"The dogs?" I asked. "What dogs?"

"Beats me," he said. "All I know is that every time this guy walked along the beach, all the dogs took off like bats out of hell. They seemed afraid of him."

"So you saw the victim before this morning?"

"Oh, sure. He walked his own dog every morning. But like

I said, any other dog made sure they never went anywhere near him."

"Maybe they were afraid of his dog, not the man?" I suggested.

The shark smiled, showing those fearsome rows of teeth again, making me feel extremely faint. "You tell me, buddy. You're the detective, not me."

After we thanked Bruce and were making our way back to the beach, I thought about what the shark had told us. "Now why would dogs be afraid of Greg Lonsdale?" I asked.

"It's probably like you said," Brutus intimated. "They weren't afraid of Greg but of Barney."

"Who would be afraid of that cute little Pomeranian?" said Harriet with a laugh.

She was in an excellent mood, after the compliments she had received from Bruce. He might not be a paying customer, but he most certainly was a fan. And if he told other sharks about her, she might even be able to make a career as a shark singer—if such a thing exists.

But she was right. What dog would be afraid of Barney? It strengthened me in my resolve to have another chat with the highly-strung Pomeranian. Maybe there was something he hadn't told us the first time. And since he would only talk to Harriet, she would have to run point once again.

"But maybe don't sing to him," I suggested.

I probably shouldn't have said that, for her jolly mood vanished instantly, like dewdrops on a sunny day.

"What's *that* supposed to mean, Max?" she demanded.

"Well, we want him to answer our questions, not be struck dumb by the beauty of your performance," I hastened to say.

Her smile broke through the clouds again. "Why didn't you say so? Of *course* I won't sing. We need him to work with us, not swoon when he hears my beautiful singing voice."

"Excellent save, Max," Brutus whispered with a grin.

My legs, which had been a little wobbly as we headed out to meet Bruce, were feeling a lot more stable now that we were returning to the resort. I know a detective needs to be able to talk to anyone, but there are exceptions. Good thing we'd had Harriet with us. Which just goes to show the old saying is really true: music soothes the savage beast.

CHAPTER 36

As we traversed the boardwalk, we tried to engage any dog we met in conversation, but the moment they understood that we wanted to canvass their views on Greg Lonsdale, they made some excuse and hurried off.

"It seems Bruce was right," said Brutus. "They're all afraid of the guy, even though he's no longer with us."

"I don't understand," I said. "Greg is dead, so why don't they want to talk to us about him?"

"Maybe they didn't like him?" Harriet suggested. "Or maybe they don't like us?"

"We should talk to Fifi or Rufus," said Brutus, referring to our neighboring dogs. "Though it's highly unlikely that they would have known Greg."

"No, we need to talk to the dogs that are here at the resort," I said. "They knew Greg and they should be able to tell us what's going on."

But try as we might, we simply could not find a single dog who wanted to go on record and tell us their views on the topic of the dead comedian. Before long, we had arrived back at the resort, and the first persons we ran into were Gran,

Scarlett, and Denice. Instead of looking for the thief, the three old ladies were lounging by the pool having a swell time. All three of them were swigging cocktails, and judging from the color of their cheeks, they had been at it for a while.

"On the house," said Gran as she held up her cocktail. "This is the good life, isn't it, ladies?"

"It sure is," Scarlett confirmed. "I hope to be working for the resort for a very long time to come. Not only do they know how to treat the people who work for them, but they have promised to pay us a reward, too."

"We've never been paid before," said Gran.

"No?" said Denice. "Nobody has ever paid you for your services?"

"Nobody!" said Gran. "We work and work and work, keeping our community safe and secure, and what do we get in return? A lot of flak from my son. My own son!"

"It's true," Scarlett confirmed when Denice gave them a look of surprise. "Alec does *not* like the watch."

"He *hates* the watch," Gran specified.

"He doesn't like it when we interfere in his investigations," Scarlett explained. "And so he wants to stop us from doing what we do best: catching criminals in the act of being criminals."

"I think you're doing a great job," said Denice. "And if I wasn't leaving in a week, I'd love to join you on your patrols. It sounds like a real hoot!"

"It *is* a hoot!" said Gran. "*Everything* we do is a hoot, but do we get any recognition? None!"

"We did get a medal," said Scarlett. "From Charlene—that's our mayor," she added for Denice's benefit.

"Yeah, that's true," said Gran. "We did get a medal. But no money. And if you get to choose between a medal and money, I'd pick the cash every single time."

"Me too," said Denice. "Cash is king, baby."

"Cash is king!" Gran cried as she pumped the air with her fist.

"They're very cheerful, aren't they, Max?" said Dooley as we moved along.

"It's the cocktails," said Harriet. "Humans are always cheerful when they're drinking cocktails."

"Especially when they don't have to pay for them," Brutus added.

"I don't like cocktails," said Dooley. "I don't like the taste."

"They're probably not good for you, so you shouldn't drink them anyway," said Harriet. She took a deep breath. "And now let's go and see Barney, shall we? I feel a song bubbling up, but I'll try and restrain myself."

"If you can't restrain yourself," said Brutus, "we can always return to Bruce. Now there's a shark who truly appreciates your talent, sweet cheeks."

"He does, doesn't he?" Harriet gushed. "Oh, he's such an *amazing* personality! Can you imagine meeting a shark who adores Barbra? I mean, of all the sharks, who do I meet? The one shark who's as big a fan of Barbra as I am. Talk about a happy coincidence!"

"Too bad he couldn't help us," said Brutus. "Now if only he had crossed paths with the killer as he dumped Greg's body, that would have solved the case and we could all go home."

"We can't go home until Marge and Tex go home," I reminded him.

"And until Gran, Scarlett, and Denice have caught the thief," Dooley said.

"So many cases, so little time," said Brutus. "When did we get to be in such high demand, you guys?"

"Since people started thinking Hampton Cove is the new Cabot Cove," I said, referring to Jessica Fletcher's hometown, where the crime rate probably was the highest in the land.

We had arrived back at the resort and trudged up those stairs again to find the suite where Barney was hopefully still laid up, hiding from the world and mourning his human's demise.

The door to the suite was closed, but that didn't stop four determined cats from gaining entrance. All we had to do was apply our secret weapon in the form of Odelia. We had found our human downstairs, in a meeting with the Wheeler family. She seemed glad of the respite, for she immediately excused herself when she saw us appear and followed us up the stairs.

"Anything of importance?" I asked.

"Nothing," she said. "They said that Greg was a model guest. Never any trouble. Until yesterday, when that waiter accosted him, but then they blamed the waiter and not Greg. I asked them to reconsider, and they said they'd think about it. I told them that it wasn't the waiter's fault. Looks like Greg was on his best behavior when he was staying at the resort. Even his shows were pretty tame and family-friendly. That, or they're lying through their teeth and don't want to wash their dirty laundry in public."

"It's possible that Greg *was* on his best behavior when he was staying here," I said. "The whole chaotic personality he often displayed must have caused him a lot of trouble, so he must have learned to tone it down over the years."

"Possibly. Though from what we learned these past couple of hours, he seemed to have made an enemy out of every single person he met, so he didn't tone it down that much."

She applied the badge she had received to the door panel, and the door clicked open.

"At least the thefts have stopped," she said.

"No more thefts?" I asked, surprised.

"Since Gran and Scarlett have teamed up with Denice and

have been staking out the roof," she said, "there have been no more thefts. Looks like the thief is lying low, knowing he's being watched."

"Huh," I said. "How about that?"

We had told Odelia about the shark, and she agreed that it was a strange thing that all the dogs would be afraid of Greg, but she couldn't offer an explanation either. Especially since Greg had a dog himself, so he didn't seem to pose a major threat to dogs. If anything, he was a friend to the species.

I glanced around the suite, but no matter how hard we tried to locate Barney, there was not a single trace of the Pomeranian.

"He probably moved into the suite next door," said Odelia. "Like Elaine, Clyde and Lloyd. Elaine demanded they change suites immediately, so the dog must have joined them."

I nodded as I studied once again the rows of books that Greg had brought along. One of the books suddenly caught my eye, and as I studied the title, it set a series of little wheels in motion in my noggin. Or at least that's how it felt.

And as I glanced up at Odelia, she smiled. "Don't tell me. You've just had an idea?"

I nodded slowly. "I think so. Though the idea is so far-fetched I'm pretty sure it's nonsense."

"Try me," she suggested. But when I did, she had to agree that it *was* nonsense. But if it wasn't, I'd just hit on something that might just explain exactly why Greg Lonsdale had been killed—and especially the way in which he had been killed.

Now if only we could find Barney…

CHAPTER 37

We found Barney hiding under the bed in the suite where his humans had relocated to. Even though it probably wasn't entirely kosher, Odelia had applied her badge to the door and it had opened immediately. First, she had knocked, of course, but when nobody answered the door, she figured that it was more important that we talk to Barney than any trouble our trespassing might cause.

"Hey Barney," said Harriet as she peered under the bed. "Remember me? Harriet."

"Oh, hi, Harriet," said the Pomeranian. "How are you doing?"

"I'm fine," she said. "You probably won't believe this, but I just sang two songs for a shark, and he liked it!"

"You sang a song for a shark?" asked Barney.

"That's right. And he loved it! Said it was the most beautiful singing he'd ever heard. How about that, huh?"

"I don't think I've ever met a shark," said the little doggie. "Though if I did, I'm not sure I would have it in me to sing a song. I'd be too scared. Sharks eat dogs, don't they?"

"Sharks eat anything," she said. "But this shark was an old shark, and he wasn't hungry. He did tell us that a lot of dogs were scared of Greg," she said, when I gave her a gentle shove to make her hurry up and get to the point. The last thing we needed was for our interview to be cut short when Elaine Lonsdale walked in, or Clyde, or Lloyd.

"He said that, did he?" said the doggie after a pregnant pause.

"He did. Though I'm not sure what he meant by that. Greg loved dogs, didn't he? I mean, he adored you, for sure."

"And I adored him," said Barney softly.

"Obviously he was a good person," said Harriet. "A person who loved dogs."

Barney nodded. "He loved dogs alright. He was crazy about them."

"So crazy that he liked to… eat them?" I suggested.

For a long moment, Barney didn't speak. But then finally he said in a small voice, "Yes."

"Greg liked to eat dogs?" asked Brutus.

"He did," said Barney. He sighed. "How did you find out?"

"He has a book on his shelf about William Buckland," I said. "The man who was famous for having the lifelong ambition to eat a specimen of every living creature. And he did. He ate elephants, kangaroos, mice, rats… and dogs."

"Greg was a big fan of Buckland's," said Barney. "Called him a genius and a free thinker. And so he set out to follow in his footsteps. Only he gave it a twist. He wanted to eat every dog breed there is on the planet."

"Which is why he traveled to so many countries that have dog on the menu," I said. "The Philippines, Vietnam, China…"

"It was his passion," said Barney. "And he always took his own set of carving knives. He liked to do everything himself: to catch the dog, cook the dog, and then eat the dog."

"But then why didn't he eat you?" asked Brutus.

"He'd already eaten my sister," said Barney, "and since he didn't want to eat the same breed of dog twice, that meant I was safe."

And then he suddenly burst into tears. I had a feeling he wasn't crying for the loss of his human, but the loss of his sister.

When he was all cried out, I asked, "Do you have any idea who killed him, Barney?"

"No, I don't. I wasn't lying when I said that I wasn't with him when he died. I was next door, in the suite, with Elaine."

"So Elaine was with you when her husband was killed?"

"She was."

"Did she know about Greg's particular hobby?" asked Brutus.

"I don't think so. Greg didn't tell a living soul, knowing that it would spark controversy and that people might not understand."

"You got that right," Brutus grunted. "Imagine if people found out that he liked to eat dogs. He could kiss his career goodbye."

"Elaine thought he was addicted to drugs, and he didn't disabuse her of that suspicion. He felt it was safer that way. As long as she didn't suspect him of being addicted to dog meat it was fine with him. The only person who knew the truth was his supplier."

"The hot dog guy," said Harriet.

"Yeah, that was the code they had agreed upon. Every time Greg was in the mood for some dog meat—" He made a face. "—he contacted his dealer and asked for a hot dog."

"Literally," said Brutus.

"Or whenever the hot dog man had a particular breed that Greg hadn't eaten yet, he'd send him a message."

"Do you have a name for this hot dog man?" I asked.

"His real name is Demetrius. I don't know his surname, though."

"Did he deliver a hot dog last night?" I asked.

"Probably he did. Greg got these cravings, and he had Demetrius on speed dial."

"But Demetrius probably lives in LA, right? So how did that work when Greg was out of the country? Or on Long Island?"

"Demetrius is well-connected. And supplying dog meat to Greg isn't the only illegal activity he engages in. All he has to do is contact one of his associates to make the drop."

"I'm so sorry you had to go through all of that," said Harriet with feeling. "That must have been so hard for you."

"It *was* hard," said Barney. "Especially since from time to time Greg made me watch. He even offered me a piece of meat sometimes. Dog meat. He said it tasted great, but I didn't want any part of that."

"What happened to your sister?" asked Brutus.

The dog's face screwed up into an expression of regret. "He had adopted the two of us, and it took us a while to understand what kind of man we were dealing with. He tossed for us, you know. It was a flick of the coin that decided my sister's fate. By the same token, it could have been me."

"Why didn't you run away?" asked Brutus.

"I wanted to many times," said Barney. "But it was almost as if Greg felt guilty for what he did to my sister, so he treated me like a prince. I don't think any dog ever had it as good as I did. And yet it never made me feel better about what happened to my sister. But to run away? I'm not brave. I don't think I'd survive in the world outside. At least I knew what I had with Greg. And I knew I was safe with him. Once he had sampled a certain breed, he didn't want seconds. One of each was his creed, and he religiously stuck to it."

"You were afraid that if you ran away you'd end up with another dog butcher," I said.

He nodded. "On the surface, Greg was a respectable man, a friend of dogs. But secretly he killed us and he ate us. So who's to say that other humans are different? For all I know, they're all the same. They're all dog killers."

"I don't think so," said Harriet. "I'm sure that most humans are perfectly decent and treat their pets with respect."

"Does your human eat cats?" asked Barney.

"No, she doesn't," I said.

"How can you be sure, Max?" asked Brutus. "Maybe Odelia does eat cats, and has eaten our particular species and so she doesn't want to eat us. Maybe she has eaten a Persian, a big black cat like me, a Ragamuffin and… whatever it is that you are."

"I doubt it," I said. "If Odelia ate cats, we would have found out by now, after living with her all this time."

"Yeah, I guess so. Still, Greg was able to keep his secret from everyone, even his own family."

"He couldn't keep it from me," said Barney.

"Oh, Barney," said Harriet. "Come here."

After some hesitation, the dog emerged from his hiding place and we gave him a heartfelt hug. He burst into tears again, which caused Odelia to also pick him up. He was trepidatious at first—she might be a secret dog eater—but after a moment he must have realized that Odelia doesn't have a mean bone in her body, and allowed her to hold him.

"Okay, so now we know Greg's big secret," said Harriet. "But we still don't know if it's connected to his murder."

"Yeah, we still have no clue who killed him," said Brutus.

Dooley had been studying me and smiled. "I think Max knows. Don't you, Max? You know who killed Greg and why, right?"

I nodded. "I think I have some idea, yes," I confirmed.

CHAPTER 38

"It's so odd that nothing has been stolen since we got here," said Scarlett as she carefully peeled an orange.

"That's why they pay us the big bucks," said Vesta as she stirred her hot chocolate.

That wasn't necessarily true, but it didn't matter. At least there was someone out there who appreciated their services, and that was more gratifying than any monetary reward.

"I think the thief is probably scared of us," said Denice, who was nibbling on a chocolate croissant. "He knows that there is a force to be reckoned with and it's got him spooked. And so he's decided to down tools for the present."

"The problem with that," said Scarlett, "is that the moment we leave, the thief will probably start up again."

Vesta shrugged. "There's an easy solution for that. It just means that the Wheelers should keep us here indefinitely. I mean, it's a small price to pay for their peace of mind and the safety of their guests."

"Do you really want to come and live at the resort?" asked Scarlett. "Like, forever?"

"I wouldn't mind," she said. "I like it here. I like our room, I like the food, I like the pool, I even like the entertainment. Well, except the guy who was killed, of course. I hate those insult comedians."

"Yeah, give me a good singer any time," said Denice. "Those comedians just think they're funny, but mostly they're not funny at all."

"I hope they'll bring on someone like Taylor Swift," said Scarlett.

Vesta scoffed. "They'll never be able to afford her."

"No, I think Taylor Swift has outgrown these kinds of gigs," said Denice. "But they could get some local talent. I'll bet there's plenty of bands who'd love to come on stage."

"The Argent has some amazing shows," said Scarlett.

"Then maybe we should move to The Argent," said Vesta. "They also must be dealing with thieves from time to time. So if we offer our services, and tell them how successful we've been here at the Hampton Cove Resort, they won't hesitate to offer us the same conditions—or even better ones."

"They might actually pay us those big bucks you mentioned," said Denice. She sighed. "It's been so much fun, hanging out with you guys and going on these stakeouts. Probably the most fun I've had in years. Too bad I'll be heading home soon."

"But why?" asked Vesta. "Maybe you could extend your stay. Or we could have a word with the Wheelers and tell them that since you're now an integral part of the watch, they should comp you your room."

"I wouldn't want to burden them with my presence," said Denice. "I'm not a professional neighborhood watch person like you guys."

"But you've learned a lot from watching us at work,

haven't you?" Vesta insisted. "Well then, that's all the credentials you need. You can tell the Wheelers that you've been trained by us—the one and only Hampton Cove Neighborhood Watch. I'm sure they'll be happy to offer you the same conditions they're offering us."

"Just do it, Denice," was Scarlett's advice.

"Maybe I will," said Denice. "It's true that I've learned a lot since I've started working with you. And it's been so much fun!"

For a moment, the three old ladies enjoyed their respective treats and each other's company. "I wish you could stay," said Vesta. "It would be so much fun if we could consider you a permanent member of the watch. We have Wilbur Vickery, of course, and also Francis Reilly. But it's not the same thing."

"They're men," said Scarlett. "And we all know what men are like."

"Oh, I do," Denice assured her. "They're so heavy, aren't they?"

"The problem with men is that everything always has to be about them," said Vesta. "And that's why I like you, Denice. You're so modest and so kind that I feel as if we've known each other all of our lives."

"I feel the same way," said Scarlett.

"Well, I'll think about it," said Denice. "I have been considering moving to a warmer climate, on account of my arthritis acting up from time to time. Though I never considered the Hamptons, on account of the cost."

"Give it some thought," Vesta said. "And let us know. In the meantime, if you want us to put in a good word for you with the Wheelers, just give a holler. Like I said, we'd be happy to have you. And I'm sure the Wheelers would be amenable to offering you the same conditions they've offered us."

Vesta watched as four cats and her granddaughter walked into the cafeteria, accompanied by Chase. She wondered what they were up to. They had been busy with the investigation into the death of that comedian, who hadn't actually been funny. She waved them over. "Hey, you guys," she said. "How are things with the investigation?"

"We're getting there," said her granddaughter. "We have some idea what might have happened, but now we have to prove it, which is always a different matter altogether."

"Do you need a hand from us?"

"Aren't you busy with that thief?" asked Chase.

"Nah," said Vesta. "He seems to be laying low at the moment."

"Ever since we arrived here, in fact," said Scarlett.

"I think it's Denice," said Vesta as she patted her new friend on the back. "She's our good luck charm. Aren't you, Denice?"

Their friend gave her a modest look. "I'm sure that's not the case," she said. "I'm not even a professional, like you guys are."

"Oh, but Vesta and Scarlett aren't professionals, either," said Chase with a wink at Vesta.

She lightly slapped his arm. "Oh, shush, detective," she said. "Nobody likes a tattletale."

Vesta noticed that Max had been studying Denice closely and now sidled up to her. He lowered his voice and said, "How much do you know about Denice, Gran?"

She couldn't answer without drawing attention to the fact that she could talk to her cats, so she simply shook her head as a sign that she didn't know a great deal about their new friend.

"If I were you," he said, "I would go through her room at your earliest possible convenience. I think you'll find a lot of very interesting stuff there. Look under the bed."

And with this mysterious message, he was off after Odelia and Chase.

"Do you really think they've caught the killer?" asked Scarlett.

"Oh, absolutely," said Vesta as she studied Denice for a moment. "If my granddaughter says she's close to collaring a killer, she's not lying. She's very clever that way." Though to be absolutely honest, it was probably Max who had provided her with the telling clue. He was the clever one in the family. Some might call that blorange cat a genius, and they'd be right. She made a decision and wiped her lips with her napkin. "Will you excuse me for a moment?" she said. "I need to pay a visit to the little girl's room. I'll be back in a sec."

And as she hurried off, leaving Scarlett and Denice to chat amicably amongst themselves, she glanced back, and when she saw that they weren't looking, hurried out of the cafeteria and up the stairs. It was hard to believe, but if Max said they should take a closer look at Denice, he probably had his reasons.

Arriving on the fourth floor, she made a beeline for Denice's room. Using the universal key she and Scarlett had been supplied with, she opened the woman's door and entered, carefully closing it behind her. Remembering Max's words, the first place she inspected was the bed. Lifting the mattress, she was surprised to find several boxes hidden there. Opening one of the boxes, she found that it was filled to the brim with items of value—the kind of items that she knew had been reported stolen in the past couple of weeks.

"Oh, my God," she muttered as she checked another box and then another. She saw jewelry, watches, smartphones, tablets, lots and lots of cash…

Looked like Max was right. The person who had assisted them in trying to nab the thief… *was* the thief!

She looked up when she heard a noise behind her. Unfortunately, she was too late to dodge the baseball bat that came swinging at her head.

Moments later she was down and out for the count.

CHAPTER 39

When Vesta woke up again, she was on the floor, her face against a soft surface that she soon realized was the carpet, and suffering from a splitting headache. She was also unable to move because she had been thoroughly trussed up. When she looked up, she saw that her good friend Denice was packing up, shoving all the stuff she had stolen into a suitcase.

The woman must have realized that she was being watched, for she suddenly stopped and looked down at her. A tight smile appeared on the familiar face, which had undergone a complete transformation. Gone was the doe-eyed innocence that had attracted Vesta to the woman in the first place—the soft and gentle demeanor. In its stead, a hardness and cunning had emerged that Vesta hadn't known the woman was capable of.

"I'm not going to ask how you found out—simple curiosity, probably," she said, "but I *am* going to tell you to keep your nose out of my business if you know what's good for you. I'm going to give you a choice, Vesta dear. Either you keep your mouth shut and live, or you won't and you will be sorry. Is that understood?"

"All this time," said Vesta, "you were the thief?"

"Of course," said the woman simply.

"Is your name even Denice?"

"According to my passport, it is," said the woman curtly. "And now you better keep quiet while I finish packing. Looks like I won't be sticking around after all."

"Why did you stop stealing? Was it because you thought we were on to you?"

"Not you, silly," said Denice. "But those relatives of yours. With your granddaughter and that husband of hers snooping around, I figured it was probably a good idea to lay low for a while. And also, with you and Scarlett insisting on those silly stakeouts, I had to be careful what I did. You may be the most incompetent neighborhood watch commander in history, but even a broken clock gets it right twice a day, so I just figured it was better for me to wait until you had cleared off again, which I knew you'd do eventually, as you're one of those people with a short attention span and you'd get bored soon enough."

"Incompetent or not, I did catch you, didn't I?"

"You didn't catch me, dear heart," said Denice sweetly. "I caught *you*, remember? When I saw you sneak out of the cafeteria, I figured something was up, so I followed you."

"And tried to kill me."

"Oh, puh-lease. That little tap on the head? A head as tough as yours needs a much bigger bat to sustain any real damage. No, I just needed to incapacitate you long enough to make my getaway, but it looks like I should have hit harder."

"What did you do to Scarlett?"

"She's probably still sipping from her cappuccino, sweet innocent dumbo that she is." She laughed, a nasty rasping sound that Vesta heard for the first time. "You two really are something." She continued packing, and Vesta continued trying to get out of the ropes that Denice had used to tie her hands. But try as she might, she couldn't free herself. At least the woman wasn't homicidal, or she wouldn't be among the living right now. But she was darned if she was going to let her get away with the loot. Not on her watch!

The only thing she could think of was to keep her talking until help showed up. Hopefully, Scarlett would realize something was amiss and come looking. It was her only hope. "So how long have you been at it? 'Cause I don't think this is your first rodeo."

"Oh, no, I have a lot of experience with this type of deal," Denice confirmed. "Usually I'm in and out in a couple of days. Any longer and things get hairy. Only this time I was having so much fun with the two of you, I decided to stick around a little longer. Just to see what would happen. My mistake," she added ruefully.

"So you admit you had fun with us."

"I admit I had fun watching you bumble around and make absolute idiots of yourselves."

"What's your real name?"

The woman produced that horrible rasping sound again. "As if I'm going to tell you!"

"I won't tell anyone else."

"Yeah, right. Your entire family consists of cops, honey, so you can't fool me."

"So all these long nights talking and enjoying each other's company, telling stuff about our personal lives—that was all lies, was it? Pretense?" The woman didn't respond this time, and Vesta wondered if she had struck a chord. "They say that when you're lying it's best to stay as close to the truth as possible. So I'm guessing that you really are a widow, and that your thieving spree only began in earnest after your husband died?"

Denice turned on her, a vicious expression on her face. "They killed him, you know. Turned him away from a life-saving operation simply because we couldn't afford to pay. If we'd had money, he would be alive today. And so after the funeral, I vowed I'd stick it to all of those rich jerks and make sure that kind of thing would never happen to me again."

"You didn't just steal from the rich," said Vesta. "You stole from everyone here, and a lot of people have saved all year to be able to spend a week at the resort."

"Oh, spare me the sob stories," said Denice as she slammed the suitcase shut and locked it. "If you can afford a week at this resort, you can also afford to lose a few baubles or a smartphone. And now I'm afraid it's time for us to say goodbye. Forever this time."

For a moment, Vesta was afraid that she would actually bash her head in, but when she picked up the two suitcases and made for the door, to her relief, her estimation that Denice was a thief but not a killer had been correct after all.

"Not so fast!" suddenly a voice spoke from the door. It was Scarlett, and she was blocking Denice's departure.

"Oh, get lost," said Denice viciously. But as Vesta craned her neck to look up, she saw that Scarlett wasn't alone. Behind her, Vesta could see several police officers who hurriedly entered the room. Among them were Chase and Odelia. Chase did the honors by slapping a pair of handcuffs on Denice's wrists.

"Elissa Kram," he said, "you're under arrest for third-degree grand larceny."

"Elissa Kram?" asked Vesta, much surprised.

The woman gave her a dirty look. "As if Vesta Muffin is such a great name. A ridiculous name for a ridiculous person."

"You're not wrong," Vesta agreed. One of the officers had sprung to her assistance and was untying her ropes. "But this ridiculous person made sure that you're going to prison for a long time... Elissa."

"Oh, go to hell, Vesta," said Elissa before she was led away.

Vesta sighed. "And to think I thought she was such a great friend."

Scarlett had hurried to her side and was helping her up. "She was probably too good to be true. The perfect friend is probably a thing that doesn't exist."

"*You're* the perfect friend," said Vesta as she leaned on Scarlett's arm. She touched her head. "Ouch," she muttered.

"Did she hurt you, Gran?" asked Odelia.

"She knocked me over the head," she said. "But as she herself indicated, I have a pretty hard head. I'm sure I'll be fine."

"Best to have it checked out at the hospital," Scarlett advised. "Make sure you didn't suffer a concussion."

The four cats had also arrived, and when Marge and Tex and Grace walked in, it looked like the entire family was present and accounted for.

"We heard what happened," said Tex.

"She was hit over the head, Tex," said Scarlett. "Better check her out."

And so Tex did look at her head, looked deeply into her eyes, and did a couple of tests to determine if she had suffered a concussion. In the end, he determined that she was fine but still said she should have it checked out at the hospital, just to make sure. A scan of the brain should suffice.

"I'm not having my brain scanned," she said. "I'm fine. Absolutely fine." And she would have walked out of the room if not for a sudden dizzy spell that took hold of her, causing her to go down again. This time, she was caught by her daughter, her granddaughter, and Scarlett. Just before the lights went out again, she realized that maybe she wasn't fine after all.

CHAPTER 40

It was a good thing that we found Gran when we did, or the thief would have gotten away. Unfortunately, our human had received a nasty bump on the head, and an ambulance had been called to take her to the hospital. Tex said that in all likelihood, it was nothing to be concerned about, but the look on his face told us that he was concerned anyway. The difference between body language and actual language was obvious.

"I hope she will be fine, Max," said Odelia as we watched the ambulance take off with Gran on board. She, too, looked concerned, and she wasn't even a doctor.

"I'm sure she will be," I said.

The weapon used to give Gran's head that whack had been found. It was a baseball bat, which is not something that should be used on an old lady's head. But then Denice Sutt, or Elissa Kram as her real name turned out to be, had been desperate not to be caught. She had plenty of stuff tucked away under the mattress and wanted to secure her haul when Gran had made the discovery.

"How did you know it was her, Max?" asked Harriet.

"Well, it was Gran telling us that the thefts had all stopped from the moment she and Scarlett had arrived. Which got me thinking. How would the thief know that Gran and Scarlett had been asked by the Wheelers to look into the thefts? Only the Wheelers knew, and surely they wouldn't pass the information on to the thief. The only other person who knew that they were actively setting a trap for the thief was Denice, and so it got me wondering if perhaps she wasn't who she said she was."

"It was certainly very clever of her to befriend Gran and Scarlett," said Brutus. "And she must have had a lot of fun staking out the roof and trying to catch... herself!"

"She played all of us for fools," I agreed. "And I think she thanked her lucky stars that she had discovered that Gran and Scarlett were, in fact, looking to catch her."

"I guess nobody suspects an old lady," said Harriet. "Especially an old lady who looks as sweet and innocent as Denice did."

After I told Gran that she should take a closer look at Denice's room, I had started to worry that I had put Gran's life in jeopardy, and so I told Odelia, who told her husband, who had started looking into this Denice Sutt a little closer. It wasn't long before he had discovered that her real name was Elissa Kram and that she was, in fact, a notorious repeat offender who had been arrested many times in the past for the same type of offense.

And so we had set off to arrest the lady and had found her on the verge of making her getaway after incapacitating Gran.

"How did she manage to get into the rooms unseen?" asked Harriet.

"She stole people's room keys when they were lounging by the pool," I said. "Then checked their rooms and absconded with any items of value she could find."

"But why wasn't she caught on camera?" asked Brutus.

"It's the invisibility coat!" Harriet cried. "I told you guys it exists!"

"Elissa Kram has a history of bribing security people to look the other way," I said. "So if I'm not mistaken she promised Mauricio Whitfield a percentage of the proceeds."

"So the reason she doesn't show up on the security footage?" asked Harriet.

"Is because Mauricio turned off the cameras when she told him to."

Harriet looked disappointed. "I really thought she had magical powers."

"Magical powers to make people do her bidding," I said. "Like many professional criminals she can be extremely charming and persuasive when she wants to be."

"And swing a mean bat when she doesn't," Brutus added dryly.

"Okay, so that's one criminal caught," said Odelia as the ambulance turned the corner and disappeared from view. Tex had decided to ride with his mother-in-law, while Marge kept an eye on Grace, who was sad that her great-grandmother had been injured.

"Let's take a closer look at our killer," Chase agreed.

And so we entered the resort again, this time eager to close the second case that had brought us to the resort. It had taken some time for Chase to make the necessary inquiries, but in the end, all the information he had received led to the same conclusion: that my hunch had most likely been correct. And so we headed up the stairs, en route to the room of Greg Lonsdale's killer.

Chase wanted to gain access to the room with his master key, but Odelia preferred to knock.

"He'll get away, babe," Chase argued.

"He won't be expecting us," she returned.

"And what if he is? I don't want to chase him up and down the resort."

"He won't try to get away, because he won't be expecting us," she said.

In the end, she won out, and Chase applied his fist to the door. "Police. Open up," he said.

A noise could be heard inside the room, and as Chase put his ear to the panel, he cursed lightly. "He's opening a window."

"He probably needs some air," said Odelia, but she didn't sound as sure of herself as she had before.

And since Chase isn't one to make the same mistake twice, he applied his key card to the door. The light turned green and he shoved open the door and slammed into the room… just in time to see our quarry jump off the balcony!

CHAPTER 41

"Oh, dear," said Odelia.

Chase merely groaned and set off in high pursuit of the suspect. At least by trying to evade capture, the man had inadvertently signaled guilt. As they say: an innocent person doesn't run from the cops.

"Maybe we should…" Brutus suggested.

"I think Chase has the situation well in hand," I said. So instead of assisting the detective in his effort to capture the possible killer, we took up position on the balcony with Odelia and followed the chase from our vantage point.

"I hope he catches him," said Odelia. "Otherwise, he'll blame me."

"He won't blame you," I said. "After all, you couldn't have known that he would try to get away."

"Chase knew," she said.

"Chase always thinks the worst of people," said Brutus. "And that's because he's a detective. You think the best of people, and that's to your credit."

"Thanks, Brutus," she said. "That's very sweet of you."

The suspect had managed to jump down from his balcony

to the one below, and from there had made his way to the ground, with Chase right on his tail. The two of them were now running full tilt in the direction of the pool, which even at this early hour was already filling up with people. I could see that Marge was there with Grace, and also Kimmy and Kitty, the twins, who were entertaining a group of kids. All of the chaise lounges were occupied, and as the killer passed by, most of the guests at the pool barely looked up.

"He's heading for the beach," said Harriet.

"Oh, I do hope Chase catches him," said Dooley. "Such a bad man shouldn't be allowed to get away, right?"

"No, he shouldn't be allowed to get away, Dooley," I said. "But I'm sure that Chase knows that and that he'll be able to get him."

The duo had reached the beach, but instead of running parallel to the ocean, for some strange reason, the killer was heading straight for the water.

"He's going to try and swim away," said Harriet.

"But why?" asked Brutus. "Does he want to reach Portugal? If so, that's a long swim."

"I'm sure he's not thinking straight," I said. "With Chase on his tail, all he can probably think about is trying to stay ahead of him."

"Or maybe he's an expert swimmer," said Dooley, "and he's hoping that Chase isn't and that he'll be able to get away like that."

"If so, he's in for a surprise," said Odelia. "Chase is an excellent swimmer. He can outswim anyone, and most definitely this little twerp."

The twerp had reached the first waves and was plunging headfirst into the surf, with Chase still hot on his tail. The cop also dove in, and now they were swimming as fast as they could, thrashing in the waves.

"They're turning it into a triathlon," said Brutus.

"What's the third discipline of a triathlon again?" asked Harriet.

"Um, it's swimming, running, and bicycling," I said. "Right?"

"That's correct," said Odelia, who was biting her lip in extreme tension. It wasn't a given that her husband would be able to successfully conclude this mission. After all, he was up against a vicious killer, so there was a certain danger attached to this pursuit.

As we watched, suddenly I thought I saw a familiar presence. "Look, it's Bruce," I said, pointing to the fin I had seen pop up amongst the waves.

"I hope he won't eat the killer," said Dooley. "He should be brought to justice, not eaten alive."

"He won't eat the killer," I said. "Bruce isn't interested in eating humans. He told us so himself."

"No, he's got plenty of food," said Harriet. "He doesn't need to feed on humans."

Still, it was a complication that made things even more tense. And as we all watched, it looked as if the killer was heading straight for the big shark.

"He's going to bump into Bruce," said Dooley.

"Bruce isn't going to like that," said Harriet. "He struck me as a peaceable old shark who likes to be left alone."

"He's probably enjoying the early morning sun," said Brutus. "And if this guy suddenly bumps into him, he won't be happy."

As Dooley had predicted, the killer was so intent on getting away that he wasn't looking where he was swimming, and suddenly he bumped into the shark, who was bobbing there and enjoying those sunrays that are so beneficial to one's health and well-being.

"Ouch!" said Brutus. "He did it! He's gone and bumped straight into Jaws!"

"I wouldn't call Bruce a 'Jaws' type of shark," I said. "I think he's a very nice old shark, not dangerous at all."

But the killer didn't seem to agree, for he was now swimming back to shore, having been spooked by his chance encounter with the shark. And who would be waiting for him but Chase! When he realized he was effectively stuck between a rock and a hard place, or rather a police detective and a shark, he had the good sense to give up. Moments later, the killer had been collared by the cop, and they were both making their way back to shore.

"Bruce is accompanying them," said Dooley.

"That's probably the strangest thing I've ever seen," said Odelia. "Are you guys sure he's not dangerous?"

"He won't eat Chase," I assured her. "He's a fine old gentle-shark and he won't harm a hair on Chase's head."

"He's a very clever shark," said Harriet, "with great taste in music, and so he must have decided to lend a helping hand to Chase and assist him in escorting the prisoner."

When they had arrived close to the beach, the shark seemed to bid Chase adieu by wiggling his fin and then returned to the deeper waters where he felt most at home. Chase emerged from the ocean with the killer in tow, who seemed to have lost a lot of his pep.

"Okay, time to head down," said Odelia, well pleased that the chase had ended well for all concerned—except perhaps the killer.

As we left the room, several officers poured in to go over the premises with a fine-tooth comb and secure any possible evidence that could be used against the killer. I pointed to a picture of the man's dead dog. "Better take that," I told Odelia. "It's key evidence."

She nodded and instructed the crime scene people to make sure they collected the framed picture.

"After all," I said, "that dog is the reason this whole thing started."

CHAPTER 42

Colin Hackney was seated in interview room number one, across the table from Chase and Uncle Alec. All the fight seemed to have gone out of him as he told a story of heartache and revenge. It was a familiar story, but usually these types of tales revolve around a human loved one who has been killed. In Colin's case, the loved one was a Cesky Terrier named Janice, now deceased.

"I loved that mutt," he said with a lopsided grin. "I'd never owned a dog before, but when I first laid eyes on Janice, I was a goner. She was the loveliest creature I'd ever met, and it was love at first sight. She never left my side after I picked her up from the breeder. She came from a litter of seven pups, but according to the breeder, she was the sweetest of them all, and he was right. Janice was a sweetheart. She followed me around everywhere I went. So even though I wasn't used to traveling with a dog, I started taking her with me, as I couldn't bear to part with her, and I got a feeling she couldn't bear to part with me."

"Is that her?" asked Uncle Alec as he picked up the framed picture we had secured from the man's room.

He nodded. "Yeah, she died five years ago, and I haven't been able to replace her, even though many people told me to. Even my own sister. She tells me it was just a dog, and I should simply get another one like her. But Janice wasn't just a dog. She was very clever and had a sunny and loving disposition." He wiped away a tear. "I just wish I had never told Greg. That's when it all started to go wrong."

"Greg also took a liking to Janice?" asked Chase.

"He did, yeah. From the moment he found out that I had bought a Cesky Terrier, he kept hounding me to meet her. Said it was one of the rarest breeds in the world, and he'd never seen one for real. And seeing as Greg was my most successful and famous client, I didn't see the harm in introducing him to Janice. Little did I know that Greg wasn't just a famous comedian. He was also a monster."

"He loved dogs," said Uncle Alec. "As food."

"Yeah, Greg ate dogs," said Colin. "It was his big secret. Even I didn't know about his secret hobby, and as his agent, I spent a lot of time with the guy. Negotiating deals, sifting through job offers, socializing outside of work. I knew his wife, his kid—we even went on vacations together. And yet he never told me that his one big passion in life was dogs."

"So what happened to Janice, Colin?" asked Uncle Alec.

"I'd asked Greg to babysit her. I had to go out of town for a couple of days for a conference, and I didn't want to take Janice, as I'd be locked up in a conference room all day, and I didn't want her to be stuck in my hotel room. So I made the mistake of asking Greg to take care of her. He'd been suggesting that he would love to babysit. That he was just as crazy about dogs as I was about Janice. He owned a dog himself—Barney. And we had introduced the two mutts, and they seemed to get along great. Barney used to have a sister, but she had died, and Greg said that Janice must have reminded him of her."

"Greg had eaten Barney's sister," said Chase.

Colin nodded as he dragged a hand through his mane, which was still wet from his swim in the ocean and run-in with Bruce. "Yeah, I didn't know about that. If I had…" His voice trailed off, and he stared at the picture of Janice. "It was the second day of the conference when I got a panicky text from Greg that Janice had run away. I was surprised, as Janice wasn't disobedient. She was sweet and docile. Running away wasn't something that I associated with her. And then when I returned after the weekend and went to pick her up, he said that she still hadn't returned. He'd called the police and they had searched the entire neighborhood, but no one had seen her. We even put up flyers, me and Greg."

"And all the while, Janice was already dead," said Chase.

"Yeah, he had eaten her. On a bed of sautéed onions and spring potatoes. He said she tasted great. Like lamb, with a hint of mutton."

"How did you find out?"

"It took me long enough," said Colin with a weary sigh. "Like I said, it was Greg's most closely guarded secret. One that he didn't share with anyone. Except for his dealer. A guy called Demetrius. He was the one who supplied him with dog meat on a regular basis. The thing is that Greg once sent me a text that was meant for Demetrius. Said he had a sudden craving for a hot dog. So I sent him a text back that we could get a hot dog if he wanted to. He must not have noticed that the text came from me, for he told me to bring the hot dog to the house. And so I did. He must have realized his mistake eventually, for by the time I showed up, Demetrius also arrived, with a cooler containing the hot dog. Though in his case it was actual dog meat. The guy seemed to be laboring under the misapprehension that I was au courant of Greg's sick predilection, for he told me that the dog he had been able to supply was a very rare breed indeed. A Lagotto Romagnolo. It was quite a big dog, and he joked that I'd have to help Greg to stow him away. I didn't know what I was hearing, and when Greg came out and understood that his secret was out, he wasn't too well pleased. He covered it well, and invited me in. And that's when he revealed to me that he was a follower of William Buckland, with a twist. Buckland wanted to eat every animal that walked the earth, and Greg wanted to eat every dog breed. And since LA is full of celebrities, and they all have dogs, Demetrius kept him well supplied."

"Did he tell you about Janice?"

"He didn't, but I suspected. And when I confronted him, he admitted that he hadn't been able to resist the temptation to eat my dog. He seemed to think it was no big deal, as it was just a dog, and in his estimation dogs are like chickens: meant to be eaten."

"But you didn't see it that way."

Colin shook his head. "Nope. I most certainly did not see it that way. In fact, I was furious and threatened to report him to the cops. He had to laugh at that. Said that if I did, he would end my career. He was my most important client, and without him, I wouldn't have a job at the agency. He was right, of course. But I didn't care. At that moment I decided that putting Janice's murderer behind bars was more important than my career."

"So did you go to the police?"

"I would have, if he hadn't knocked me out cold," said Colin bitterly. "When I came to, I found myself locked up in his basement. For a while, I thought he was going to eat me, as he didn't seem to have any qualms about that. But in the end, he made me promise that I wouldn't report him. If I did, he'd have Demetrius find me and kill me, before going after the rest of my family, and kill them all. And I had no doubt in my mind he wasn't kidding. He was a dangerous man. Completely mad, of course, and probably a psychopath."

"You could have reported him and asked for protection," said Uncle Alec.

"First of all, who would have believed such a crazy story?" asked Colin. "It was my word against a very powerful person. Greg would have said that I was angry because he had fired me, and even if the police would have believed me, Greg's threat still stood, and there was not a doubt in my mind he planned to make good on it. This Demetrius fellow is a convicted killer with ties to organized crime. Originally Greg had hired him as a bodyguard, but when he discovered the guy's unique skill set and absolute lack of a conscience, he started using him as his personal dog catcher. The man is extremely good at what he does, whether it's killing dogs or people, so the last thing I wanted was to wake up one morning with Demetrius breathing down my neck, a knife to my throat."

"So why did you kill Greg now?" asked Uncle Alec. "After all these years?"

"After the incident, he fired me as his agent, and as a consequence, I was let go from the agency. So I retrained as a pastry chef, and I was reasonably happy. Try as I might, though, I couldn't forget what happened to Janice. And so when I ran into Greg here at the resort, it all came back to me. I overheard him talking to Demetrius, ordering a hot dog, and that's how I discovered they were still up to their old tricks. And so I vowed to put a stop to this butchery once and for all. Make sure they never hurt another dog again."

"You made Greg eat his own leg," said Chase.

Colin shrugged. "I figured he might appreciate a taste of his own medicine. So I sliced off parts of his leg and fed them to him. Contrary to what I thought, he didn't enjoy it."

"And then you killed him."

"That, I did. And I don't regret it. That man had to be stopped, and I'm glad I was the one to do it. The only good thing I've done in my life. Stop a dog killer. The only part I'm sorry about is that I didn't do it sooner. I should have killed him when he confessed that he had murdered my sweet Janice." His voice broke and tears trickled down his cheeks.

CHAPTER 43

We were back at the resort, where Marge and Tex were enjoying their final days as honored guests of the Wheeler family. Bea Wheeler had personally thanked Odelia and Chase for catching a murderer and also a thief, thereby ridding the resort of a black mark.

The whole family was gathered by the pool, even Gran, who had recovered remarkably fast from her ordeal at the hands of Elissa Kram. The doctors had scanned her head and found nothing out of the ordinary—no indication that she had sustained anything other than a slight concussion. They had told her to rest, and Gran was determined to do just that —by the pool.

As a consequence of Colin Hackney's actions, Greg Lonsdale's dog was now without a master. However, that hadn't lasted long, as Clyde had decided to look after Barney—a much better master than his dad ever was.

Colin was in prison awaiting trial, and I had a feeling that the jury would be especially lenient with him, considering the story he would tell the court about a man who was quite mad. If only he had gone to the police when he had discovered what had happened to Janice, a lot of dogs could have been saved.

Demetrius Burbage had also been arrested and would never supply hot dogs to anyone again. Killing a dog might not carry as big a sentence as killing a man, but it was safe to assume that his dog-murdering days were over—and a good thing, too. Cats may not always have a dog's best interests at heart, but that doesn't mean we want to see them slaughtered and eaten.

"One thing I don't understand," said Harriet, "is how Colin's sleep app didn't register that he was up and about and murdering Greg when he was supposed to be fast asleep."

"Because those apps can be rigged," I said. "And that's what he did. It was all part of his plan to get rid of Greg once and for all. A plan he worked hard to make foolproof."

"He shouldn't have put that picture of Janice on display," said Brutus. "That's what gave him away, isn't it, Max?"

"It was," I confirmed. "It made me wonder if there might be a connection between the fact that Greg liked to eat dogs and the death of Colin's dog. Turns out there was a link."

"A simple background check would have shown that Colin used to be Greg's agent," said Harriet. "And that he had lied about that."

"He probably had some excuse prepared. The most important thing was that he didn't draw any suspicion to himself in the early stages of the investigation. By the time Chase discovered there was a link between Colin and Greg, he would have skipped town."

By the same token, Chase would have discovered that Colin Hackney had rented Weston Kerby's boat the week before and had gleaned the code and knew how to take out the boat. These were all things that would come out in the later stages of the investigation and, while not conclusive evidence of the man's guilt, might have put him in the frame.

"I wonder if there are people like Greg out there who do the same things to cats as he did to dogs," said Brutus. "I mean, are there any cat eaters in the world, do you think?"

The four of us had taken up position underneath Gran's chaise lounge, the only place where we were safe from that relentless sun beating down on our humans. Grace was playing in the pool with the other kids—even Timmy, who seemed to have become her best chum now—and was having a ball splashing in the water, as all kids do.

"I hope not," said Harriet. "Imagine people murdering cats and eating them. That's too gruesome to contemplate."

"I think there are people who eat cats," said Dooley. "If there are people who eat chickens, ducks, and lambs, why not cats? As I'm sure there are also people out there who eat other people."

"Cannibals," said Harriet knowingly. "I wonder if you can call a cat-eater a cannibal."

"Only a cat who eats another cat is called a cannibal," I said. "Any species that eats members of its own species is a cannibal."

"Like a dog that eats dogs?" asked Dooley. "Or a bird that eats birds?"

"Exactly."

We all thought about this for a moment and then collectively shivered. "Imagine eating a cat," said Brutus. "That's just... gross."

"Isn't it?" said Harriet. "Like I would eat you, and you would eat Max, and Max would eat Dooley, and Dooley would eat me."

"I wouldn't be able to eat you, Harriet," said Dooley. "Not if I'm being eaten by Max. Unless he's only eating a part of me, and the rest of me is still alive to eat a part of you."

"You mean like we would all eat each other's hind leg or something?" said Brutus.

"Or an ear," said Dooley. "Ears are crunchy, aren't they?"

I gulped. "I do *not* want you to eat my ears," I told Brutus.

"I wouldn't mind nibbling on your ears, love bug," said Harriet as she gave her mate a slight nudge. "Just a little nibble, mind you."

"I wouldn't mind nibbling on *your* ears," he said.

"Oh, you guys," I said. "Get a room."

"We will," said Harriet, and much to my surprise, she and Brutus strolled off in the direction of the resort.

"I was only joking!" I yelled after them.

"I wasn't!" Harriet yelled back and giggled.

It looked like she and Brutus were going to enjoy one of the main pleasures of taking a vacation: quality time with a loved one.

And then it was just me and Dooley. We followed Grace's adventures in the pool for a few moments, supervised by Kimmy and Kitty, who seemed to have risen to the occasion and were actually getting better at handling a group of kids. My understanding was that they hadn't enjoyed the job when their mom first assigned it to them, but now they did. Assisting them was Clyde, who seemed to have developed a strong liking for Kimmy—though it could have been Kitty, of course. And much to the young man's surprise, she seemed to like him too.

"Holiday romance," said Dooley now that he had followed my gaze and guessed my thoughts. "It's sweet, isn't it?"

"It sure is," I said, "especially after the kid found out that his dad was a monster."

"I hope nobody will hold it against him," said Dooley.

"I'm sure they won't. After all, he's not a monster, his dad was."

"Kimmy sure doesn't seem to hold it against him."

The two teenagers shared a sweet kiss, and all the kids in

the pool whooped and hollered, even Grace, who was possibly the loudest of them all.

"Oh, can you get those kids to shut up?" asked Gran, whose head was still hurting to some extent.

"They're kids, Vesta," said Scarlett. "You can't get them to shut up."

"Yeah, I know," said Gran. "So how about that reward, huh?"

"What reward?" asked Marge from the next chaise lounge.

"The Wheelers have told us that we can stay here every year from now on as a reward for helping them get rid of this thief."

"That's very generous of them. So they were pleased with the way things have gone?"

"Absolutely pleased," said Scarlett. "Turns out this thief had been terrorizing resorts and hotels up and down the coast for years. And now that Elissa is finally behind bars, more and more businesses are filing complaints against her."

"Notorious thief," said Gran sleepily. "And we caught her. Well, actually Max caught her." She reached underneath her chaise lounge until she found me and gave my head a pat. "Thanks, buddy. You did good."

"Does that mean we can also stay here for free once a year, Max?" asked Dooley.

I rolled my eyes. "I guess so, but why would we want to?"

I mean: sun, sand, and surf. Who wants it, right? Not me!

I closed my eyes, and moments later was fast asleep.

Until I felt a slight nudge in my side.

"Max?"

"Mh?"

"If a cat eating another cat is called a cannibal, then what do you call a dog who eats a cat?"

"I'm not sure dogs like that exist, Dooley," I said sleepily.

"But dogs are always chasing cats, Max. So what do they do when they catch us?"

"Give us a chance to get away so they can chase us again? It's all part of the game, Dooley. Dogs don't really want to catch us. They just want to play."

Gran, who had overheard our conversation, decided to add her two cents. "You're taking too charitable a view of things, Max," she said. "I'm sure that if a dog does catch a cat, he won't play catch and release. At least not certain types of dogs. So next time a dog tries to catch you, you better run, all right? Take it from one who knows."

"Have you ever been bitten by a dog, Gran?" asked Dooley.

"Have I ever! I married him!"

"You married a dog?"

"Absolutely."

"But that's terrible!"

"Tell me about it."

"So what happened?"

"He died. Which is probably the best thing that he ever did in his life. Well, he also gave me two lovely kids. So I can't complain. He may have been a dog, but without him, I wouldn't be here, so I guess he did something right. And now please let me rest, all right? Your gran has a splitting headache, courtesy of another dog. Though I should probably say bitch."

"Gran!"

"A female dog is called a bitch, Dooley," I pointed out.

"Oh, right," said my friend.

For a while, no one spoke, but then Dooley must have processed the information that he had gleaned from the conversation, for he nudged me again. "Max?"

"Mh."

"What happens if a bitch chases a cat?"

"Um… no idea," I said.

"She bitch-slaps him."

"Haha. Very funny, Dooley."

"Here's another one. What happens if a cat chases a bitch?"

"He, um, cat-slaps her?"

"How did you know?"

"Just a wild guess."

"Can you guys cut down on the chatter?" asked Gran. "I would like to get some rest now, please."

"Yes, Gran," said Dooley.

"Yes, Gran," I murmured, grateful for the intervention, as I was pretty eager to get in some nap time.

For a few moments, all was quiet, except the chattering from the kids in the pool, which was actually more relaxing than annoying, I found. Then Dooley gave me another nudge.

"What is it, Dooley?" I said reluctantly.

"What do you call a bitch tricking a bitch, Max?"

"No idea," I confessed, quickly tiring of this game.

"A bitch-up!"

"Ha. Ha."

"Maybe I should be a comedian, Max. Like Greg Lonsdale? I think I could do it. All it takes is getting up on stage and telling a bunch of jokes."

"I'm sure there's more to it than that, Dooley."

"I wouldn't insult people, of course. Or cats. Or dogs."

"Good for you," I murmured.

"I might have my own hot dog man, though. But only if he delivers actual 'hot' dogs, not actual hot 'dogs,' if you know what I mean."

I sighed.

"Too soon?"

"Too soon, buddy."

"I'm sorry, Max. That was in poor taste."

"It certainly was."

"It's hard to be a comedian."

"I thought you said it was easy."

"I guess I've matured as an artist."

I smiled. And as Dooley thought up some new jokes—in good taste or bad—I finally got that nap I had been craving. Unfortunately, I dreamed of being stuck in the middle of a huge hot dog bun and being lowered into the mouth of a giant shark.

I woke up with a start, and since I wasn't sure if there was any substance to my dream, I decided to crawl up onto Odelia's chaise lounge.

"Odelia?"

"Mh?"

"You would never turn me into a hot dog and eat me, right?"

"You mean a hot cat, don't you?"

"Odelia!"

She smiled. "Of course not, Max. I love you too much to eat you."

"That's ironic," said Gran. "I love Dooley so much I *could* eat him."

Dooley emerged from underneath the lounger and stared at her. "Gran!"

"Just kidding, little buddy," said the old lady.

"Well, it's not funny!"

"You have no sense of humor," said Gran.

His face fell. "But I want to be a comedian."

Both Gran and Odelia laughed, proving that perhaps Dooley was a natural. Though judging from the look on his face, he had no idea what he had said that was so funny.

As he curled up next to his human, I curled up next to mine, and we all dozed off.

It wasn't long, though, before I became aware of a persistent itching sensation, and when I opened my eyes, I discovered a tiny speck on the chaise lounge. Upon closer inspection, it wasn't a speck but a bedbug. When he spoke, I recognized him as Rico.

"I told you we'd be back, Max!" the tiny bug cried triumphantly.

"But… this isn't a bed, Rico," I said. "What are you doing here?"

"What am I doing here? Having the time of my life, buddy! After you got us kicked out of the resort, I had to find a new way to feed my family. Like Madonna, we had to reinvent ourselves. And that's when it hit me: what is the one place where people spend even more time than a bed? A chaise lounge! It's the new frontier! The future of bedbuggery! And we have you to thank for it! So say goodbye to the bedbug and hello to the chaisebug!"

As I looked around, I saw that all the people present were scratching themselves. And not just the people, but the cats, too, and the dogs. The chaisebugs were taking over!

I closed my eyes in dismay.

Oh, dear. What had I done!

THE END

Thanks for reading! If you want to know when a new Nic Saint book comes out, sign up for Nic's mailing list: nicsaint.com/news

EXCERPT FROM PURRFECT BULLY (MAX 92)

Chapter One

"How many times do I have to tell you?"

Brian looked up. He'd been busy carving a nice wooden sculpture of a turtle, and this interruption in his thought processes, such as they were, irked him to some degree.

"Huh?" he said, in that eloquent way he had of expressing himself.

"I said…" His mom seemed to think better of repeating herself, and instead yanked the knife from his hands and placed it on the table. "Have you finished your homework?"

"Well…" He thought for a moment, but then had to admit that he hadn't.

"And why not, if I may ask?"

"Because… I have to finish my turtle?" he suggested.

The turtle was a present for his uncle Dave, and since Uncle Dave's birthday was next week, he felt it was probably a lot more urgent to finish the turtle than to spend his precious time on such an inconsequential thing as making

EXCERPT FROM PURRFECT BULLY (MAX 92)

sure that his homework was done. After all, homework could wait, but Uncle Dave couldn't.

"Go and finish your homework," said Mom, who, like all moms, seemed to operate on entirely different logic. She was pointing to the door and it was clear that she wasn't in the mood for any discussion. And so he sighed and did as he was told.

"Uncle Dave won't be happy," he said as he placed his foot on the first step.

"Uncle Dave knows that his nephew's future is a lot more important than any turtles," said Mom, proving to Brian that hers was not the kind of flexible mind his teacher Mrs. Gibson had talked about at length when discussing the great geniuses of past and present.

How could Mom not see that his future wasn't going to be determined by the homework that he made today but by the promises he kept? Ever since Uncle Dave had become aware of his talent for wood carving, he had been pestering him to create a turtle just like the many turtles he had made before for other members of his family, all of his friends, and even for his sister, even though she had taken one look at the thing and had dropped it to the floor and unceremoniously kicked it under her bed, never to be seen again.

Clearly, she wasn't as appreciative of his talent as Uncle Dave was.

And as he entered his room and took a seat at his desk, suddenly he got a bright idea. The kind of idea that Mrs. Gibson would surely have seen as a sign of genius. Not that he was any kind of genius, but still. It showed that he had a knack for thinking outside of the box, another aspect of geniuses Mrs. Gibson said was very important. She never did mention what box this was, but then maybe she was keeping that revelation for the next lesson.

He got up and tiptoed into his sister's room. Crouching

EXCERPT FROM PURRFECT BULLY (MAX 92)

down and looking under Jodie's bed was but the work of a moment. Much to his disappointment, he didn't see any sign of the turtle that languished there, and now he wondered what she could have possibly done with the thing. As he started looking around, he became aware that his sister's room was a lot cleaner than his. In fact, it wasn't too much to say that Jodie was probably what Mrs. Gibson would call a neat freak—a topic she had discussed at length in a different lesson not that long ago. According to her, neat freaks took a good thing and gave it a bad reputation. It was obvious that keeping your room clean was a good thing, but taken to the extreme, it suddenly turned into a bad thing. How this was possible, Brian didn't know, and he'd been afraid to ask, as Mrs. Gibson didn't appreciate it when her students asked a bunch of questions. He also wondered where she drew the line between a regular neat person and an obsessive neat freak. But a hunch told him that Jodie had definitely crossed that line.

As he lifted a pillow, he found himself staring at a diary, and as he picked it up, he immediately recognized his sister's flowery handwriting. Even though he wasn't all that interested in what his sister entrusted to her diary—girls always made such a fuss over these things whereas boys knew it was just a load of nonsense—he still opened it and started to read. It wasn't long before he became aware that not all was well in the World of Jodie Brocket. In fact, things were pretty rotten if these scribblings were to be believed.

But before he could get deeper into the matter, he heard the front door open and close and immediately tucked the diary back where he had found it and tiptoed out of the room.

His sister might not be the worst sister in the world—for one thing, she never ever called him bad names or even hit him over the head like some sisters of his friends at school reportedly did—but she probably wouldn't like it if she found her brother leafing through her diary and reading her personal notes.

Returning to his room, he discovered that he had all but forgotten about Uncle Dave's turtle. Gone was the urgency he had felt in connection to delivering to that man the turtle he had expressed a wish to accept. In its stead, thoughts of his sister's predicament now loomed large and ominous. And since he was still Jodie's brother, a new task emerged on the horizon: rescuing her from a fate that to him seemed worse than death.

And since he wasn't an actual sleuth or even a caped crusader, like many of the superheroes he admired so much, all he could think was that he needed to enlist the assistance of someone who did have the necessary qualifications to deal with this type of life-and-death stuff. In other words, the one person he knew who could help him out.

Chapter Two

I had been soaking up a few rays when my attention was drawn by a loud lament seemingly coming from one of my friends nearby. When I looked up from my pleasant position on the lawn, I saw that it was, in fact, a small turtle uttering the lament. I was surprised to see the turtle, as I had never seen it before, and turtles are not a fixture in our home.

"Hey, little buddy," I said, eager to establish that I didn't pose a threat to the creature. I may not have met this particular turtle before, but that didn't mean I wasn't going to welcome it with open paws into our backyard, so to speak.

As I saw it, Odelia must have decided to gift her daughter the turtle as a present. A pet to call her own, in other words. Kids are always being taught about the different members of the animal kingdom at school, and Grace must have learned about the turtle from her teacher and decided that she wanted one for herself.

"This is an outrage," the turtle muttered.

"What is?" I asked, curious as to why the turtle would be muttering these strange words.

"Why, the fact that they're forcing me to do all this slave labor, of course," said the turtle, and seemed to gesture to the house as it spoke these words.

I glanced up at the house, but since I didn't see anyone who could possibly be responsible for imposing slave labor on a turtle, I was at a loss as to how to respond.

"They're making you work hard, are they?" I asked.

"They sure are," said the turtle. "Which is exactly why I decided to make a break for it." He directed a sort of pleading look at me. "Can you help me find refuge, cat?"

"Max," I said, deciding that maybe now was a good time to start on those introductions that are so essential in establishing good relations with a new acquaintance. "And what's your name?" I asked when the turtle didn't seem to be on the verge of being forthcoming with a name.

"Max," said the turtle.

"Yes, that's right," I said. "My name is Max, and I live here. And what's your name?"

"Max," the turtle repeated.

I frowned. I don't mind pets being obtuse, but it does pose a sort of barrier to furthering that essential sense of bonhomie I like to see in my associations with a new friend. "Yes, I think we've established that my name is Max," I said. "But what I would like to know is your name, if you see what I mean."

"Max," the turtle said, like a record that was stuck. "Quite a coincidence, isn't it? That we should both share the same name?"

EXCERPT FROM PURRFECT BULLY (MAX 92)

I brightened. I finally saw it all. "Your name is Max also?" I asked, therefore.

"Yeah, though in actual fact it's Maxwell the Third. My dad was Maxwell the Second and his dad—"

"Maxwell the First?" I ventured.

He gave me an odd look. "How did you know?"

"Just a wild guess."

"My friends all call me Max, though. Maxwell is such a mouthful, don't you find?"

"I do," I confirmed. "If I may ask: these people who make you work like a slave, who are they, exactly?"

"I'm not sure," said the turtle. "The guy is named Ted, and he claims to be my owner, though it's still not clear to me how that works, exactly. From a legal standpoint, I mean. As far as I can tell, it's not legal to possess a person and call him your personal property. I mean, there must be laws about that sort of thing, wouldn't you agree?"

"Oh, absolutely," I said. "Though it's also true that pets don't exactly feature in these laws. The laws about not being allowed to own a person don't apply to pets but to humans, as they're the ones who make these laws."

The turtle stared at me. "What are you saying, Max? That this Ted fellow is legally allowed to treat me as his personal property?"

"In a nutshell? Yes."

The turtle shook his head. "I don't think that's fair, do you?"

"Fair or not fair, it's the way things are, I'm afraid, Max." I still found it a little strange to call another pet by my own name, but then I guess names are not exclusively assigned to one particular pet. Just as different humans can be called the same name, the same goes for us.

Dooley shot out through the pet flap and plopped down next to me. He was still licking his lips, which told me that he'd gone in for some refreshments and had found them. "Hey there, little buddy," he said as he spotted the turtle. "You're a turtle, aren't you?"

"Excellent powers of observation, cat," said the turtle with a touch of sarcasm. It was obvious that he wasn't in the best of moods.

"Dooley," said Dooley. "And what's your name?"

"Max," said the turtle.

Dooley stared at him, then at me. "Yes?"

"That's my name," said the turtle.

Dooley gawked for a moment, but then got the picture—and a whole lot quicker than I had, I have to say. "Your name is Max?"

"That's right. Just like your large orange friend over there."

"Blorange," I muttered in an effort to rectify a common misconception.

"But..." Dooley looked from me to the turtle and back again. "But how is that possible?"

"Names aren't the exclusive property of one single person, Dooley," I explained.

"But you're so different," he said.

The turtle smiled. "You can say that again. In fact, we couldn't be more different." Then his smile vanished again. "So how about it, Max? Can you suggest a place for me to stay? It would have to be where I can lay low for a while and won't be found by that horrible Ted."

"You don't like Ted?" asked Dooley.

But the turtle decided to ignore him. "Maybe *you* could put me up?" he said, giving me a pleading look. "Just until I can arrange things. The thing is that I kinda lost track of my brothers and sisters, so I don't know where they are. That's the trouble with these pet shops. They take you in wholesale and then sell off the different members of your family one by

EXCERPT FROM PURRFECT BULLY (MAX 92)

one. The upshot is that you all get separated and might not be able to find each other."

"So... where are your brothers and sisters, you think?" asked Dooley, who seemed fascinated by this rare glimpse into the life of a species that we weren't familiar with.

The turtle shrugged. "I have no idea where they are. They might be in Canada for all I know, or Mexico, having been taken across the border by the people they've been sold to."

"Where is this pet shop that sold you located?" I asked.

"Why, here in Hampton Cove," said Max. Then, anticipating my next question, "But that doesn't mean anything. This place is visited by tourists all the time, and so one of them could have taken my sister Shirley, another my brother Lance, and another one still could have adopted my older brother Rhett and my two other sisters Ginger and Irene. Effectively splitting us up." He sighed deeply. "They should institute a rule that if people want to adopt a turtle, they have to take us as a family—all or nothing."

"Yeah, I can see how that must be frustrating," I said.

"Frustrating! It's a disgrace, that's what it is." Dooley suddenly emitted a giggle, and the turtle gave him a dirty look. "You think this is funny, do you, Dooley?"

"Oh, no!" said Dooley quickly, trying to suppress his mirth. "It's just that—what are the odds that you would have the same name as Max?"

The turtle rolled his eyes. "Still harping on the same topic, I see."

"You have to admit it is a big coincidence," said my friend.

"I'm not admitting to any such thing," said the turtle. He seemed out of sorts, which wasn't surprising considering the fact that he might never see his brothers and sisters again.

"Okay, if you like, I will ask my human to put you up for the time being," I said.

"And hide me from Terrible Ted?" he added hopefully.

EXCERPT FROM PURRFECT BULLY (MAX 92)

"And hide you from Ted," I agreed.

"Has Ted been very terrible to you?" asked Dooley.

"He has," the turtle said curtly.

Dooley shook his head sadly. "Ted is an accountant. He's used to working with numbers, not pets. He used to be awful to Rufus also. But I think he has learned his lesson after Rufus ran away from home once, and now he doesn't treat him as badly anymore."

"Rufus?" asked Max. "Who is Rufus?"

"Why, Ted's dog, of course," said Dooley. "He's a good friend of ours," he added. "Even though he is a dog, we all like him very much."

The turtle frowned. "That's the trouble with being kept in a shed, you see," he said. "You aren't allowed outside, and so I haven't met any other members of Ted's household. In fact, I didn't even know that the guy had a dog."

"What did Ted make you do?" I asked.

"Sit for him," said the turtle.

"Sit for him? What do you mean?"

"Just what I said. I had to sit for him while he tried to capture my likeness in clay. I don't know why, but he seems to have developed this obsession with trying to replicate the way I look in dead material. All I can say is it was a lot of hard work. Turtles hate to sit still for hours at a time, see. We like to move around, dynamic creatures that we are. Always up for some action—that's the turtle way. But every time I moved, Ted expressed his displeasure and threatened to take away my food if I didn't do as he said."

"Oh, but that *is* terrible," said Dooley, who hates it when his bowl is empty. "He can't do that to you!"

"Like I said, it was pure torture. Which is why I escaped the first chance I got. And now I'm here, talking to you guys." He darted a glance over his shoulder. "I just hope he won't come looking for me. I'm pretty sure he won't like it when he discovers me gone. He said I was an integral part of his plan."

"What plan?" asked Dooley.

"Beats me. He didn't think I was important enough to confide in. All I know is that I'm glad I got away, and I'll never have to go back to spend time with that horrible man."

Poor Ted, I thought. He'd probably hate it if he knew that his turtle was saying these awful things about him. But then I guess when you threaten to deprive a turtle of food if he doesn't do as he's told, you can expect some kind of backlash. So Ted only had himself to blame that Max would have escaped the shed where Ted kept him.

I could only imagine that this was the garden shed and that Ted had decided to use it for some experiment, the likes of which didn't bear thinking about.

"Let's get you into the house," I suggested, "before Ted comes looking. We don't want him to find you and drag you back to his shed to carry out these heinous experiments."

The turtle looked extremely grateful as he followed us into the house through the pet flap. I felt a warm glow spread through my chest at the thought that I had saved this tiny creature from being worked to the bone by a Ted Trapper who had obviously gone berserk.

Chapter Three

Marc Oldoland was taking the mail out of the mailbox when he saw it—a dark van with tinted windows slowly cruising along the street. A deep frown puckered his brow. It wasn't the first time he'd seen that van. As he tried to get a look at the driver, the reflection from the sun made it quite impossible to identify the person. He got the impression it was a man, and he was wearing a baseball cap, though it could just as well have been a woman.

"Not with me, you don't," he said, and hurried back into the house, where it didn't take him long to retrieve his phone and step outside again. He was just in time to see the van turn the corner. He held up his phone and managed to snap a shot, and when he checked it, saw that he had managed to catch the license plate on the van.

Satisfied, he held the phone up to his ear. Moments later, he was in communication with Dolores Peltz, who manned the front desk at the police station.

"What is it this time, Marc?" asked the woman, not sounding all that happy to hear his voice.

"That van was back just now," he said. "Cruising down the street, all suspicious-like, just like the last couple of times. And this time," he said with a note of triumph in his voice, "I managed to snap a picture… of the license plate!"

There was silence on the other end, which wasn't Dolores's habit, and then her snappy response came. "Why don't I connect you to one of our officers?" Without waiting for his response, she put him on hold, subjecting him to some of that horrible muzak the station used for this purpose. Impatiently, he tapped the phone against his chin, and when he heard a tired voice ask him to state his name and his business, he immediately launched into his spiel again. When he finished explaining to the person on the other end that he had quite possibly managed to catch a picture of a van driven by a couple of crooks intent on who knows what, the officer, whose name was Wilson, didn't seem overly impressed.

"So you saw a van drive down the street, and you think they're up to… what exactly?"

"How should I know?" he said. "You're the police. You figure it out."

"Sir, as far as I know, it's still not illegal to drive along the street in a van."

"But it's got tinted windows! Now if that ain't suspicious, I don't know what is!"

The officer sighed deeply. "Was the windshield tinted, sir, or the front side windows?"

"Well... no. Or maybe a little. I couldn't get a good look at the driver, though."

"Then they didn't do anything wrong. The windshield and front side windows of a vehicle operated in the State of New York cannot block more than thirty percent of the light. Seventy percent of the light must pass through. In your estimation, was that the case, sir?"

"Why... yeah—I guess. But it's the way he drove, see? All slow like, as if they were looking for something. Probably casing a house or houses. Probably they're part of a gang of burglars and they're going to break in one of these nights."

"And you know this how, exactly?" asked the cop, who was not the brightest bulb in the shed as far as Marc was concerned.

"Why, common sense!" he cried. "Look, I've got the license plate right here. I managed to snap a shot of it just as it disappeared around the corner. Can I read it to you? You can look it up in that database of yours. I'll bet it's connected to all kinds of illegal activities."

"I'm afraid we don't give out that kind of information to the public, Mr. Oldoland," said the cop.

"I didn't mean you have to give me his name and address," he said. "But you can look it up and then arrest the people involved, can't you? Be proactive for a change?"

"I'm afraid..."

At this, Marc got so worked up that he promptly tapped the big red button on the screen and ended the conversation. "No use," he muttered under his breath as he scrolled through his list of phone numbers. "No use whatsoever." It didn't take him long to find the number he was looking for, and so he pressed it. When the familiar voice answered, he perked up a great deal. It was obvious to him now that he should have called Vesta Muffin in the first place instead of wasting his breath on that useless and incompetent police force they had in this town—all paid for with his precious tax dollars, no less.

"Yeah, Vesta," he said. "Marc Oldoland. I just got off the phone with the police, and they're refusing to take me seriously. I hope you've got more sense."

Vesta listened patiently for him to finish his story, then said, "Can you send me that picture? I'll take a look if you want."

"I'm pretty sure they're going to hit my block one of these nights. They've been casing it for days now. And the cops aren't doing anything. On the contrary, they're feeding me all this stuff about privacy laws and it not being illegal to drive a van. But it's the *way* these people are driving their van, Vesta. You can see that, can't you?" he added hopefully.

"Absolutely," said Vesta, much to his relief. "It's exactly this kind of thing we should be seeing more of, Marc. Community spirit, you know. People like you reporting suspicious activities are what crime prevention is all about. And if the police can't see that, it means we'll just have to do it ourselves, like the responsible and concerned citizens that we are."

"Oh, thank God there are people like you active in our community," he said, and meant every word. "Otherwise we'd all be sunk!"

"Just send me that picture and I'll see what I can do," she promised.

"Can you have it checked by the cops?"

"Absolutely," she said, and that didn't surprise him one bit. After all, her son was chief of police, her granddaughter was married to a cop, and Vesta was in charge of the watch.

EXCERPT FROM PURRFECT BULLY (MAX 92)

"I want in on this," he said.

"What did you just say?"

"I said I want in on this. This is my block, Vesta. I've lived here all my life. And if these thugs are going to target me or my neighbors, I want to do my bit to help protect us from these crooks. So if you're going on patrol tonight, I want to ride with you guys. At least," he added cautiously, "if you think that's a good idea."

He didn't know how Vesta ran her neighborhood watch, but he'd heard stories, and those stories said that she ruled the watch with an iron fist. But that didn't bother him. He had been robbed in the past, and he was prepared to follow Vesta's lead if it prevented that kind of thing from ever happening again, either to him or one of his neighbors.

"Sure you can ride with us," she said, much to his surprise. It had been a spur-of-the-moment thing, but he was glad she had said yes. "I'll pick you up at ten," she told him.

"Can… can Rafi also come?" he asked.

"Who's Rafi?"

"My Chihuahua," he said. "I don't like to leave him alone in the house. He gets scared when I'm not there."

"Oh, all right. The more the merrier. I just hope Rafi doesn't have a thing against cats."

And with these mysterious words, she hung up. Then he remembered that Vesta often patrolled with her cats in the car. She seemed to think they were a great help in fighting crime. Or maybe she just liked the company. Patrolling probably got tedious after a while.

As he returned to the house, he wondered if he shouldn't install one of those alarm systems that scare off intruders. But since his budget didn't stretch that far, he'd have to do it himself with a kit he picked up at the hardware store. He wasn't sure it would be sufficient, but since it was all he could afford, it would have to do.

EXCERPT FROM PURRFECT BULLY (MAX 92)

And so he grabbed Rafi from the couch and moments later was on his way into town to pay a visit to Franklin Beaver, the fellow who ran the hardware store, hoping Franklin could instruct him on how to install the deterrent to end all deterrents. If these people thought they could target him a second time in a row, they had another thing coming!

ABOUT NIC

Nic has a background in political science and before being struck by the writing bug worked odd jobs around the world (including but not limited to massage therapist in Mexico, gardener in Italy, restaurant manager in India, and Berlitz teacher in Belgium).

When he's not writing he enjoys curling up with a good (comic) book, watching British crime dramas, French comedies or Nancy Meyers movies, sampling pastry (apple cake!), pasta and chocolate (preferably the dark variety), twisting himself into a pretzel doing morning yoga, going for a brisk walk, and spoiling his feline assistants Lily and Ricky.

He lives with his wife (and aforementioned cats) in a small village smack dab in the middle of absolutely nowhere and is probably writing his next 'Mysteries of Max' book right now.

www.nicsaint.com

Printed in Great Britain
by Amazon